For my cousin and best friend,
Jean Florentino Stokowski (1931–2015)

ACKNOWLEDGMENTS

Thanks as always to my critique partners: Nannette Rundle Carroll, Margaret Hamilton, Jonnie Jacobs, Rita Lakin, Margaret Lucke, and Sue Stephenson. They are ideally knowledgeable, thorough, and supportive.

Special thanks to Linda Plyler, retired postmaster with a thirty-year career in the postal service. I received the full benefit of her professional experience as a training and development specialist in a large city and as a postmaster in a one-woman office in a small town. Linda is also an award-winning quilter whose "zip code quilt" received national recognition and media coverage.

Thanks also to the extraordinary Inspector Chris Lux for continued advice on police procedure, and to the many other writers and friends who offered critiques, information, brainstorming, and inspiration; in particular: Gail and David Abbate, Sara Bly, Mary Donovan, Ann Parker, and Karen and Mark Streich.

A special word of thanks to writer and musician Betty Moffett of Grinnell, Iowa, for her generous assistance with the music of the Ashcots! Any wrong note is my fault entirely.

My deepest gratitude goes to my husband, Dick Rufer. I can't imagine working without his support. He's my dedicated Webmaster (www.minichino.com), layout specialist, and on-call IT department.

Thanks to Bethany Blair and Jen Monroe for their expert attention, and to the copy editors, artists, and staff at Berkley Prime Crime for all their work on my behalf.

Finally, my gratitude to my go-to friend and editor, Michelle Vega, who puts it all together. Michelle has been a bright light in my life, personally supportive as well as superb at seeing the whole picture without missing the tiniest detail. Thanks, Michelle!

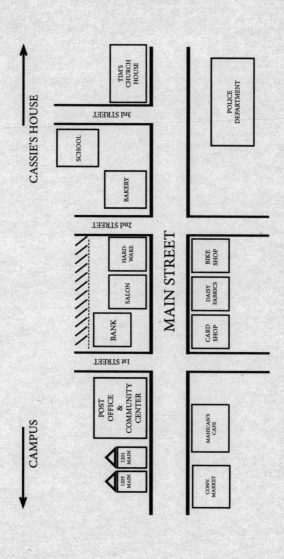

1

Winter weather is hard on flags and the poles that display them. It had taken me a while to bring my predecessor around to this reality and convince him that the North Ashcot Post Office needed to upgrade its image and its equipment. Finally, on this freezing February morning, I was able to hoist a strong new double-ply polyester Old Glory to the top of a pole with a smooth, wire-centered rope and the latest in pulley assemblies.

For the past few months, discussions on this topic between old Ben Gentry and me had been frequent, and of the same format.

"The American flag is not equipment, like computers or a piece of machinery, Cassie," Ben would say, his lanky form making itself comfortable at my desk. "It doesn't need updating."

"Yes, it does," I'd respond. "The pole has cables and

a rotating top that are old and worn, and the banner itself is made of a flimsy fabric that has been abused for years by New England weather. It all needs to be kept in working order."

"It's an unchanging symbol of identity and national pride," Ben would counter, in a glowing non sequitur. "And it reminds people that we're here to serve, no matter what winds of change are blowing around us."

He might as well have lifted his chin, held his hand to his heart, and sung the national anthem. Maybe he'd been humming it to himself and I'd missed it.

In the end, I'd appealed to his sense of patriotism and invoked the name of John Paul Jones, Revolutionary War hero. Jones was famous for his alleged cry of "Surrender? I have not yet begun to fight," and for many firsts involving our flag. He's said to have hoisted our first national flag, the first time it was ever flown, on board the first ship of the Continental Navy. That was a lot of firsts, and the way to Ben's heart. "What would John Paul Jones do?" had worked to bring Ben around to a new flag, if for no other reason than I'd shown some appreciation for history.

Each time this and other issues of postal management came up, I was able to hold my tongue and refrain from reminding Ben that he'd retired, that the nameplate on the counter read CASSIE MILLER, POSTMASTER, NORTH ASHCOT MA POST OFFICE, and that I had no obligation to listen to him.

But Ben was also a friend and the first to step up when I needed help or a temporary replacement in what was ostensibly a one-woman postal service to more than three thousand citizens in the beautiful, woodsy Berkshires of Massachusetts. I had no doubt that I'd be calling on him soon, as we were approaching the busy time of Valentine's Day, second only to Christmas in the volume of mail that passed through our small Colonial building. Even Mother's Day took a backseat to Cupid's arrow.

One more breath of twenty-degree air, and I cast a last upward glance at our new flag, my gaze reaching the top, higher even than the arrow on our weather vane, and hurried out of the cold to enter the post office building through its side door. I was greeted by the sounds of music coming from the community room, which ran the length of the east side of the building, one thin wall away from me and my place of business. A group of local musicians, loosely organized, had been bumped from their usual rehearsal place in the school auditorium as the crumbling North Ashcot Elementary underwent much-needed repairs.

After some negotiation, the Ashcots, as they were known, had won access to the community room for an hour or so in the morning, before I opened the doors to post office customers, and for a couple of hours in the evening, as needed, after the post office closed. The reason for the stepped-up rehearsal schedule was the upcoming Valentine's Day dinner dance at the senior center that served both South and North Ashcot, located a few blocks away from my post office, on Fifth Street.

This morning, I heard the soft notes of a folk tune dominated by the guitars and an instrument that reminded me of a flute. The latter was actually a tin whistle, according to Quinn Martindale, whom I sometimes called my boyfriend, depending on who was listening. I'd gotten to know the players through Quinn, our local antiques dealer when he wasn't strumming his own dobro (more than a guitar, he claimed) with the group. After normal retail hours, which was paperwork time for me, I was likely to hear the Ashcots' louder, more upbeat strains.

I checked my watch and saw that I had enough time for a morning Skype session with my best long-distance friend, Linda Daniels, who still managed a human resources program at Boston's main postal facility. In the days when we worked together, people often mistook us for sisters—the two tallest women in the building, five-nine and marathon fit, distinguishable only by our hairstyles: hers short, blond, and neat; mine long, dark, and too curly to ever label *neat*. Linda and I had met in college and traveled the same career path until mine brought me back to the town where I'd grown up.

Because I'm a slow learner, I thought I could share my Stars and Stripes excitement with Linda.

"Why would you wait for Ben's permission for a new flag setup in the first place?" she asked. "You've been the official postmaster out there in the boonies for nearly two years." She was off by six months and spoke the words as if it was about time I moved back to the city, where we could once again share our morning lattes and scones in person.

I chose to ignore her "boonies" characterization—Linda felt deprived when she couldn't get to New York for a weekend of shows, shunning even Boston's considerable theater scene. Reminding her that North Ashcot was closer to New York than Boston was a waste of time.

She'd strike back with something like "Albany doesn't count."

The longer I stuck it out in North Ashcot, the less bad-mouthing I suffered from her, but this morning for some reason Linda was not happy and I bore the brunt of her displeasure. As usual, she was dressed in a power suit and I felt like an adolescent in my regulation blue-striped shirt and small scarf. She sat with her back to her window, the better to remind me of her great view of Boston's financial district.

I could never make it clear to Linda how small towns worked, how the chain of command and way of life were different from the protocols in the state capital. But I tried once more this morning to explain that as postmaster for more than twenty years, Ben deserved a certain degree of respect. "He's from an era when things were supposed to last forever," I said. "Including flags, along with clothes and shoes."

Linda broke down and smiled. "I guess he wouldn't be familiar with the built-in obsolescence of televisions and cell phones?"

Linda was the poster girl for state-of-the-art electronics. For years, I'd been the beneficiary of her obsessive need to upgrade. My latest acquisition was a new tablet and stylus that I was still getting used to.

"Ben is suspicious of my tablet," I said, "just as he was when I bought a microwave. He's afraid the electrical pulses are going to mess up our postage meters."

Linda laughed, as I hoped she would so I could take advantage of a light moment. "Something wrong today,

Linda?" I was ready for something as serious as a breakup or as frivolous as missing a sale at her favorite shoe store.

"Just a sec," she said, leaving her computer. I heard the familiar sound of a door closing. She came back to the camera, breathing heavily, as if worn out by the trek to the doorway. "I guess you could call it a job crisis, since I hate to call it *midlife* before I'm even thirty-six years old. I may have hit the career ceiling here and I don't know what's next."

"Wow."

"I know. Wow. I guess you thought I was here for life, happily ever after."

"I did. Was it something in particular that brought this on, or—"

"I don't know. Maybe I see how things are going so well with you. You have no complaints—you've even won old Ben over—and here I am, dreading coming in to work every morning to an in-box full of same old, same old." Linda shuffled papers on her desk and held them up, one at a time, with a summary statement. "Health benefits review. Changes to the handbook. ADA implementation. EEO compliance. *A*, *B*, *C*, *D* . . . The whole alphabet needs reworking."

I gulped. "I had no idea, Linda. And I'm so sorry. But in case you think it's all sweetness and light here, the only reason I don't tell you all my problems is to keep you from nagging me about returning to Boston."

"Do I do that?"

"Yes, and I'm not that confident. I'm afraid I'll give in. I'm not as settled here as I might make it seem."

"Wow," she said, and we laughed at the symmetry.

With all our defenses down, we made the most of the few minutes before my retail day began, airing our problems, offering quick advice, promising to deal with everything in more depth soon.

Our litanies of dissatisfaction played out to background music from the Ashcots in the room next door. I recognized the voices of Mercedes Davis and Dennis Somerville singing about a chain gang, if I heard correctly, with heavy guitar accompaniment in the background. I'd heard the musicians often when they played at the coffeehouse and at special events and especially loved their original compositions. Which reminded me. There was a special event on Saturday.

"Why don't you come here for the weekend?" I said to Linda.

She groaned. "You're inviting me to a senior dinner dance on Valentine's Day? Are you really trying to depress me?"

"It's not a senior dance. It's for everyone, just in the senior center, which is our largest venue."

"Is there a sign outside that says 'Senior Center'?" she asked.

I laughed but didn't acknowledge her point. "Quinn will be playing for the first part of the dance," I said. "The guitar people are taking turns so no one is tied up for the whole evening. So you and I will have some time alone. Unless you have a hot date back there? Someone you're keeping from me?"

She chuckled, a wry sound. "Hardly. I'm between guys, as you know. My timing is always impeccable." Linda looked up to where I knew the clock hung on her wall. "More later. I'm so lucky. I have a committee meeting now." She put on a clearly false smile and we signed off.

I felt sorry for Linda's plight, and regretted my own lack of gratitude for things that were going well for me. I had two close friends in Quinn and the chief of police, of all people, and on most days I enjoyed my job. But the call hadn't put me in the mood for a glass-half-full moment.

My flag-waving cheerfulness had dissipated even before my retail day started.

2

I realized the music had stopped and a few of the musicians were filing past my front doors on the way to their cars. I waved to Joyce Blake and Dennis Somerville, both in their forties, math and physics professors, respectively, who ignored my greeting, walking with angry faces angled toward each other, their mouths going simultaneously. I wondered if they were arguing about black holes or something equally well beyond the layman's reach. More likely their syllabi, according to Quinn, who was privy to some of their squabbling, and who was among the missing this morning.

Dennis must have arrived early for rehearsal, since he'd captured the best available parking spot, curbside. A big man, Dennis had no trouble maneuvering his bass guitar, stowing it in the trunk of his car. To my surprise, he walked toward my doors, perhaps to apologize for not acknowledging me. *LOL,* I thought, in the parlance of the day.

Mercedes Davis and Shirley Peterson came within view. The women were, respectively, a history professor and a retired administrator from the same nearby community college where Joyce and Dennis taught. The two women lugged their guitar cases in silence and gave me cheerless nods. The youngest member of the ensemble, Brooke Jeffries, a financial officer in South Ashcot, whizzed by, head down, her penny whistle sticking out from her jacket pocket. Arthur Chaplin, next in view, carried his mandolin case over his shoulder, in the manner of kids and their backpacks. He headed into the post office, sporting as dour a look as I'd ever seen on a performer.

Not even the musicians were joyful today.

I was only five minutes from admitting the regular morning crowd to the lobby and, ultimately, to my counter. Or should I say, the *onslaught was upon me*? It was never a good sign for the week ahead when I was worn out before I opened the doors.

I finished preparations and did my best to welcome a long line of customers, many stomping their feet as if to shake off nonexistent snow. Or to blame me for the freezing weather.

Another disappointment awaited me. Monday regulars Carolyn and George Raley, keepers of exotic little animals, were not in the lobby. I remembered that they were scheduled to head south to Florida for a warm two weeks with their son and his family. No sweet Llarry the Llama to be weighed in today on my scale, the most accurate in town; no long-tailed baby genet with zebralike stripes to wiggle on the counter. Only grumpy Mr. and Mrs. Bertrand with complaints about their post office box.

"It's too high for me to reach," the matronly Mrs. Bertrand groused this time. "And I can't get my hand into the back corners to dust it out. And my, does that box need dusting! I guess the rental fee doesn't include maintenance."

I put on my best apologetic expression. "I thought you didn't want to bend down so much for the last box you had," I offered, straining to remember that the customer was always right.

"That one was way too low," Mr. Bertrand said. "We're not thirty years old anymore, you know."

I wondered if they were ever thirty. I tried in vain to picture the Bertrands young and happy. I gave them as much time as I thought reasonable with so many others waiting, then suggested they look at a list of the available boxes and choose the one they liked best.

"I guess we have to do her work for her," Mrs. Bertrand said to her husband, who was quick to nod, then shake his head in disbelief. I was sure "Young people today" was on the tip of his tongue.

Dennis Somerville approached with a complaint of his own. He'd received a few crank letters in the past week, purportedly from students, and wanted me to put a stop to them. He plunked three envelopes on the counter. "These are all about my alleged unreasonable homework assignments or my tough grading policies with thinly veiled threats to report me to the college oversight committee."

Unlike the Bertrands, Dennis spoke softly, elbows on the counter, perhaps embarrassed to have the world know that he was perceived by some in his classes to be a less than stellar teacher.

I looked at the plain white envelopes, all size ten, standard business size, all with appropriate stamps and postmarks. The handwriting on the envelopes was all in cursive, and in no way distinctive, unless you considered that cursive itself was on its way out. I pointed this out to Dennis. "There's nothing I can do about these, unless you're reporting a threat."

Dennis heaved a sigh. "I told you. They're threatening." He put special emphasis on the last word. "They're making a case for the college grievance committee. They're claiming I'm in violation of good instructional practices, or some other mandate."

"I think the threat has to be a little more—"

"You *think*? Aren't you supposed to *know*? Aren't there federal regulations about this? Don't you have a postmaster inspector general or something like that to investigate this kind of thing?"

"We have a chief postal inspector," I said. "But the threat has to be bigger. Like a threat to your person. Or to the country." I stumbled through, hoping I was right. I'd never been asked to intervene in a college classroom dispute, but I couldn't imagine typical student complaints constituted a case for our postal inspectors. I resolved to visit the U.S. Postal Inspection Service section of my handbook the first chance I had.

Dennis stabbed a finger in turn to each of the conspicu-ously blank upper left corners of the envelopes, still keep-ing his voice to just above a whisper. "Isn't there always supposed to be a return address? Aren't you supposed to reject mailings with no return address?"

"Only in special cases," I said, again straining to recall that section of the USPS code. To the best of my knowl-edge, a return address was required for Priority Mail and other special services mailings. Not for an ordinary first-class letter.

Another heavy sigh from the physics prof. I thought his attitude alone could be considered cause for grievance from his students, although I'd never known him to be out of sorts. "Okay, but I'm not through with this. I can read the postal code"—here he sneered and raised his voice—"as well as anyone." He took out his wallet. "Just give me a roll of Forevers. I guess you can do that much for me?"

I was relieved that Dennis didn't open the envelopes and demand that I read the letters. I suspected he pre-ferred to keep the exact contents to himself. I handed over stamps, a receipt, and change for a one-hundred-dollar bill. I didn't dare perform the usual check for the accep-tance of a Ben Franklin, lest Dennis start in again on post office policies. He left without checking the post office box he managed for the Ashcots. Something was defi-nitely off. Dennis was usually a calm sort, and certainly never as belligerent as I'd seen him today. I guessed hate mail from your students could do that to a teacher.

A few customers later, I was surprised to see Mercedes Davis in front of me. And no Arthur Chaplin, whom I'd seen enter the building, in the line. "Art held a place for me while I went to my car," Mercedes explained, lifting a produce-type box onto the counter. "I had to stow my guitar and pick up our flyers and a mailing for my husband's business." Mercedes, the designated secretary for the musicians' group, and for her husband, it seemed, was a frequent customer. Today an obviously grandchild-made knitted cap covered her wavy white hair. The bowl-shaped hat had been stitched together with yarns of conflicting colors, many of them neon bright, severely clashing with her otherwise carefully planned outfit.

"Did everything go okay at rehearsal today?" I asked. I nodded in the direction of the community room, my hands busy with the mailing. After working with the USPS since college, many of those years at the service desk, I'd become a master at multitasking. I'd learned early on that there was a fine line between friendly banter with a customer and a conversation that meant the next person had to wait an extra thirty seconds for his turn.

"Oh, you noticed the mood in there?" Mercedes asked, mimicking my nod toward the ad hoc music room. "Some days are like this, where everyone has some agenda that has nothing to do with the sheet music, if you know what I mean. Today, Brooke had to defend her bank for holding up Arthur's son's loan application; Joyce and Dennis were at it, as usual, over whether first-year calculus should be required before the physics class or vice versa, as if it mattered; and forget Greg—he's been out of it ever since his wife left him."

More than I needed to know, but I mumbled a "Tsk-tsk" and decided to let her go on chattering until I checked out the last of her husband's international forms. I wondered if all this intrigue and infighting had been going on in the background the last time Quinn and I heard the group play together at Mahican's coffeehouse. If so, they certainly covered it up well and seemed to be at one with their music.

Mercedes looked around, at the same time tucking away stray, curly strands of pure white and off-yellow hair, most of which was pulled back from her face. The grooming gesture was a diversionary tactic, I guessed, while she assured herself that there was enough distance between her and the next in line at the PLEASE WAIT HERE sign. She leaned toward me and whispered, "I shouldn't be telling you this, but there's a rumor that Missy left Greg for Touchstone. You know, the clown in *As You Like It*."

It took me a few seconds to remember that Greg Overland, the group's drummer, was also the drama coach at the community college. Tall and well built, Greg had the powerful voice of a trained actor. Now Mercedes was letting me in on the not-so-secret news that one of the main characters in the college production of Shakespeare's *As You Like It*, the lovable court jester, had wooed and won over Greg's wife.

I noticed some shuffling in the line and heard a few loud, heavy sighs, all code for "Hey, we're waiting to do business here."

"Sounds like there's a lot going on," I said to Mercedes. I handed over her receipt. "I hope the day gets better for you."

"Thanks. Actually, I have a favor to ask, Cassie. Quinn

says you're an expert on post office history, going back to the Victorian era in England and the early Pony Express days in this country. Would you be willing to give a talk to my class? I'm covering that period, and there's only so much you can do with Victoriana that hasn't been done a million times before."

I'd expected—hoped—the favor would be something like ordering extra stamps with images of musicians, or waiving the requirements for bulk mail so the Ashcots could use the service for its flyers. I wasn't ready for a personal challenge like public speaking. "Sorry, Mercedes, no personal business at the counter," I said, giving her a big smile and my most apologetic look.

"Oh, right. No problem. As long as you're willing, we can discuss the details over lunch. Okay?"

"Okay," I said.

Before I could qualify that I meant "Okay, let's not do business at the counter," not "Okay, I'll give a talk," Mercedes chimed in. "Great. I'll bring sandwiches around noon." She was gone in a flash, trailing wisps of bright pink yarn from her hat, leaving my smile in her wake for the next customer.

If that next patron, a burly man in a red and black lumber jacket, noticed how overwrought I was, he didn't mention it. He was too busy with his own complaint, and the effort of slamming a package on the counter. "This was shoved into my mailbox and, as you see, has been damaged by you people."

I examined the mailing label. "This was addressed to you in South Ashcot?" I asked.

"That's right."

"And it reached the correct mailbox in that town?"

"That's right. It was shoved into my box and damaged, obviously."

"I'm very sorry, sir. But I'm not sure why you're bringing it here. As you know, we don't even have home delivery in North Ashcot. This needs to be handled by your post office in South Ashcot. I'm sure they'll take their responsibility very seriously and make this right."

He glared at me and waved his large arms around, encompassing the lobby and possibly out to the flagpole. "Isn't this part of the United States Postal Service?"

"Yes, sir, it is, and I regret that your package was damaged, but—"

He leaned over and stabbed the cancelled stamps. "And are these stamps not part of the United States Postal Service?"

"Yes, sir, they are, but—"

"Then I expect you to make this right."

I looked at the line of frustrated customers and at the clock. If I was going to be able to fit in a corrective phone call to Mercedes, I needed to move the line along. I grabbed a form that could pass for a receipt of merchandise and scribbled my name on the bottom line. "Of course, sir," I said, handing the lumberjack the slip of paper. "Leave it with me and I'll take care of it."

He slapped his beefy hand on the counter, grinned in a way that made me cringe and several customers turn away, and walked out of the lobby. A young woman with a toddler in her arms covered her child's eyes as the lumberjack walked by her, and collective grumbling began in earnest.

Truism: When people witness rude and/or creepy behavior toward a clerk, they rally, expressing sympathy and support beyond what they would otherwise offer the person behind the counter.

"Unbelievable," said an older man.

"Bully," said another.

"You might know he's not from around here," said a woman with a cane.

"What do you expect from South Ashcot?"

Others were more severe.

"You should just trash the package," I was advised.

"Give it to me and I'll crush whatever's in there."

"Then he'll really know what 'damaged' means."

I tried not to encourage the laughs that these suggestions brought.

The truth was that I had no idea what I was going to do with the mystery shipment, other than pass the buck to Ben.

I turned my attention to the line, but while my hands were busy stamping letters, weighing odd-sized packages, and answering questions about the next rate increase and the availability of a popular celebrity stamp, my head was swimming with other tasks I needed to do, impressions I needed to correct.

The last guy in line was another man I was acquainted with. Hank Blackwood used to play acoustic guitar with the Ashcots, but left under unpleasant conditions according to Quinn. (Who was where today, by the way?) A falling-out with Dennis Somerville, if I remembered correctly. Hank had retired from teaching math at the college around the same time that he left the Ashcots.

"Remember me?" Hank asked. His short frame disappeared behind the counter for a moment while he bent to pick up a stack of parcels.

I smiled. "Good to see you again, Hank."

He seemed pleased that I remembered his name and took advantage of being the last in line to get me caught up with what he'd been doing since he left the group. The overall impression he wanted me to have was that he was better off now, playing with a group down in Pittsfield.

"It's more of a drive, of course, but the people are nicer."

I smiled and said how glad I was for him, and weighed his packages as quickly as I could.

"The North Ashcot group takes things too seriously," Hank said. "Over in Pittsfield, things are more relaxed."

"I'm glad it's working for you," I said again.

"Yeah, it's not rocket science, you know?"

By the time Hank left, I felt my face would be stuck in a fake smile, never to return to its normal configuration. I also wished I'd paid more attention to the customer service training modules I'd been subjected to over the years.

Finally, around eleven o'clock, I had a break to call Mercedes. No answer, but I was able to leave a message and explain that I couldn't meet her for lunch. I made a point to mention that I had a prior meeting with Sunni Smargon. I refrained from using Sunni's title; everyone in the county knew that Sunni was the chief of police. Surely, Mercedes wouldn't expect me to bug out on the highest-ranking cop in the NAPD. The fact that Sunni and I had planned to share quilt blocks during our important lunch was immaterial.

Next I sent a brief text to Quinn.

I left it at WHERE R U? since my real question to him was too long for a text: *Why in the world would you suggest me for a talk on the history of the post office, or on anything, for that matter, since you know I hate public speaking? And is this why you're afraid to show your face this morning?*

I did recall a conversation I'd had with Quinn when I was going through a reading phase that included post office history and lore. I'd been fascinated by a book on the once-eminent Sir Rowland Hill, whose pamphlet "Post Office Reforms" in the mid-1800s instituted reforms that opened the British postal system to the masses. Before that, an elaborate and expensive method of delivery was in effect. Sir Rowland had unleashed a revolutionary postal network for sending business and personal letters that allowed Victorians to transcend geographical boundaries and changed postal services around the world. Or so his biographer claimed.

I loved to share bits of history with my friends, but addressing a group of strangers, albeit all college students, was outside my wheelhouse. I wasn't an expert on postal history, and even if I were, I was anything but an expert speaker. I'd flunked debating in high school, begged off orals in college in favor of a written thesis, and lost a night's sleep worrying about giving a maid-of-honor toast at my cousin's wedding. I was the poster girl for fearing public speaking more than death.

I had to admit I'd never expressed my fear explicitly to

Quinn, but I felt he should know me well enough to have figured it out. Why else refer to him as my boyfriend?

Before I finished my internal monologue on the day's anxieties, my phone rang, startling me, since I'd already begun another text, to Linda. I wanted to set up a time when we could talk at length about our mutual not-quite-midlife crises, and to pin her down for a visit to North Ashcot this coming weekend.

Mercedes's number came up on my screen. I accepted.

"I'd love to join you and Sunni," she said. "One of my favorite people. Well, two of my favorite people." She chuckled at her wit. "I'm trying to line Sunni up for a talk, also, on the development of a Victorian-era police force. You know, 'the peelers' as they were called, or 'bobbies,' after the home secretary at the time, Sir Robert Peel."

No, I didn't know. I did know that Mercedes was planning to retire at the end of this school term. Was she planning a de facto retirement sooner, by enlisting guest speakers for her classes?

"We usually just bring our lunches and eat in my office," I said.

"That's fine with me," Mercedes said.

Why was I having such trouble making myself clear to Mercedes? "I'm afraid we have some private business today, Mercedes. But another time. Oops, I'm getting another call. Talk to you later."

I couldn't believe I pulled that on Mercedes. On anyone. But I needed time to check out what Quinn had told her and to find out whether Sunni was also on the roster. Mostly, I didn't like Mercedes's presumptuous attitude.

I was happy to see a customer approaching the counter,

as if that validated my fib to Mercedes. And, at last, I had a fun patron. I said hello to "Moses" Crawford, reputed to be the town's oldest citizen, and accepted his mailing, in a large, decorated box, sold in the lobby, that weighed practically nothing. Moses sent a birthday balloon filled with helium to each of his far-flung great-grandchildren, amounting to at least one a month. I wondered if he ever checked on the condition of the balloons on arrival.

"Thanks, Moses," I said, and handed him change for a twenty. "This is the most fun I've had today."

"Poor Cassie," he said, stroking his straggly beard. "Maybe you should come with me to the Valentine's Day dance."

"Aw, too bad I'm booked, Moses," I said, wondering if I was right. Quinn still hadn't shown up.

"That's okay. I'm sorta double-booked myself."

I had no doubt the charming old man was telling the truth.

3

When Sunni entered the lobby with a long face and a halfhearted greeting, I knew the day was back on its downward spiral. I tossed her a key and she locked the front door behind her.

The chief of police pushed on the low swinging door between the lobby and the retail counter and entered my work area, the only civilian (in the USPS sense) allowed to do so. Another reason I didn't want to invite Mercedes to lunch today. It would have set a bad example for the rest of North Ashcot's citizens. Or I imagined the awkwardness if I had her sit on the other side of the counter.

Sunni removed her hat, shook out her auburn locks, and lowered her small body onto my extra desk chair. "Another one this morning," she said.

"Another break-in?" She nodded. "Oh no."

While I'd been dealing with angst over the small

tribulations of life behind a service counter, my good friend had real problems to deal with. For the past two months, the usually quiet town of North Ashcot had seen a sharp rise in crime. It was getting so that the police briefs in the local paper were taking up more column space than the community events listing or the letters to the editor. In fact, many of the letters included cries of police incompetency and expressions of fear for the safety of our citizens. Not everyone knew, as I did, how hard Sunni and her four officers were working to find the person responsible for the upset.

Sunni had the newspaper open to the page that listed house break-ins and vehicle crimes. The addresses were strung out across several lines of text: Houses hit were on Squire Road, Bennington Street, Wisteria Lane, Ravenwood Avenue, Park Circle. Vehicle break-ins occurred on Forest Lane, Crescent Circle, Gilmore Court, and Proctor Avenue. The standard "if you have any information" line seemed small and ineffective at the bottom of the column.

"Who even has a car radio these days?" Sunni asked, stabbing the paper with her finger. "Doesn't everyone listen to music digitally? It used to be the biggest problem in this town was loud stereos after ten o'clock at night or before eight in the morning. This almost makes me long for some old-fashioned shoplifting or the occasional cat in a tree."

I looked at the addresses again. "These locations are all over town," I said.

"Yeah, I know. East, west, north, south. All hours of the day and night."

It was true that the crimes were what might be called minor—home robberies and car break-ins. A few personal assaults. Nothing major like a television set had ever been taken. There were slight injuries, only a broken nose or two, but when it was your home, your car, or your bruised face that was the reality, all bets were off as far as perspective was concerned. It was a terrible situation for the residents of North Ashcot.

"This guy seems to know everyone's schedule. He hits during the one hour that no one is home—which is a good thing, in a way—and he seems to know where extra cash is stored and how to open a locked glove compartment. Sometimes it's daylight, sometimes dead of night. He's like a superhero, only the opposite."

I took the leftover cheese and rice casserole that I'd promised Sunni from the small fridge in my work area. I now added one more reason for eliminating Mercedes from the lunch equation. There wasn't enough food for three. The deck was stacked against the needy history professor.

"Maybe it's not one guy, but some kind of team," I suggested. "With recon people and lookouts."

"We've considered that. He, or they, never leaves fingerprints or any kind of forensics. And there's not a lot of damage. He takes a few valuables and cash and leaves."

"No cigarette butts or candy wrappers to send to the crime lab?"

"Nuh-uh. No hair and fibers. Anyway, you'd be amazed how seldom a case is solved by hair and fibers, except on television." Sunni busied herself with nuking and serving the casserole on my best plastic dinnerware. She took in a deep breath and uttered a satisfied "Mmm" at the cheesy aroma. "I'm famished. I hope this is Quinn's doing."

I should have been insulted that Sunni liked Quinn's cooking better than mine, but it was no contest, since I never cooked if I could help it. I'd managed to find a nice guy who also enjoyed playing chef.

"Speaking of Quinn—has Mercedes Davis asked you to give a talk at the college?" I asked. "Never mind why Quinn is connected to that question, by the way."

"Yeah, she has. I've been putting her off for years."

"That works?"

Sunni smiled. "I guess we're not being very community minded."

"At least you have a fascinating job."

"Huh. I guess it's my fault Mercedes thinks so. One time I mentioned how interesting it was that in the early days, cops had other chores to do around town, like lighting the lanterns on the streets. And they weren't armed, but they carried rattles, an adult version, in case they needed to raise an alarm." She paused, a small frown creeping across her brow. "And, you know, I think it was Quinn who gave me a book on the subject, which is why it was fresh in my mind whenever it was that I talked to Mercedes."

It wasn't surprising that Quinn would give Sunni a volume on police history that he happened on, in his never-ending search for merchandise for the antiques store he managed. He was always on the lookout for things someone might want, most of the time passing them on free of charge.

"I'm going for the big-ticket items eventually," he'd

say to me. I realized his gifts were good sales strategy, but it was also his nature to be generous, even if he knew you were never going to invest in a Louis XVI armoire.

"Did you intend for Mercedes to ask you to give a talk?"

Sunni sputtered. "You're kidding."

There was no time for me to clear things up, however, since Sunni's cell phone went off. She glanced at the screen. I heard a heavy sigh, and then she stuffed a large chunk of casserole into her mouth and thrust her thumb toward the door. She managed a thank-you before following her thumb through the exit.

I hoped the call was one that would improve her day, not make it worse.

The afternoon passed uneventfully, the most interesting first-class mail being addressed to Darling, Mississippi; Romance, Arizona; and Juliette, Georgia. The pink envelopes were brought in just before closing time by three teenagers from Ashcot High School, serving both South and North Ashcot. The girls approached the counter together and explained their strategy to me, as if I wasn't well aware of the practice.

"We do this every year," said teenager number one, her long, straight brown hair hanging over a fake fur collar. "You just address your valentine as usual to your guy of the year"—a giggle—"and then put it in another envelope and address that envelope to the postmaster of a town named, like"—she tapped her envelope—"Juliette, Georgia, which I'm doing this year. Last year I did Honeyville, Utah."

"Yeah, we all know that last year you sent a valentine to a different guy," said teenager number two, causing another eruption of giggles.

"I did Loveland, Colorado," teenager number three offered. She held up her bright pink envelope. "Mine are always extra postage, too," she said.

"The post office in that town mails it for you with their postmark," the first teenager said, trying to be very clear, seeming unaware that she was speaking to a USPS employee, and one who was instrumental in marketing the practice several years ago. I remembered the project—signing up cities to emulate Valentine, Texas, which had a postmarking service going back more than thirty years. I'd read that they typically received about eighteen thousand special cancellations in a given year.

"You have to remember to put 'valentine re-mailing'" on the outside, said teenager number two, a slightly different shade of long, straight brown hair pulled over her ears.

I nodded and pretended to be learning a lot, but I felt obliged to issue a warning. "You know it's a little late to be doing this. Usually, these post offices require a lead time of a couple of weeks."

The only short-bobbed teenager shook her head. "Nuh-uh. We do this all the time."

"Okay," I said, stamping the last of the three cards.

"It won't be a problem," said another.

"Okay," I said again, and handed each girl her change.

"Besides, we don't know who we're going to send to that far in advance," another offered, prompting more giggles.

Oh, the confidence of youth. All was fine with me; I'd covered my bases. I noted that all of their valentines were over the one-ounce limit and, thus, our initiating committee's idea that the gimmick would pay its own way had come true. Not only was the USPS getting an extra mailing, but most valentines, with their ribbons, puffy hearts, and three-dimensional Cupids, would require extra postage.

Out of the corner of my eye, I saw a familiar figure waiting for the excited teenagers to finish their business. Quinn Martindale leaned his long frame against the end of the table that held the USPS forms and other supplies. He caught my eye and touched his Ashcot's Attic cap. I couldn't read the subheading, but I knew it by heart. *Where everything new is old.*

Quinn had come to the Berkshires from California nearly a year before I returned to the home of my youth. In some ways, we bonded over being outsiders, for different reasons. That connection had gone as we both gained acceptance and felt more comfortable, but a new one had formed and we were now officially dating. So much so that my fridge was full of concoctions by Quinn, and his home was acquiring various covers and wall hangings as I took up quilting, the sport favored by our mutual friend, the chief of police.

When the girls left, Quinn came to the counter and leaned over. The day was looking up.

"New jacket?" I asked, noting that he was making strides in building his winter wardrobe, unnecessary in his part of California.

"It's a castoff from my boss. You know I hate to spend money on clothes."

"So you weren't out shopping all morning?"

He shook his head. "Sorry I didn't keep track of my phone. I was with Fred at this great site in Brimfield. The place was amazing. Furniture, dolls, books, military items. Fred's thinking of arranging a special sale at the Attic on the stuff we picked up."

I pictured Quinn and his boss in ecstasy over the little Massachusetts town with the big antiques show, said to be the largest outdoor antiques show in the world. But the date was wrong. The show's dates were in spring and summer.

"But it's February," I said, as if I'd caught him in a lie.

"It was a private sale," Quinn said. "Fred got a call from a buddy down there, that there was a big event—an estate on the edge of town came up for sale. Everyone's had their eye on this place forever, and finally . . ." He shrugged, a sheepish look taking over his handsome features.

"Finally, someone died," I said.

"Well, yes, but that happens a lot in the antiques business. I mean, well, you know what I mean. The timing was good because the heirs didn't want to wait for the big show in the spring. And it was good for our customers, too, because the Brimfield show can be overwhelming for a layperson. They count on us to scout for them. We've had this one customer who comes back to us every summer, looking for a certain watch, and now I think we have it. It's a Tudor that actually has papers to go with it. It's very rare to have documents that . . ."

I hadn't meant to frown, but I found my mind drifting toward my own agenda.

"I'm going on and on," Quinn said, raising his eyebrows and tilting his head. "Your turn."

"Do I look bored?"

"A bit."

"Only because I've been wanting to ask you—have you been talking to Mercedes Davis?"

"Uh-oh." Quinn stepped back from the counter, where he'd been resting his elbows. He looked toward the door, hoping, I knew, for someone to interrupt us, like a last-minute customer. No such luck.

"So you did offer me up?"

"I thought it would be fun for you. You always say you like it when you get to do something different besides stand here all day."

"What I meant was I'd like to visit one of those unusual post offices I tell you about."

"Like the mail boat that's operating as a floating postal zip code along the Detroit River?"

"Yes, like that." It was true that I'd been thinking about visiting that area ever since I saw a video on their "mail in the pail" system—a diesel motor ship glided up to a larger vessel; then a bucket attached to a rope was lowered to collect letters and packages. How cool was that? "Or it might be fun to see the country's smallest post office, in the Florida Everglades, just seven by eight feet. Or go to Hawaii, where you can just write an address on a coconut and—"

"I get it," Quinn said. "But you'd be a great speaker.

You're always looking up post office facts and figures, reading stories, like that blog with all the odd stories. Like the town where, when the postmaster is out of town, you pick up your mail at his dad's auto body shop."

"All that reading is for my own pleasure, not research for a speech. Besides, Mercedes is teaching the Victorian era, of which I know almost nothing, except what's in that Sir Rowland Hill bio you gave me."

Quinn let out an exaggerated "Ahem." He gave me a winning smile. "I could help you out there."

Of course, I should have thought before I spoke. Quinn knew Victoriana the way I knew post office lore. The red brocade love seat in his small house was a testimony to his excellent shopping skills, and the (almost) matching balloon fabric armchair provided seating fit for a papal visit.

My phone cut off further discussion. "Sunni," I said to Quinn, showing him the screen, as if that would be enough for him to understand why I'd accept the call.

"Closing up?" she asked.

"Almost." I told her about my visitor. I was ready to bring her into the conversation about the Mercedes Davis requests, but she rushed in.

"How soon can you be here?"

"Be—?"

"At the station."

"Ten minutes if I need to."

"You need to," she said, and hung up.

I made a quick call to Ben to close up and grabbed my jacket.

My best guess was that since I'd seen Sunni at lunch-time, her day hadn't gotten any better. Maybe I could help.

Quinn offered to drop me off at the North Ashcot Police Station, a couple of blocks from the post office, straight through the town's main shopping district. We passed the card shop, fabric store, and bike shop, all within minutes of closing their doors for the day. There wasn't much to do after dark on Main Street. Now and then, like this evening, I thought about the contrast with Boston, less than three hours away, where I'd spent most of my adult life, where the clubs and coffee shops in my old neighbor-hood would just be coming alive.

Quinn's words called me back from Faneuil Hall, with its plethora of restaurants and live music venues. "While you're being grilled by the chief"—he grinned—"I'll pick up some supplies and get the grill started at your house."

Now that I was back in the present, I was too nervous about this strange summons to the PD to fully appreciate Quinn's humor, but I thanked him for trying.

"Tell Sunni there'll be enough for her, too," he added.

"Thanks. I'll call you when I'm done."

It had taken me a while to get used to Quinn's manner, the gentle and supportive way he treated me. One might even say he spoiled me. I had Linda to thank for being able to accept the change. She'd seen me through my failed engagement to Adam Robinson in Boston. Adam's idea of treating me to dinner was to take me to a five-star restaurant, in a dress of his choosing, either to impress his wealthy clients or to woo potential new ones. I'd finally admitted to myself that his dumping me was the best thing that could have happened. So what if he notified me of the breakup through text messages? More evidence of his lack of class.

"What do you think the chief wants?" Quinn asked, driving up to the curb and pulling me back to the present once more.

"I have no idea. She cut lunchtime short when she got a call. I presumed it was another robbery. I haven't heard anything from her since."

"Yeah, Fred and I were talking about that. So far we've been lucky. I guess no one wants old stuff, but then no other shops have been robbed, either, that I know of. Maybe they realize there would be better security at a place of business."

I had a sudden thought. And gasped. "What if my house has been broken into? What if that's why she wants me here?"

Quinn shook his head. "She would have met you at your house."

"Let's hope so," I said, and got out of his SUV.

The police department building was redbrick with white trim, not much different from the post office except that it was two stories, shabbier on the inside, and housed a small jail in its basement. The main attraction was Sunni's state-of-the-art coffeemaker, which she had put into service in time for me to catch the aroma of a delicious dark roast as I approached her office.

Greta Bauer, the tall UMass graduate who was Sunni's newest recruit, waved me in. "She's waiting for you," she said, her tone noncommittal.

An NAPD mugful of cappuccino was waiting for me, along with the chief of police, half sitting on the front of her desk. Was this coffee treat a good sign or a bad one? I wondered. Was this the prelude to informing me that all my earthly possessions were now in the hands of the crooks who'd been terrorizing North Ashcot?

I took the seat in front of Sunni as directed and waited as she picked up from her desk a slip of paper encased in plastic. "Here's why I needed to see you," she said, handing me the paper.

My eyes focused on a receipt, three inches wide and about ten inches long. Only one product was listed, a cash purchase for which a one-hundred-dollar bill was used. The rest of the strip contained boilerplate with tracking information, a notice about a self-service kiosk, a URL for ordering products online, a warning that all sales were final, and other messages, including THANK YOU FOR YOUR BUSINESS and HELP US SERVE YOU BETTER, with a plea to take an online survey about the shopping experience today.

I couldn't have imagined a more caring, friendly receipt. I thought of the two customers I hadn't served well today—Dennis, with his student complaints, and the unnamed lumberjack, with a damaged package. Add to that my refusal to serve the college community by sharing my knowledge, and I was batting zero for customer service. I needed to make some changes to our automated receipts, or change my attitude.

Printed at the very bottom of the long strip was CUS-TOMER COPY. At the top was the name and address of the North Ashcot Post Office and today's date. In between, covering much of the text, were red spatters.

I ran my fingers over the red splats and felt a shiver even though there was a layer of plastic between my skin and the splats. I gave Sunni a questioning look.

"Yes, that's probably blood. The receipt was found on a body of a murder victim."

I gulped. It wasn't only Sunni's day that had gotten worse since lunchtime. I placed my mug on the floor near my chair, knowing I couldn't trust myself to keep it upright otherwise. "Dennis Somerville has been murdered?"

It was clear that the winning candidate for worst day of all had gone to my customer, musician and physics professor Dennis Somerville.

4

I turned to the window in Sunni's office, looking for answers in the darkening sky. I'd arrived at the police station expecting to hear the news that my home had been broken into, some of my belongings stolen, a window broken, or a carpet ruined. All of that paled in comparison as I thought of Dennis Somerville, who'd lost not just a set of china or a DVD player, but his life. It seemed the North Ashcot home invaders—I thought of them now as a team—had ratcheted up to murder.

Sunni had given me a moment to compose myself, but I noticed her eyes had widened, a surprised expression still on her face. "Do you recognize every receipt you hand out?"

"No, but this one's from this morning, and it's the only hundred-dollar bill I handled today, so . . ." I shrugged.

"Well, you're right. It's Dennis Somerville's. His body was found this afternoon. A neighbor called it in. She noticed his front door was open and went in to check."

"I can't believe it. I just saw him." I uttered a nervous chuckle and held out the plastic-enclosed receipt. "Obviously, I just saw him. Sorry. He bought a roll of Forevers," I said, and heard a similar uneasy chuckle from Sunni. *How could anything be remotely funny at this moment?*

Sunni straightened and walked behind her desk, a mahogany fixture scarred from years of service. She arranged a pad of paper and pen in front of her and prepared to write. "From the time stamp, it looks like you were among the last to see him."

My head snapped up. A chill went through me as I eyed the blood spatters, most likely right next to my fingerprints. By now I was used to the way Sunni could go into cop mode at the drop of a hat. I always knew she'd eventually come back as my friend, the woman who had welcomed me when I first came back to town, who'd introduced me to quilting and brought me into her group, but I knew enough not to mess with her official persona while she was on the job.

"Does that mean I'm a suspect?" I asked.

"Should it? Make you a suspect?"

"I assumed it was the home burglars."

"Should you be a suspect?" Notwithstanding her petite figure and lovely red hair, Sunni in uniform and all that implied was scary.

"I . . . No, no, no."

She put her hand on my shoulder, a calming gesture. "I'm not worried about you, but we'll be checking the cameras in the post office, just for completeness. I assume they're in working order."

"Uh-huh." I was grateful that I'd been able to talk Ben into an upgrade of our security system. Too bad his agreement had had to depend on a scary incident during my first months as postmaster.

Sunni took the receipt from my hand. I was glad to be rid of it. "This transaction occurred at nine eighteen. That's not long after you opened, right?"

"Right. I opened at nine."

"Can you tell me what Dennis was like this morning?"

"What he was like?"

"How did he seem to you? Nervous in any way? Looking around? Jittery?"

I thought back to Dennis's first appearance in my line of sight, arguing with Joyce Blake as they left the rehearsal; then as he stood in front of my counter, complaining about his hate mail. "He was having a bad day, except for parking."

"What?" Sunni was understandably confused.

"He plays with the Ashcots. He must have arrived early for rehearsal, because he had the best spot in front of the building. After their rehearsal, he put his guitar in the trunk of his car and then came into my lobby."

"And then?" she prompted, her tone suggesting I move on to something more significant.

"Before that, as he was walking toward his car, he was arguing with a colleague at the college. Joyce Blake also plays guitar, but not the big bass version. They're in the same department at the community college. Well, she's in math and he's in physics, but they're sort of combined."

"Could you hear what they were arguing about?"

"Nuh-uh. I could just tell from their body language. But Quinn says Dennis and Joyce are always at odds about the math and science curriculum and the catalogue. I thought it was funny that their classes and schedules are all lumped together in the same department. I guess it's a small college."

I took a breath from what I realized was useless rambling, and dared take another moment of Sunni's time to reach down for my coffee. I needed both my hands to manage a sip. Although Sunni had essentially cleared me already, I felt a chill wind wash over me and zipped up my jacket. More stalling, as a guilty person might do. Was I guilty? Could I have done something to prevent Dennis's murder? Kept him longer at the counter, for example? Maybe if I'd engaged him and tried to help with his mail, he wouldn't have walked in on the robbers.

"You okay?" Sunni asked.

I nodded. "Just flustered, I guess."

Sunni's phone rang, but she ignored it. Maybe Greta would take care of it, I thought, as if it mattered to me. Sunni tapped her pen on the pad in front of her.

"Eventually, he approached your counter . . . ?" she prompted, not as impatient as she might have been. She put the bloody receipt behind her, out of sight, and I relaxed a bit.

"Yes, he came into the lobby and waited in line a short time. When he got to the counter, he wanted to show me some letters he'd received from students. He assumed they were from students, but there were no return addresses, so he couldn't be sure, except they were criticizing his teaching practices. He didn't actually show me the letters, just the envelopes."

Sunni took notes while I described Dennis's plight over the threat of having to appear before a grievance committee. "How did he take it when you couldn't help him?"

"He was a little upset, I guess." I cleared my throat. "A lot upset, truthfully. Then he just asked for the roll of stamps and gave me a hundred-dollar bill. He grumbled some more, then took his change and his receipt and left." I realized I'd moved to the edge of my seat. I sat back now, finished with my report. "How did he die?" I asked. "Did he refuse to cooperate with the robbers, trying to protect his home?"

Sunni rolled over my questions and continued with her own. "Did Dennis mention any possibilities as to who he thought wrote the letters? Did he name any students he thought might have been involved in the mailings?"

"No, nothing like that. Isn't this related to the robberies? I assumed—"

"Usually, a person would have someone in mind, some clue, or warning before getting nasty notes. Or if it was a group, maybe he'd know who the ringleader might be," Sunni said, trying to shake something loose from me.

"He didn't say anything like that. You can't tell me how he died? Or where he was found?"

"We'll be releasing information shortly."

"Do you already have a suspect? I guess not, since you brought me in."

"You're the best thing we have to a material witness, Cassie, someone who interacted with the victim close to his time of death."

"I wish I knew more."

"You might, without being aware of it now. I'm going to ask you to think about Dennis Somerville's time in the post office. Try to remember who else was there, any interaction he may have had with someone other than you. Anything he might have said. Did he talk to someone in line, take a phone call? See if anything else occurs to you, then let me know."

"Of course, of course," I said, dreading the idea of going over the matter again.

I blew out a long breath, as if reliving a few minutes of post office business had already taken a lot out of me. As indeed it had.

I walked the short distance to my car, keeping my head down against the cold wind, and stuffed my hands in my jacket pocket. I'd left my hat and gloves in my car this morning and wished I had them now. Snow had been predicted, but there was no sign of it yet. Dennis Somerville had been murdered, I told myself, so what if a freezing storm blew through? So what if power lines came down or a car was battered by a falling tree? Nothing compared to what had happened to Dennis Somerville.

I crossed at Second Street and passed the still-open salon where the last customers of the day were kibitzing with Tracy and Becca, two of the stylists. Even through the closed door, I could hear the soft rock the owners favored. *Life goes on,* I thought.

When I reached my building, I saw that the lights were out and Ben Gentry was leaving by the side door. Ben had closed up for me, as attested to also by the absence of Old Glory outside. Although he never admitted it, I suspected Ben had a police scanner. No doubt he knew about Dennis and also knew that Sunni had called me in.

"I figured you'd be glad to just go home when you were done at the PD," he said, pulling on thick gloves.

"You're wonderful, Ben," I said, managing a brief hug before he waved me away.

"Course. Terrible thing, with Dennis Somerville, huh?"

I nodded. "It was one thing when it was just robberies, but this . . ."

"Yup. Well, you go on, now. And if you want to sleep in or something in the morning, let me know."

"Thanks, Ben. I'll be fine."

But not too soon, I thought.

On the way home in my car, I replayed this morning's interaction with Dennis Somerville again and again. Not because of Sunni's request, but because I couldn't clear my head of our brief, unpleasant encounter. I saw Dennis hoist his guitar case from the street behind his car. He was such a large, fit man that the task seemed effortless. Maybe that was why he thought he could overpower the robber, tried to be a hero and capture the person who'd been making us all double-lock our doors and add to our home security systems. Maybe he'd seen only one, when in my mind, there was a group. No wonder he'd lost the fight.

Dennis's guitar case was navy blue with some kind of gold braid trim around the edges. Had I mentioned that to Sunni? Might that be an important detail? I'd also noticed that the inside of his trunk had a large cooler that Dennis had to move in order to accommodate the guitar. Was that another detail I should have mentioned?

My cell phone rang, filling my car with a Bach tune, then Quinn's voice when I touched the screen to answer.

"Dinner's ready," he said.

"I'm on my way now," I said.

"I know. I talked to Greta. She said you left ten minutes ago. I was worried. I would have picked you up, but I couldn't leave the roast, you know." He laughed, as he always did when he knew he sounded like a 1950s housewife.

"There's a roast?"

"Well, no, but you won't go hungry."

"I'm sure I won't." In fact, I doubted I'd be able to eat at all. "I'm pulling onto Birch Street now."

"Coffee and appetizers waiting."

For a minute, I was able to let go of the Dennis Somerville murder and be thankful for the life I still had.

I could smell tarragon chicken as I climbed the steps to my front porch. I looked at the ages-old Nantucket pine swing Quinn had found for me, its seat now covered with a thin layer of ice. Why did everything have to be so cold tonight? Quinn opened the door before I could think of getting out my key. He hugged me and led me to my favorite easy chair, treating me with great gentleness and compassion.

"I don't know why this is hitting me so hard," I said,

flopping onto the seat. "It's not as if Dennis was my best friend."

"What's the point of calling anyone a friend if they're not all best ones?"

"I didn't think of that." I accepted a napkin holding a cracker and a hunk of Gouda and set it on the end table next to me. I thought of times I'd worked with Dennis. He was in charge of the arrangements for using the community room and the official renter of the post office box for the Ashcots. "I wish I could have helped him more."

"What could you have done?" he asked. From his tone, a rhetorical question. But I answered it anyway.

I briefed Quinn on Dennis's problem mail. "We have facilities and services beyond my little counter where I give out stamps and the little wall where I stuff post office boxes. Not everyone knows that the USPS has forensics laboratory services. They do things like analyzing paper and ink, restoring impressions on paper, detecting altered or counterfeit writing. Linda has been involved in lots of these cases. She's even been able to return money to people who were fleeced of their life savings by mail fraud."

"Have the postal inspectors handled lots of cases of teacher-student relationships, where students don't like their grades?"

"No, but—" The doorbell cut me off. Only then did I notice that the dining room table had been set for three. "I forgot we're having company."

Quinn nodded and opened the door. "I hope you don't mind," he said.

"She'd better not mind," said the chief of police as she entered my living room.

"We can't have our top cop going hungry," Quinn said.

"As long as she's not going to arrest me," I said, and accepted another warm embrace, counting my blessings.

Sunni made it clear that she had to eat and run, but not before dessert. "It's going to be an all-nighter," she said. "I promised Greta I'd bring her a doggy bag. Do you mind?"

"Not at all," Quinn said. He went to the kitchen to fill the take-out order. Since he'd shopped, bought, and cooked the food, I didn't feel that I had to add my permission.

I'd picked at my chicken and passed on the rich-looking mound of mashed potatoes. "It's horrible," I said. Fortunately, Quinn seemed to understand that I wasn't referring to his cooking.

"You're thinking you could have prevented Dennis's murder, aren't you?" Sunni said.

I nodded. "You said it yourself. I was one of the last people to see him."

"What could you have done?"

"Uh-oh. Don't get her started," Quinn said, returning with containers for Greta. He made one more trip and came back with apple pie and dessert plates. He hadn't tried to hide the pink box from the great bakery in town. "I leave the baking to the pros," he often said.

"I could at least have offered to look into our policies on mail fraud," I said. "Maybe Dennis's letters came under the heading of official hate mail." I gave Sunni a summary of the role of the USPS forensics lab, as I'd done for Quinn.

"Does the USPS handle teacher-student relationships?"

"My question exactly." Quinn beamed, pleased that his thinking was in league with that of the chief of police, I guessed.

"Most of Linda's cases were about deceptive ads, like lotteries, mail theft, that kind of thing," I admitted.

"In all honesty, can you say that Dennis's letters might have been something of interest to a national forensics lab? Or that they had anything to do with his death?" Quinn asked, directing his questions to both Sunni and me, his head ping-ponging between us.

"It doesn't matter. The point is that I didn't even try to find out. Instead, I just dismissed him. I threw up my hands and said, 'Not my job.'"

"Cassie—" he began.

I held up my hand. "And, if you must know, yes, there's a chance that I did contribute to what happened. What if the burglars were almost finished? And just then Dennis comes home. If I'd asked him to wait while I checked out his case, then he wouldn't have stormed out, angry and frustrated over his post office experience, ready to take on even a burglar."

Sunni shook her head. "That's some creative thinking, Cassie, even for you."

"Meaning?" I was ready for battle, but when Quinn chose that moment to take his seat and put his hand on mine, I knew I'd better take a breath.

Sunni had finished her pie in record time and now pushed her chair from the table. "I wish I could say more. But let me tell you this much. Dennis's murder was not a matter of bad timing. It's very unlikely that he walked in on a robbery."

"I get it," Quinn said. "It doesn't fit the pattern, does it? They've always had impeccable timing at knowing when the owners would be away."

"That's right. Except for one time. They were interrupted in one of those new condos over on the west side and they dropped everything and ran."

"They didn't hang around and wrestle with the owner," Quinn said, thinking it through. "And they certainly didn't kill him."

Sunni shook her head. "No, they didn't. And the owner thought it might be kids, they moved so quickly."

"You said 'they.' There was more than one burglar?" Quinn asked.

"I'm using the universal 'they,'" Sunni said. "The homeowner heard a noise in the back bedroom and saw a couple of chairs turned over, but by the time he got back there, whoever it was had gone out a window. So, no, we're still not sure whether we have one or more perps, except that it seems it would take at least one accomplice to coordinate and carry out so many incidents."

I'd been thinking things through, also, and had my own theory. "Then it's possible Dennis's murderer was the one who wrote the letters he showed me. All the more reason I should have investigated."

"Is that true, Sunni?" Quinn asked.

Sunni shrugged. Something in her eyes gave me the clue I needed.

"You have those letters in custody, don't you?" I said, realizing they would have been taken away by her crime scene guys.

She shrugged again.

"Blink once for yes, twice for no," Quinn said.

But I already knew the answer.

I convinced Quinn he didn't need to help with the dishes. "Cooks don't clean up" had been our rule, and I saw no need to change it tonight.

Besides, I wanted Quinn to leave. I needed time to think about everything. Especially what Sunni might or might not have been implying about the student or students' letters. It was clear that Sunni had brought me into her office this evening not only because I'd had dealings with Dennis today, but because she'd found the letters and thought there might be some connection.

I decided it was time to have a serious, rational talk with her about what the USPS could do to help. Maybe if I approached the idea without whining about bearing some guilt, she'd be more inclined to let me work with her.

But not tonight. I'd give her time to get caught up. I also ruled out returning to the post office to pick up the piles of handbooks and manuals stored in my desk. The most I could do now was try Linda, but I had to be satisfied with leaving a message.

I got ready for bed, turned on the television in my bedroom, and caught the late-night local news. I listened intently as a well-groomed young woman stood in front of an oversize map of North Ashcot and gave her report.

"A series of home invasions turned deadly today in North Ashcot when an instructor at the community college was found shot to death in his home. Apparently, Dr. Dennis Somerville"—the background shifted to include an image of Dennis in a jacket and tie, undoubtedly a staff photo—"came home to find a burglary in progress."

Finally, another detail. Dennis was shot. No surprise that reporters had their ways of getting questions answered when, ahem, best friends of the chief couldn't.

The somber voice continued. "Police say that the forty-seven-year-old physics professor surprised the burglars and . . ."

I turned the set off. How do you know? I asked it, and waited for sleep.

Unnecessary worries swirled in my head, refusing to be replaced by woolly sheep jumping over fences. Who would take over Dennis's physics classes? Did schools have backup teachers ready to step in at times like this? How was Dennis's son holding up? If I remembered correctly, he was in college out of state. I'd seen him during school vacations when he sometimes played with the Ashcots. Dennis's wife, Charlene, a nurse, had died a few years ago.

Since the campus wasn't a crime scene, I doubted they'd close it for very long, perhaps to accommodate a tribute of some kind, however. I thought of the argument Dennis had had with Joyce Blake from the mathematics side of the department. Was she feeling as awful as I did, stuck forever knowing that her last interaction with Dennis was contentious?

The only thought that relaxed me was that there was

still time for me to help find who killed Dennis, burglar or no burglar.

As I drifted off, a plan took shape. I wanted to write it down so I wouldn't forget, but in my semisleep state my arms were as heavy as a mailman's sack and I couldn't reach the pad of paper. I'd have to remember.

5

On Tuesday morning, Ben sent me a text. Not a phone message, which meant his lovely young niece, Natalie, was visiting. He offered me the morning off if I needed to recover from Dennis's death. I knew that part of his motivation in wanting to work the desk was to keep the truth of his official retirement from Natalie. After all, Ben had known Dennis much longer than I had, so it would be he who would need recovery time. But the three of us—Ben, Natalie, and I—had been maintaining the ruse that Ben was still in charge. It was fine with me.

I texted back my thanks and was only too happy to have time to put my plan into action. For once, I remembered a plan that had come to me, practically fully formed, in last night's half-dream state.

I wasn't sure whether Mercedes and the other Ashcots

would be rehearsing this morning, or perhaps simply meeting to discuss their future without their bass guitarist. In any case, I didn't want to show up at the community room attached to the post office, lest Ben see me and change his mind about subbing for me. I called Mercedes instead and asked her to meet me at Mahican's coffee shop, where Ben had not and would never set foot. "Too uppity," he claimed. "With all the fancy names. Macchiatos, freddos, whatever. Coffee's coffee." And that was that.

Quinn called to check up on me as I was leaving for my nine o'clock with Mercedes.

"I'm doing okay," I said. "Ben's filling in for me."

"Anything I can do for you?"

I paused, not wanting to share my plan with Quinn, but needing his help. I tried for a middle ground. "I'd like to talk to you about antiques."

"Ha. I think I can do that. What kind of antiques?"

"More like the history of things. Or a period in history. Remember that bronze bust you found for me, of the British postal reformer, Sir Rowland Hill? We were talking about how expensive it had been to send mail in England at the time. Up to a day's wage for a working-class guy, right? Until Hill worked to introduce inexpensive postage. And they cheered for him on the opening day of the Penny Post. So interesting."

"January 10, 1840," Quinn said, unable to resist joining me in a discussion that related to history, with a piece of trivia on the side. He then broke into a heavy sigh, followed by a long pause—things that told me he knew what I was up to, even across telephone lines. "You're not going to do anything stupid, are you?"

"Whatever do you mean?" I asked, feigning grave offense.

"Oh, I don't know. Can you spell *investigate*?" he asked, emphasizing each syllable.

"I'm not a cop," I said. "I just realize that I need to broaden my interests, and you're such a great resource for that."

"And you say Ben will be at the office, so you have the whole morning free?"

"Uh-huh."

"You're going to tell Mercedes you'll give that talk for her at the college, aren't you?"

I was stunned but thought it was worth a try to stall a bit longer. "That's quite a leap."

"So you can nose around the campus. Where the late Dennis Somerville happened to work." He took a breath. "Cassie."

"I guess I'm predictable, huh?"

"I know I can't stop you. Can you promise me that you will be careful?"

"Of course." I'd have promised anything. I couldn't wait to get started on my plan.

Mercedes joined me at the café downtown, wearing one of her signature cold-weather capes. With her severe hairstyle and a bright, flared garment covering her stocky body, she drew mixed appraisals from the patrons of Mahican's. It was clear that she didn't mind the attention. I thought it likely that with a name like Mercedes, and her interesting, slight overbite, she'd had a dramatic start in life.

"Well, that was awful," Mercedes began, draping her cape over the back of a chair. "It was more of a funeral than a rehearsal." She sat down heavily and blew out what seemed like an exhausted breath. "Everyone's in shock over Dennis."

I nodded in understanding. "Are you going ahead with your appearance at the Valentine's Day dance?"

"The consensus is yes, so far, but we thought we should talk to Dyson, Dennis's son, to see how he feels about it. He's probably a wreck. And there's his sister-in-law, Charlene's sister, but I think they haven't been on speaking terms."

"She's not local, is she?"

"No, she and her husband live out West somewhere. I know that Dennis could be difficult. He had his ways and I think one of the reasons for their estrangement was his inability to meet his in-laws halfway."

"I wasn't aware of that."

"Charlene was close to her family and it seemed there was always something that Dennis had a problem with, every holiday or celebration. He had no family himself and didn't seem to feel any obligation to honor Charlene's. There were years when they didn't see each other at all. I never got the whole story."

Rather than comment, I took a bite of blueberry muffin. I was always taken aback at how quickly after death, a person's life and character became the object of great interest and discussion. The saying about not speaking ill of the dead is seldom followed.

Mercedes had started in on her apple turnover, a specialty of the house. Something Ben would love, if he could get past the nonfat lattes "with room." When she picked up her chatting, Mercedes switched off Dennis's personal life and moved to his murder. "I can't believe it, Cassie. I have to admit I haven't paid attention to those robberies that have been going on all over town. You always figure it's not going to impact you or any of your friends, so you bury your head. And then something like this happens." She let out a long, exasperated sigh.

I couldn't decide how to evaluate Mercedes's responses. She'd come in upset, then lapsed into criticism of her deceased friend and his ability to relate to his in-laws. I chalked everything up to shock and to the fact that we all express our emotions in different ways. Good thing it wasn't my job to judge.

I didn't disabuse Mercedes of her assumption that Dennis's murder was tied to the string of robberies. For all I knew, she was right. I had only innuendo from Sunni and my own imagination that said otherwise.

While Mercedes and I were talking, other musicians had entered the café and made their way to the counter. Now Joyce Blake and Shirley Peterson came to our table, both without their guitars, and pulled up chairs. The pair were polar opposites on any pop psychology scale, with Joyce a tell-it-like-it-is complainer and Shirley a perpetually optimistic smiler. Although I'd been counting on discussing my proposed postal history talk with Mercedes, I didn't feel I could dismiss the other two women. Besides, maybe Dennis's coworkers at the college could shed some light on the letters that preceded his murder. I hoped my companions couldn't tell that I was operating in investigator mode. As I saw it, my desire to help in bringing Dennis's killer to justice was part of my sorrow and regret over his death.

"Poor Dennis," Shirley said, propping her elbows on the table. "Dennis was the best teacher." This was Shirley's first year of retirement from teaching high school biology, and she'd taken up the guitar in earnest. "He was so patient. Once I retired I wanted to learn the guitar and he was so generous to me. I feel so awful about what happened."

"You can imagine how I feel," Joyce said, still wrapped in a long winter coat and a scarf in a clashing color. With Joyce nothing ever matched. When she was onstage, she could have been the long-haired girl in any of the seventies bands I'd seen on videos, with rainbow-colored ribbons in her hair. "The last time I saw Dennis, yesterday morning, I was chewing him out over the curriculum. As if it was a matter of life and death whether calculus is or is not a prerequisite for physics. I said some stupid things."

"That's not all you should remember," Shirley said. "You two worked together well for years."

Mercedes and Shirley continued to assure Joyce that she should forget that last argument and try to focus on the better memories. I decided not to share my own final, contentious interaction with Dennis. I wondered if any of the three women knew of the letters he'd brought to me. I thought back to who was in the post office when Dennis showed them to me. I remembered that he'd come to the counter immediately following the Bertrands with their post office box crisis. Mercedes came after Dennis, but there had been a few other customers in between, so she might not have heard his low-volume rant. I suspected she would have mentioned it if she had.

When the barista called their names, Joyce and Shirley took their coffees to go and we uttered good-byes all around, adding on "take care" each time.

I'd hoped Mercedes would pursue her request for me to give a talk to her class, but apparently Dennis's murder and other events of her life had taken over her thoughts. I'd have to broach the subject myself. I couldn't think of a smooth segue except to get up for refills and come back as if I'd had a sudden idea.

I plunked a fresh coffee in front of Mercedes. "Are you still interested in having me speak to your class about postal history?" I asked.

Mercedes's expression brightened, not merely from the coffee, I hoped. "Of course, of course. I'm delighted. I thought you were brushing me off yesterday."

There was nothing like being wanted, and Mercedes's response was almost as rewarding as an attaboy from the postmaster general. "You caught me at a busy time, but I think I can fit it in," I said.

I felt Mercedes could see right through my pretense. Didn't everyone in town know I had essentially a nine-to-five job, with Ben to help, and one hobby that I'd just taken up—quilting, at the behest of the chief of police? I was new to the quilting group and hadn't become as obsessed as Sunni or some of the other members, who bought fabric the way I bought takeout when Quinn wasn't around to cook.

In short, I had lots of free time.

"Great," Mercedes said. "How soon can you be ready? We meet Tuesdays and Thursdays. I'd hoped you could take this Thursday's class."

I gulped. I'd been thinking more like May or June, but, of course, the sooner I got to campus to look around Dennis's environment—my real purpose for the trip—the better. "I can do Thursday, but I'm wondering if you'd mind if I visited the room ahead of time." I screwed my face into a nervous wince, hardly faking. "It would make me less nervous."

Mercedes waved her hand. "No problem. We meet at eleven this morning. Though I don't think there's going to be much class work going on today. I fully expect the dean to call an assembly to announce some kind of service for Dennis." She took a gulp of coffee and swallowed hard. "Can you be there a little before?"

"That works for me."

"Good. You can stay for a few minutes, or as long as you like, and get a feel for the class."

I ran the timeline in my head. If I didn't have to be at my real job until one, that would give me at least an hour on campus. "Perfect. I'll drive over myself and meet you."

Mercedes took out a notepad and drew a quick sketch of the campus, marking an X on the building I'd be visiting, Mary Draper Hall. "I'll see you there," she said. "I'm so glad you're up for this. And remember, it doesn't have to be restricted to Victorian England. The U.S. was around then, too." She laughed and flung her cape over her shoulders, just missing my coffee mug, and left the café.

Everything was going as planned. I'd managed to arrange to be on campus twice in the next couple of days. Now all I had to do was make good use of the time there.

And prepare for a lecture to a group of college students. I shuddered, hoping it was a friendly, intimate group. I'd forgotten to ask the size of the class. I was committed now in any case, all for the sake of speedy justice, I told myself. No wonder I had to order a third cup of coffee.

Mercedes suggested I allow a half hour to drive to campus and park. I still had time to call Quinn.

"Are you busy?" I asked.

"Oh yeah, February in the Berkshires is brimming over with tourists, wanting to see the bare trees."

"Their loss. They don't realize how beautiful birches are in winter."

"Neither did I until I moved here. Birch trees don't do well in the drier parts of California."

"Since Ashcot's Attic is not crawling with foliage fans, is it okay if I come by the shop and talk about my class? I meet them on Thursday."

"You're not wasting any time, are you?"

"I can be at the shop in ten minutes. Does that work for you?"

"Why do I have the feeling I'm aiding and abetting a potential felon?"

"That's harsh."

"Obstructing justice."

"That's usually a misdemeanor, like telling a state trooper your speedometer is broken and that's why you might have been speeding. A felony would be—"

"Okay, and a misdemeanor doesn't worry you?"

"I see what I'm doing more as participatory democracy."

"Wow."

"I knew you'd understand."

It was closer to fifteen minutes by the time I gathered my February outerwear and made my way to the antiques store that Quinn managed for its nearly retired owner. Geography was in my favor, since his store was on the way to campus. The way I was scheduling my morning off, you might think I was a busy executive instead of a simple postmaster who at times took on the role of detective.

Ashcot's Attic, housed in a two-story, two-toned green building with a front right on Main Street, offered a broad range of antiques. *Cluttered* was the operative word for any antiques store, I imagined, and Quinn's place near the edge of town was no exception. Large mahogany and walnut glass-fronted cabinets butted against each other, vying for attention for their contents: metal toys, novelty salt and pepper shakers, elaborate ceramic figurines, trays of costume jewelry. A row of bone china cups sat precariously along the ledge of a bookcase that towered over nonmatching, plush easy chairs. I imagined the dust of centuries weighing them down. I spied a small pine end table with a shelf and single drawer, which I'd contributed to the inventory, from Aunt Tess's estate. I told myself once more that I didn't need it.

Neatly printed signs throughout the store advised that the professionals of Ashcot's Attic would happily conduct an on-site home sale, taking full responsibility for categorizing, staging, cleaning, appraising, and displaying items attractively, to help maximize sales. They would do all the advertising, including Internet and local newspapers, and an extensive customer and client e-mailing. Such a deal.

I'd already taken advantage of the Attic's services. I'd returned to my hometown after all those years in Boston to take care of the aunt who raised me. I now owned that house, where I grew up. When Aunt Tess died soon after my return, Quinn had helped me sort through her belongings, keeping what had sentimental value, passing on the rest.

"Still thinking about that pine table?" Quinn asked, startling me from behind.

I recovered quickly and shook my head. "Just visiting it."

He was dressed in jeans and a plaid flannel shirt that could have come from his own racks, near the back of the store where a closet served as a dressing room. Never a suit-and-tie kind of guy, in his words, he enjoyed his comfortable sweatshirts and corduroys. Quinn invited me to a corner of the store where he had what he called an office, defined by a desk and chair on an area rug. He moved a second chair onto the rug and pulled out a large, leather-covered volume from a shelf, an illustrated encyclopedia of all things Victorian. When we were seated, he opened the tome to a page he had bookmarked.

"I found something I think you'll like. It's a reference to an amusing article entitled 'Valentine's Day at the Post-Office,' written in part by Dickens for an issue of a weekly magazine he founded."

"A perfect title," I said.

"Listen to this. 'Swains in very blue coats and nymphs in very opaque muslin, coarse caricatures and tender verses.'" Quinn read the passage from a page that showcased Dickens's sense of humor as he discussed the image of Cupid peering from behind paper roses. "There's more on darts, also," he said in closing.

"It's great, Quinn. But I'm going to try to fit in more about U.S. postal history." I brushed nonexistent lint from the sleeves of my navy blue USPS jacket—I always felt dusty in Quinn's shop. I'd dressed prepared to head for work after my Attic visit.

"Maybe you'll like giving a talk so much that you'll do more of them."

I sneered. "I doubt it. Can you copy part of that article for me?"

"Already done." He turned to another bookmarked page and read a passage about other images, like flaming hearts, all in the name of St. Valentine. And there was more, going back even further to the fifteenth century when a duke mailed his fiancée a love letter while he was imprisoned in the Tower of London.

When he started rattling off figures on the expansion of postal services in the United States—from about twenty-eight thousand post offices in 1860 to more than sixty thousand thirty years later—I gave out the loudest "ahem" I could manage.

"I thought you wanted data on the United States during that period."

"I did. I do." I looked at my watch.

"Had enough, huh?" he asked.

"For now. I have to get to the campus."

"Will you be back for lunch?"

I held up a protein bar. "On the road, I'm afraid."

I left the Attic, promising once again to be careful and to report on any progress I might make. Quinn walked me to my car and handed the Victoriana volume to me through the window.

"Carry this around. It will give you some gravitas on a campus."

"I thought my uniform would do that," I said, smoothing out the postal seal on my sleeve.

"You can never have too much gravitas," he said.

I agreed.

6

I entered the campus at the parking lot on the north side, closest to the X that Mercedes had drawn on her sketch. I hadn't been on the community college campus since I toured it with my class when I was a junior at Ashcot High. The school had prospered since I visited. At the time, only three plain redbrick buildings around a quad accommodated all the classes, science labs, and administrative offices.

Now I saw from the poster-size map at the entrance that three additional buildings had been added, all with blue solar panels; plus a swimming pool, a tennis complex, an environmental science center, and an arts center. I was confused by the presence of green dollar signs here and there on the map until I read the legend. The money symbols identified the locations of ATMs. A lot had changed in twenty years.

All the buildings were named after Revolutionary War heroes and heroines, not unusual throughout Massachusetts. I'd grown up thinking the War for Independence was the most important in history. I could remember writing essays in grammar school on General Nathanael Greene and the Battle of Brandywine; on nighttime messenger Paul Revere; and on revolutionary propagandist Thomas Paine of "Common Sense" fame. To say that the former thirteen colonies, and Massachusetts in particular, were parochial in outlook might have been taken as a compliment by my grammar and high school teachers.

Not many other souls were strolling the pathways on this cold morning, most of them seeming not much older than high schoolers, but once I passed thirty I no longer trusted my ability to guess ages with any accuracy.

The few students I did encounter were stuck to their phones. No one nodded or greeted me. I wondered if any of them had the new app Ben's niece had shown me—an app that had to do with personal safety.

"All my roommates have one," Natalie had said, zipping her fingers over her phone's screen. "It's worth the peace of mind when you're jogging, or on a blind date, or a late movie. One of my friends uses it even if she's getting in a cab alone. You get to choose contacts and messages, like 'I'm walking to my car' and then a time frame."

"And if you fail to check in, some kind of alarm goes off?"

Natalie had confirmed my guess, adding much more about "guardians" (the contacts you choose), GPS trackers, panic buttons, and direct links to emergency help lines; all features that came with a subscription.

Times had changed even more than I thought.

I located Mary Draper Hall on a sign at an intersection and followed the arrow. Mercedes had explained that the great Ms. Draper was famous for harboring, feeding, and providing clothing for American soldiers. She was said to have torn up her blankets and bedsheets and used the fabric to make jackets and shirts for the boys in the army. I figured she deserved at least a college building named after her.

My head down against a chilly wind, lost in thoughts about times when Dennis Somerville had walked these paths, oblivious of any danger coming his way, I nearly bumped into someone coming in the opposite direction. In a minute, it was clear that it was no accident—the person meant to get my attention. I looked up into the suspicious eyes of the chief of police.

"Special delivery mail?" Chief of Police Sunni Smargon addressed me with a smirk.

I couldn't quite suppress a laugh. "It's part of a new outreach program by the USPS, to improve customer relations, reaching out to the community."

"Funny, I thought we were the ones who protect and serve the community," Sunni said, running her hand over the patch on her jacket.

If I weren't so intimidated, I would have run my hand over my own patch. So intimidated, in fact, I almost forgot I had a legitimate reason for being on campus. "I'm scheduled to give a talk in a history class this week. I'm a guest speaker for Professor Mercedes Davis," I said, cocking my head in a faux pompous way.

"Of course you are."

"Really. I'm headed to Draper Hall"—I pointed to the building at the end of the path—"to check out the facilities. It's where I'll be giving my talk."

"Uh-huh."

We seemed to be at a stalemate, so I decided to waste no more time. "I suppose you're interviewing Dennis's coworkers here? Have you found anything that helps with the investigation?"

"Besides protecting and serving, we're also the ones who ask the questions."

My mouth went dry. I saw only the tiniest glint of amusement in Sunni's eyes and I didn't want to be ushered off campus, an unseemly sight for a prospective guest lecturer. "I probably should get going," I said. "I have a meeting with Mercedes in a few minutes."

Sunni cleared her throat and shuffled her feet. Her expression had turned pleasant. "Cassie, will you do me a favor?"

"Anything," I said, then realized the favor might be for me to beat it off campus.

"See if you can find out, without being too obvious, who else has seen the letters Dennis received. The ones he showed you in the post office, and especially if they have any idea who might have sent them. I'm getting this town-versus-gown feeling, where I represent the town and the faculty gowns are zipping up when they see me."

"Do you have those letters? Did you find them among Dennis's things?" *Oops.* There was that frown again. It was never a good idea to ask a police chief, or any other detective, a question. I should have known better. "I mean, of course, I'll do my best to find out and let you know."

I stopped short of saluting, and Sunni and I parted company.

I waited for Mercedes in the small lobby area at the front of Mary Draper Hall. Young men and women sat reading or talking on sofas and wide chairs. I couldn't hear conversations, but it was clear that a kind of pall had settled over the gathering. Faces were solemn; voices were soft. The only signs of ordinary life were the unmistakable rings and pings of cell phones and the reboot noise of computers.

When Mercedes arrived, we began a trek down a long well-lit hallway toward her classroom. It was clear that she was proud of her school and this relatively new building. "A whole building for classrooms," she said. "We've needed this for years. One semester, I taught an advanced seminar on the Enlightenment in the waiting room outside the admissions office."

We passed rooms of various sizes on both sides of the corridor, most with seating that was more flexible than the usual rows of desk-chair combinations that I was used to in college. I noted roundtable-style arrangements as well as some rooms that were tableless, with circles of chairs only. Most rooms had students, probably waiting for class to begin, all talking in more hushed tones than I would expect on a normal day.

"Have the students been informed about Dennis's death?" I asked.

Mercedes nodded. "The dean called an assembly at ten fifteen this morning. She'd notified the faculty first.

I was a little late for that, but I knew what the announcement was." She paused to catch her breath, as if we'd been sprinting down the hall. "A lot of the students had heard about it already, too, but the ones who come a distance didn't know."

"Is that why it's so quiet in here?"

She nodded. "I stopped at the bookstore and found everyone whispering. There were no details given, but you could tell people were sober, and also relieved that the crime hadn't happened on campus."

How considerate of Dennis's killer, I thought, choosing not to turn an entire campus into a crime scene. I was conscious of my need to query Mercedes about the letters Dennis had received, but it hadn't been easy to interrupt. I took advantage of a pause in her narrative. "You know, Dennis came to the post office yesterday, after your rehearsal."

I hoped she'd chime in with having seen him in line and heard him grumbling about his letters. Instead, she gave no indication that she'd heard me.

"A lot of the eleven o'clock classes have been cancelled," Mercedes said, continuing her own thread. "I'm going to keep my students for only a few minutes. Unless they want to talk about it. About Dennis. I think Thursday is soon enough to pick up on our course content." She turned to look at me. "That's you."

How well I knew. Since arriving on campus, I'd made an effort to notice the students, to try to see what they were reading or focusing on, as if to make friends with them before my talk. I tried to recall what I'd been like at their age. Not a happy kid. I'd lost my parents in a car crash before my sixteenth birthday and had managed to remain depressed and unsociable for a long time after. I didn't get my bearings until at least a couple of years into college. Although I maintained a decent GPA, it would have been hard to interest me in being a guest lecturer of any kind.

Mercedes and I had come to the end of the corridor, to a large tiered lecture hall, and entered on the bottom level. Steps led up to rows and rows of desk-chair combinations that filled the equivalent of another floor. The twenty or so students chatted in low voices, looking lost in the vast room. I couldn't help thinking that their professor's murder was the reason for their muffled tones.

"This room is our largest," Mercedes said. "It has all the modern features. Retractable folding wall, highly rated sound partitions, projection screens."

As Mercedes waved her arms to point out various features, more students filed in, chatting at the same hushed levels I didn't expect. I noted about an equal number of males and females, practically all in jeans and heavy jackets. They swung their backpacks, hats, gloves, and scarves over chairs and attached desktops.

"And, of course, the podium is smart," Mercedes said.

"Like a smartphone, with apps and all?"

"Pretty much. And so is what looks like an ordinary whiteboard." She pointed to a large board at the front of the room. "It's smart, also. Any program that works on your computer or phone can be used on the board, audio included."

"Impressive. Where's your classroom?"

"This is my classroom."

I felt my stomach clutch. By now the room had filled up. I tried to estimate how many students were present but lost track in my nervousness. "How many people does it hold?" I asked.

"Two hundred or so." Mercedes must have noticed my distress. She quickly added, "But there are only eighty in my class."

I drew in a gaspy breath. "I was thinking more like eight. Maybe eighteen."

Mercedes laughed, a dramatic laugh befitting her cape, which she now swung off her shoulders. "Oh my. You're not bothered by the numbers, are you?"

"No, not at all." I always stutter this way, I said silently.

"They're a very friendly group. Let me introduce you."

"That's okay. I really need to get to work," I said. "I'll be in touch."

I left the room before Mercedes knew what was happening. Lucky for me, at the same time, a small group of students had come down the steps and made their way to the smart desk to talk to her.

I slipped out and ducked into the nearest women's room. I was impressed and relieved that this one had an anteroom with a couch. Just what I needed. But what was I going to need before lecturing to eighty people? Or after?

Who knew that an institutional couch could be so comfortable? I woke up, afraid I'd overslept and left Ben alone at work all afternoon, but I'd nodded off for only ten minutes. A peculiar reaction to my stress.

I'd come close to asking Mercedes where Dennis's office was, but I lost my nerve. So far, my trip to campus was as useful as if I'd slept in, in my own bed instead of a restroom couch. I hoped the directory would be some help. I walked back to the poster-size sign at the edge of the parking lot and looked on the map. I found that faculty offices were in Patrick Henry Hall, at the opposite end of the campus. My car, on the other hand, was right in front of me. I could be home in a half hour, have lunch with Quinn, and get started on my talk. Or I could seek out Dennis's office on the off chance that I'd even be able to enter it and the still smaller chance that it would give me a clue about Dennis's death.

Decision time.

I left the building and took a seat on a wooden slatted bench near the directory. I was sure the landscape planners didn't expect much loitering on the bench in the middle of February, but it served my purpose.

Decision made.

I called Ben. "Are you about to close for lunch?" I asked.

"Yup. Going to put the sign up."

"Yes, can you use the one that says one thirty?"

"Okay. Sure you don't want me to come back?"

"I'm sure. One thirty will be fine for me. Thanks a lot for this morning." I would have loved for Ben to finish off the day behind the counter, but I knew it would be hard on him, and, more important, I wanted to save the favor for a time when I might need him more urgently.

"Did you get some rest?" he asked.

"Oh yes." If ten minutes on a restroom couch is

enough, I said to myself. "I made the most of the morning, and thank you again. Enjoy the rest of your visit with Natalie."

"Yeah, I might just take a nap while she hits the outlet stores. Oh, the chief of police came by. Did she catch up with you?"

"She sure did."

"Hmm," Ben said, but I signed off before he could ask any questions and turned back toward the buildings on the south side.

The trees were bare of leaves, and the wind whipped through the few buildings on campus. I kept my head down and my jacket closed tight, and moved my scarf up to cover part of my mouth. Typical cold-weather walking in New England. A few yards down the path, I saw a figure coming from behind a tree, headed toward me. I lifted my head and identified Hank Blackwood, former member of the Ashcots, also with a scarf up to his chin. Odd. I thought Hank had retired from teaching as well as from the music group, as he'd reminded me this morning.

"Cassie Miller, how strange to run into you here."

"I was thinking the same," I said.

"Yeah, well, I was just visiting some of my old buddies. All us professors in the math department get together once a week for coffee and talk about the latest in math developments. You know, the new papers on group theory, conformal geometry, that kind of thing. I like to keep up on things."

"That's nice," I said, making a move toward continuing my walk. Hank turned from his own path and joined me.

"It's pretty somber around here today," he said.

"It is."

"Awful thing, huh? You'd think the cops would have cracked down on that gang by now," he said.

Hank was shorter than me by a few inches and therefore had to hurry to keep up with my stride. Not that I deliberately tried to make it hard for him to accompany me.

"Gang?" I asked.

"Well, I'm assuming it's a gang doing all those robberies. I guess that's the drawback of a small town, right? So few law enforcement personnel. Pittsfield, on the other hand, has three full patrol shifts, plus a detective bureau, narcotics, you name it. I told you I'm playing with a group of musicians there, right?"

"Right" seemed the only appropriate answer, other than *Too bad Dennis didn't live in Pittsfield*, which seemed to be what Hank was implying.

Hank had run out of breath trying to keep up with me, I suspected, and paused on the path. He continued to extol the virtues of big-city life in Pittsfield. I looked at my watch and started walking again. "I'm on my lunch hour, so I'd better get moving."

"Oh, sure sorry. Well, good to talk to you, Madam Postmistress," he said, with a slight bow.

I winced. "You, too."

I stepped up my pace, berating myself. Why hadn't I queried Hank? Because I didn't like him very much? A little too pompous for my taste. Was this the short person syndrome I'd read about? People trying to make up for lack of height. It certainly didn't hold for the petite chief of police, a good six inches shorter than me and most men, but in no way full of herself.

This made me a triple failure as a good citizen or a detective: I hadn't given Dennis the attention he should have gotten as a customer, I hadn't fulfilled Sunni's request to find out if Mercedes knew about Dennis's letters, and I didn't think of asking Hank a question or two. I had one more chance. Maybe something useful would come out of my visit to Patrick Henry Hall and the site of Dennis's office.

First, I needed some food. Sustenance would be required if I was going to keep from being a quadruple failure.

7

I'd been smart enough to remember the knife and fork symbol along with the dollar signs on the poster directory. Food and money—still two important resources for college kids.

I stopped at the straightforwardly named Student Union Building. Maybe the naming committee had run out of heroes and heroines to honor, or maybe they'd come to a stalemate between Abigail Adams and Martha Washington and used a functional designation instead. A nice blast of hot air greeted me as soon as I opened the second set of doors and I stuffed my knitted cap in one pocket and my gloves in the other.

An array of food aromas also hit me immediately and I knew I was in the right place. Or the wrong place, if it was gourmet food I was after. But all I wanted was a stopgap until Quinn cooked dinner this evening. I followed the scent to the basement level, where I grabbed a prepackaged turkey sandwich and chips and sat in a corner. On a better day I might have eaten while I walked, but that would have meant removing my gloves outside. Not an option today.

It was noon and the cafeteria was crowded, the noise level high. I'd expected the cacophony in an area like this one, with high ceilings and linoleum flooring. I tuned in to the conversations closest to me. Listening for incriminating comments such as *Professor Somerville was a bad teacher.* I doubted it would happen. Even if a student letter writer were responsible for Dennis Somerville's death—more likely to me than the North Ashcot burglar—it was beyond unlikely that I'd discover it on my quick visit to Dennis's campus. On the other hand, the chief of police did ask me to investigate, I reminded myself. Sort of.

I leaned a little closer to the table next to me, but all I heard were remarks about the worst spaghetti and meatballs *ever*, and the too-high price of a bag with six potato chips. *Totally.* I fared better leaning in the other direction when a young couple expressed regret over Dennis Somerville's death.

"It's so hard to believe," the young woman said. "I mean, I didn't have him for a class or anything, but still."

"Yeah, well, it happens," the young man answered, drawing in a noisy sip of something from a straw in a large paper cup.

"It's one of our faculty members," the woman said, annoyed, as if to prod him into sympathy.

"Yeah," the young man answered, still no feeling in his voice.

I tuned them all out and pulled out my phone. I found four messages, three from Linda. I was a failure not only as a postal employee and detective, but also as a friend. I'd underestimated the level of crisis Linda had reached. There'd been a time, when we worked together, that we would have cut out of the office and found a spot to talk for hours, until whichever one of us was hurting had found a way out of it. Now all we had were snatches of Skype and texts, and it wasn't working. Add to that, it had taken me more than a year to return to Boston for a visit, attributable to the lack of confidence I had that I wouldn't just stay there, and perhaps beg my ex-fiancé to take me back.

I sent a quick text to Linda.

so sorry. rushed all morning. skype tonight?

To which she answered:

yes yes yes.

And another to Quinn.

still safe on campus.

To which he answered:

how about pot roast?

To which I answered:

yes yes yes.

I wondered where Sunni was, and whether she'd fared any better than I had. If I had any news, I'd have texted her, too, but I had to pass. I gathered my winter accessories and left the nameless building.

On the way out, I noticed large framed portraits of one Samuel Whittemore (legend: Oldest Known Colonial Combatant in the Revolutionary War) and Colonel William Prescott (legend: Famous for "Do Not Fire Until You See the Whites of Their Eyes") near the exit. I wondered if they'd been the last contenders for eponymous honoree of the building.

No other random friends or strangers intercepted me in my final approach to Patrick Henry Hall. This building was one of the originals, gray stone with arched stained-glass windows on the lower floor, as if it had started out as a church. According to the directory in the lobby, math and science classes were still held here and not in the newer Mary Draper Hall classroom building.

My interest was on the third floor, the faculty offices.

A matronly, older woman, probably sixtyish, was the gatekeeper to the floor, the kind of woman who had probably been at the job more than half her life and knew more than anyone else in the building. I hoped I could win her over and coax her into giving up a secret or two.

A placard on her cluttered desk read GAIL CHAMBERS.

She was surrounded by a computer and a variety of peripherals that seemed to have been squeezed into the space once occupied by a typewriter. No one else was around. In fact, the whole building seemed empty, except for some possible action in a closed-door classroom a few yards away. Gail peered at me over narrow glasses that hung on a beaded chain.

"Is there something I have to sign for?" she asked.

I started. *What?* Ah, the uniform jacket. I felt the gears spinning in my head. She'd seen the patriotic eagle patch on my sleeve, the emblem that carried the weight of the USPS. *Should I or shouldn't I?*

"Good morning," I said, straightening my back, holding my leather purse in front of me as if it were an official sack of the USPS. "I was hoping to get into Dr. Dennis Somerville's office for a few minutes." Pleasant but official. *Could I be jailed for this?* I wondered. It wasn't my fault that Gail thought I'd been sent by the postmaster general.

She sighed. "Dennis," she said softly, and shook her head. She looked up at me. "You know he passed away?"

"I do, and I'm so sorry about that."

"A wonderful man." Another sigh. Gail gazed into space for a moment, then came back. "Oh, I'm sorry. Did you have some business with him that I can help you with?"

"No, thank you. If I can just pick up something that I'm sure is ready for me in his office." *Blah, blah, blah.* Stumbling along. "I saw him yesterday." Finally, a truth.

"I don't know what this world is coming to when you're just minding your own business or protecting your property, and . . ." She trailed off. Apparently, there had been no update on the motive for Dennis's death, and Gail believed that he was the victim of a robbery gone bad.

"It's terrible," I said.

Gail lifted her hefty body from an old wooden swivel chair that matched her oak desk. "I'll walk you down there."

"If you can just point me in the right direction."

"It's not a problem. It's kind of a dead day around here." She drew in a sharp, loud breath. "Oh no. What did I say?"

"Maybe you should stay here and take it easy . . ."

"I'm fine," she said, starting the walk down the hallway. "The police have been here and took his computer, plus almost everything in the office except the furniture, so I don't know if what Dennis left for you would still be there."

Neither do I. Sunni had beat me to it. Kudos to her for doing her job, though it meant I couldn't look through files. But it was doubtful I'd have been able to circumvent a password, and I did feel a little better about what I was about to do.

"I'll just have a quick look," I said, hoping she didn't ask me to describe what I was looking for. "I'll bet Dr. Somerville was a very popular teacher."

"Oh yes. But he was very strict, mind you. Not like some of the others who give out A's just for effort, if you know what I mean."

I didn't, exactly, but I nodded anyway. We'd passed the one room with a class meeting and now walked by empty classrooms and offices and framed photographs on the walls of both sides of the hallway. Gail's old-lady pumps clicked on the flooring all the way, her pastel sweater set reminding me of several I'd found in Aunt Tess's closet.

I wanted badly to ask Gail if she knew anything about the nasty letters Dennis had shown me. I had a feeling that nothing got past her. Except me, right now. I decided to take a chance and edge my way toward asking her if she knew of Dennis's hate mail. She seemed a likely person for both students and teachers in the department to confide in. I thought back to the letters, closed up in envelopes. He'd given me a couple of sample phrases. Two that I remembered were "unreasonable homework assignments" and "tough grading policies."

"My niece tells me students these days are very vocal when they think a teacher is being unfair," I began. "Like giving too much homework, or grading too strictly."

"Dr. Somerville was never unfair," Gail said, bristling. I wondered if she'd switched from "Dennis" to put me in my place. She seemed like the kind of admin who considered it part of her job to keep the department's dirty laundry in-house. Not a bad trait, except when I was the one needing the scoop. I mentally cut off the topic of student evaluations and started another one I was curious about.

"I guess his regular group this morning missed him," I said.

"You mean the math and science discussion group?"

I nodded. "I know a couple of the members." *Oops. Maybe I shouldn't sound so . . . what? Unofficial?*

"The leader, Dr. Winston—he'll probably take over as department chair—called everything off today, except for an advanced seminar that's going on now. I sent a memo out last night to everyone, as soon as we heard the news."

"My mistake. I thought my friend Professor Black-wood had been here."

Gail laughed. "He still calls himself that, huh? No, he hasn't been around."

"He's not a professor?"

Gail shook her head. "He never made it to that level. He retired"—she made quotes in the air—"under a kind of cloud." She whispered this last part and seemed to wish she could take it back. "He still hasn't cleaned out his office, though we send him constant reminders."

That made Hank a liar, even a double liar if he not only didn't have a meeting but wasn't a professor. I could have predicted that. He was the kind of guy who wanted to seem important. And smart, what with that geometry reference. I wondered why he'd bother; I wasn't one who needed impressing.

We'd reached Dennis's office, a corner office as befitting a chairperson. My talk with Gail hadn't gone well after opening remarks. I sensed that she was having second thoughts about accommodating me and planned to stay while I retrieved my alleged—what? Package? Envelope? I couldn't remember what I'd called my excuse for being here. Some sleuth. I was on the road to fourfold failure. Or was it fivefold already?

"Here we are," Gail said, reaching for keys to unlock a half-windowed door that opened into Dennis's office. "The police didn't put tape up, so I guess they're finished."

No tape, no foul, I thought. Anyone could enter Dennis's office.

"I don't know why I locked it," she continued. "Out of

respect for Dennis, I guess." I took that as a warning to behave myself around his things.

Gail pushed the door open and held her arm across the glass pane while I walked in. I heard her heavy sigh. The blinds were down on both sides. Gail's doing, I was sure. I couldn't imagine Sunni or her officer darkening the room as they left. As I'd been warned, cables lay across Dennis's desk where a computer should have been. A wire in-box was empty, as was a stack of trays with labels on the side. GRP THY. E&M. THERMO. MECH. LABS. I wondered what was missing from the empty trays, but I doubted I would have understood whatever had been in the slots.

I walked toward a credenza under one of the windows, trying to look as though I knew what I'd come for. My stomach was queasy from the taste of mustard, potato chips, and an unidentifiable third flavor. Was it bad food or Gail's cross-armed stare that was bringing on this discomfort?

When Gail's phone chimed a bland melody, I let out a deep breath and walked farther into the office, circling the desk and chair, then walking along the row of files. I didn't dare open a drawer.

Gail, standing on the threshold, wasn't pleased with her caller any more than she was with me. I was more focused on finding something useful and didn't hear too much of her side of the conversation. As near as I could tell, the issue was supplies for the math department.

"I know it's only February, but we had an unusually large incoming class." Pause. "At least another case." A pause and an annoyed sigh. "Well, you are certainly welcome to leave your office and walk across the campus to see for yourself."

I felt a wave of sympathy for the person on the other end of the call. On the other hand, I'd had my share of disagreements with administrative staff over supplies and budgets.

During Gail's pauses, she had her eye on me. I took out a notebook and pretended to be tending to the post office business I'd come for. Making note of the date and time, perhaps? Keeping track of my pickups for the day? It was anyone's guess.

While Gail was speaking, I busied myself taking photos surreptitiously with my smartphone. I could only guess at the correct angle to snap the furniture and artifacts. I aimed my phone as accurately as possible at the top of the desk, the front of each file cabinet, the tops and fronts of the bookcases, the large whiteboard, the small corkboard, and the posters and certificates on Dennis's wall, all science-related except for one that featured a colorful guitar against a white background. I smiled at PHYSICS: IT'S THE LAW and barely understood PHYSICS TEACHERS HAVE POTENTIAL. I drew in my breath at PHYSICS TEACHERS HAVE PROBLEMS. Dennis had problems no one should have. I took a breath and photographed the view out each window, for completeness.

I checked out the tchotchkes on the shelves and surfaces. A bust of Einstein dominated one end of a shelf that was cluttered with wooden and plastic puzzles of many degrees of complexity. Other items that the police weren't interested in included seashells and a slide rule.

I recognized the fancy ruler only because a high school boyfriend insisted I learn how to use it, since it was "so cool" and would come in handy someday. He'd been wrong.

I aimed my camera at a Boston lighthouse snow globe similar to one I owned. I wished I could pick it up to read the name—was it North Shore or South Shore?—but I felt Gail would be on me in seconds. What I didn't see were photos of any kind, and assumed Sunni had taken them.

When I heard Gail's "Have a nice day," in a tone that said she wished the caller anything but, I grabbed the nearest thing to me. I stuffed the lighthouse snow globe in my pocket. A shrink might say I was desperate not to leave Dennis's office—the whole campus—empty-handed. Sometimes shrinks are right.

Gail clicked off her call and clomped over to me. I knew my time was up. "I'm not sure I got your name," she said. Her tone was cold, suspicious. I was surprised she didn't add "young lady."

She was right, of course. Another big decision. I could tell her that my identity was classified USPS information and run down the hall. I knew she'd never catch me. I could give her a false name, but why bother? In the end, I grabbed a business card from my purse and handed it to her. In almost the same movement, I pulled up my sleeve and tapped my watch.

"Oops, it's later than I thought. I have to get back to the office," I said, perhaps the most honest thing I'd said to Gail since we met. "Thanks for your help."

I hurried down the hall, remembering that I never did like science.

I turned left, down the short wing of the hall, toward the elevator. Two doors down on this section of the floor was an office with the same half-glass door and a sign that read H. BLACKWOOD. I stopped to listen for footsteps and heard none behind me. Gail's pumps would have made it impossible for her to sneak up on me.

I tried the door, not surprised to find it locked. I did note that the considerate Professor (or not) Blackwood had provided a way to leave a message for him. I'd seen this arrangement on other office doors in the department. Dennis Somerville had affixed a small whiteboard to his doorframe, with a marker dangling from a string. Hank Blackwood had chosen the paper and pen method, with a set of pockets for sticky notes. The setup contained a thick pad of blank notes. Though I couldn't be positive, I thought they were identical to the note Hank had left on my counter the last time he bought stamps. I would never want to be held accountable for IDing math symbols, most of which looked alike to me. The low-tech communication system included a separate pocket for leaving your note. I was tempted to leave a note, such as *Stop bothering me*, but thought better of it.

Once more hearing no footsteps—I was convinced that Gail was opening drawers and running her hand over all surfaces, trying to determine exactly what I'd done in Dennis's office—I slipped my hand down into the pseudo "in-box," on Hank's door, hoping to find something pertinent. The pocket was empty, thus ruling out sticky notes as the investigator's best lead.

I gave up and summoned the elevator, my only takeaway a small lighthouse snow globe.

Outside, the campus at about forty degrees felt warmer than the building I'd just left. In the end, Gail's cold good-bye had gotten to me. It was as if she'd figured out that my visit wasn't legitimate, and had been about to execute a citizen's arrest. Which I probably deserved. I wouldn't have been surprised if she was on the phone now, calling Sunni or the post office to verify my credentials. At this hour the office was closed for lunch and she'd get the answering machine, fortunately. Maybe recognizing my voice on the recording chip would be enough to satisfy her that at least I hadn't stolen the uniform.

I trudged north toward the lot where my car was parked, the wind seeming to pick up. My head down, the way I tended to walk in the face of even small gusts, I nearly bumped into Joyce Blake, who was also paying no attention to what was at her eye level, which was the same as mine for all practical purposes.

We both laughed and paused to exchange a few words. We remarked on the fact that the campus was so quiet, as if a blanket of snow had covered it, and adjusted our clothing accordingly—she tightened the sash on her coat and I adjusted the collar of my jacket upward.

"Did you hold class this morning?" I asked her.

She shook her head and blew out a visible breath, like the kind we had competed with on snow days as kids. "But we did go ahead with our faculty meeting. There were some forms we needed to finalize for grants we're applying for in the math department. Nobody had much heart for it. And on another note"—she smiled—"Note. Sorry. I'm glad we'll be going ahead with the Valentine's Day gig. Dedicating it to Dennis, in a way."

"I haven't talked to Quinn, but I'm sure he's happy about it, too."

"Oh, and can you believe Hank Blackwood actually asked to rejoin the group?" Joyce shook her head, her long hair moving slightly under her tight knitted cap. "The gall. As if Dennis's death cleared the way for him."

"It was Dennis who asked him to leave the group?" Quinn, not given to gossip, had never mentioned this, figuring, correctly, that I had no need to know.

"Oh yes, and no one yet knows why Hank complied. He could be very stubborn. We think Dennis had something on him, but who knows?"

It was unthinkable that someone would use the death of a friend or a colleague in that way. It crossed my mind that Joyce herself had much to gain in her department now that Dennis was gone. Hadn't there been that calculus-now-versus-calculus-later debate? I brushed the thought away. This was what happened to amateurs at detective work. Suspect everyone. Be able to prove nothing.

As Joyce and I talked, I'd pushed my gloved hand deeper into the pocket of my jacket, gripping the lighthouse globe I'd taken from Dennis's office, so afraid that it would fall to the ground where Joyce would see it. She would surely recognize it as Dennis's and be all kinds of confused about why I had it.

Much like me.

8

B ack at my familiar retail desk on Main Street, my spirits were lifted. Ben had left things in perfect order, of course, and even picked up a box of my new favorite cookies—French macaroons from our local bakery. He'd placed the box on top of the small pile of my personal mail that had come in.

A much-needed laugh came around three o'clock. When you've managed counter service for as many years as I have, you become an expert on the behavior of people who are waiting in line.

In Boston, or any big city, there are strict rules. Usually, several clerks are working, each at a different station. When a window comes open, the clerk calls out "Next," and it's like a bell going off. The person at the front of the line has a fraction of a second to beat it to the counter before there's a clamor and everyone badgers and nudges him verbally, to the accompaniment of colorful language.

"Hey, buddy, you deaf? You're next."

"Hello? Number two is open. Are you waiting for an invitation?"

"You want an escort, mister?"

The aural abuse is not unlike the honking horn syndrome in traffic when the lead car is slow to respond to a green light. I missed the action.

In North Ashcot, no one was in that big of a rush. Except for today, when a middle-aged man in a business suit, a stranger to me, expressed annoyance several times that there was only one clerk—me.

Old Mrs. Frederich was the next person in line.

"Any time before the sun goes down, huh, lady?" the man said when Mrs. Frederich didn't lift her tennis-ball-footed walker and respond to her turn in a flash.

I knew the betting would begin immediately.

"Worcester," called out Beth Keller, one of my high school classmates.

"Springfield," said Hank Blackwood, back for another transaction today.

"Bridgeport," said Edna, the school bus driver.

"Hartford," said Brooke Jeffries, the penny whistler of the Ashcots.

"Providence," said Mike from the hardware store down the street.

My guess was Albany, thirty miles to the west, population one hundred thousand, more or less, but I always recused myself from the game, citing the number of a fictitious postal regulation.

Three more guesses were entertained, then "Where are you from, sonny?" Mrs. Frederich asked the businessman in a sweet voice.

"Hartford, so what?" the man said.

Wallets came out, purses were opened, and dollar bills were handed to our very own former Miss Berkshire County, Brooke Jeffries.

"You might know, the banker won," Mike said, with a big grin.

The man in the suit caught on pretty quickly, huffed, and left the building, clutching his free Priority Mail envelopes. A loss of revenue for the USPS, but a fun time for my regular customers. Sometimes strangers from a big city broke down and enjoyed the joke; other times they ranted all the way out the door.

Brooke waved her bounty in the air. "Next term's tuition," she said. Brooke was studying for her MBA on the campus I knew so well after my morning's journey.

When Hank Blackwood came to the counter, he was in a good mood even though he hadn't bet correctly on the stranger's hometown. "Third time's a charm—right, Cassie?"

I gave him a questioning look.

"This is my third time seeing you in two days."

I smiled, as if I'd been counting also and was happy about the visits. "What can I help you with, Hank?" I asked, seeing no mail to be processed.

"A sheet of stamps," he said. "Those Forever ones."

I dug out a sheet of commemoratives with a patriotic theme. "These okay?"

"Sure," he said. "Plus, I need a sheet of those extra ounce ones."

I picked out a sheet with Abraham Lincoln's image and handed them over. Hank fished through his wallet. He looked around and saw only one other person in line—our bus driver, Edna, who was holding an e-reader. He leaned into the counter. "You and Quinn are tight, right?" he asked me, in a conspiratorial voice.

I pretended I didn't know what "tight" meant in this context. "Quinn and I are friends, yes," I said, in a normal tone.

"Well, I'm trying to get back to playing with the Ashcots. I thought maybe you could put in a good word."

"I know nothing about music," I said.

"You don't need to know music; you only need to have clout."

"I don't have that, either. I'm just a groupie following the band around." I shrugged and gave a laugh that I hoped signified the end of the conversation.

"Yeah, well, you know, he's a nice guy, Quinn. You know his shop is interested in some old stuff I have in my grandfather's attic. I should remind him of that. Plus, I know he covets that old car I drive around. Anyway, I'm sure he'll vote me back in, but just in case, I thought I'd let you know."

"Good luck, Hank," I said, catching Edna's eye and waving her over.

I was proud of myself for not reminding Hank about his claims of how much better Pittsfield was the other times we'd met. I wondered why he was so eager to return to the Ashcots. I knew for a fact that they didn't get paid, except for an occasional basket of fruit after a wedding gig.

Not my problem, I told myself. I already had a few of

my own. An empty lobby gave me a minute to review what those were as I cleared the counter of crumbs (the remains of a snack Melissa's toddler enjoyed while sitting there), stray paper clips and rubber bands, and tiny bits of adhesive paper from the edges of stamp sheets. A sticky note was doing its job, sticking to the edge of my counter. I peeled it off and saw that it must have been discarded by Hank Blackwood. There were math symbols all around the edge, and the memo was a short list: "forevers," followed by "xtra oz." Exactly what Hank had bought. I had to admit I was surprised that his trip was legitimately planned—I would have bet that he dropped in randomly to rant, and faked his shopping list. I tossed the sticky and all the other paper scraps into the recycle box under my counter.

I listed my concerns as I tidied my work area. Linda's plight, for one. I hoped tonight's Skype session would be useful and supportive. My talk, for two. It was dawning on me that I had only one day to prepare for a lecture to an entire stadium full of people, or a classroom full of kids, depending on how I looked at it. Either way, it was daunting.

And then there was the murder. I glanced down at my bottom drawer, where I'd stashed the snow globe I'd taken from Dennis's bookcase, my only physical link to Dennis Somerville. Had some invisible force been guiding my hand toward it while I was looking around his office? Or did I just want a souvenir? I could only imagine Sunni's reaction if she knew what I'd done. My only defense was that I hadn't violated a crime scene.

I checked the clock. Less than an hour until I'd be able

to close up. I sat at my desk and took out my phone, ready to satisfy my curiosity about the photos I'd taken in Dennis's office. I hoped they weren't all shots of the floor or the ceiling (it wouldn't have been the first time) or the inside of my jacket pocket.

I stopped at the clearest picture, a shot of Dennis's bulletin board. I enlarged the picture and saw notices of meetings and a memo about physics club elections, plus class assignments and conference badges. Stuck to the top right corner was a button with a probably-famous equation that meant nothing to me.

I scrolled through other photos, sending the better ones to my e-mail address for later study. When my lobby door opened and Quinn appeared, I clicked back to my home screen. No sense taking up his valuable time explaining a bunch of pictures that might turn out to be useless.

Even with an otherwise empty lobby, I didn't open the gate to my boyfriend. Rules were rules. Instead, we hugged over the counter (sometimes it came in handy to be tall). There was no explicit rule against that.

"Enjoy your trip back to school?"

"I had a delicious lunch," I said.

He pointed to the bakery box, open on my desk. "Are those cookies from the critically acclaimed cafeteria?"

We laughed and I took the hint. I offered Quinn the box, where there were still a few pastel macaroons left. "Compliments of Ben," I admitted.

He took a pale green cookie. "Was it a useful trip to the campus? Anything you can use to help the chief?" The green cookie was gone in one mouthful. He took a pink one next.

"Yes and no. That is, nothing useful." I told Quinn about meeting Joyce and Hank.

"Hank seems to think you're dying to do business with him."

"It's more Fred than me. I think the guy is more talk than truth, if you know what I mean."

"He thinks you have your eye on an antique car he drives sometimes."

Quinn made a *pfft* sound. "It's a 'sixty-six Nova. Not exactly hot these days."

"I get that impression, about the hot air, I mean." What was I doing? Gossiping when I had a class to face in less than two days. "The class is huge," I told Quinn, who was rightly confused by the lack of transition.

"Are you ready?"

"What do you think I should wear?"

He grinned. "That's your problem? What you're going to wear?"

"That's the one that's easy to take care of."

"Your uniform, definitely."

"Really?" I pulled out the front of my shirt. "Really? This old thing?"

"And your jacket. It's a sign of authority. They'll pay more attention."

"Hmm. I don't have to rush out and buy a new dress?" Not that I intended to.

He shook his head. "Now for the lecture."

I winced. "Don't call it that."

"Chat?" he offered. I shrugged.

"Oration?" he asked.

I shook my head no.

"Presentation?" He wasn't giving up.

I twisted my wrist in a "maybe" gesture.

I noticed a group of women crossing Main Street, headed my way. I recognized a couple of them and guessed they'd just come from a crafts day at the back of Liv Patterson's card shop. I let out a breath of relief when the women walked by my doors. I waved back to a couple of them. Lost revenue aside, I was ready to be done with post office business and get down to police work, which I considered my talk, or presentation, to be part of. If only Sunni knew the sacrifices I was making for her and the murder investigation.

"Okay," I said. "Presentation. Are you still willing to help?"

"Of course I'll help," Quinn said. He looked at his watch. "Almost closing time. Why don't you stay here after you lock up? Get some notes and thoughts together. Maybe take some photos of your work space."

I waved my arm and turned my body three-sixty. "Take pictures of this? I don't think so."

"Whatever. I'll go to your place and start dinner and you call me when you're ready. I was thinking of chicken and cashews."

"Wow."

"I know. Cinderella, huh?"

I nodded. "After the prince finds her slipper."

"The flag should be hoisted briskly and lowered ceremoniously," stated the guidelines in my handbook, "and any onlookers should stand at attention." There were seldom people around when I hoisted the flag in the morning or took it down for the night.

This evening, however, I saw three figures standing across the street. Main Street was pretty wide, and it was already past sundown, making it impossible to identify the onlookers or even to determine their gender, but I guessed from their postures that they were relatively young. They stood at attention, as appropriate. Did they really still teach that in schools?

The strange thing was that they kept standing there, at attention, even after the flag was down and as I walked around to the side of the building. I carried the flag through the side door and looked out the front windows. They were still standing there. I now saw their posture not as patriotic or respectful but threatening. I lowered the shades and made sure all the doors were locked. I took a breath. Dennis Somerville's murder was getting to me. Surely, there was nothing amiss in three people standing on the sidewalk. Main Street, North Ashcot, wasn't exactly the drug capital of Berkshire County.

I couldn't talk myself out of a creepy feeling, however, and decided to go home. I added my scarf and hat, but not my gloves. I left my hands free to use my phone in case I needed to make an emergency call. I shoved the lighthouse snow globe into my pocket and left by the side door, the one closest to my car. I scanned the street. The group was no longer together on Main Street, but I could tell from their retreating figures that they'd just dispersed.

I got in my car, locked myself in, and headed home. I

checked my rearview mirror more than once on the short drive, but even in our small town there was enough traffic at commute hour to ruin my chances of noticing a tail. It wasn't until I pulled into my driveway that I relaxed my grip on the steering wheel.

"You're early," Quinn said.

"I wanted to see you with your apron on," I said.

"It gets kind of creepy out there when the shops close, doesn't it?"

How could Quinn know I'd been frightened out of my own office? Was I shaking externally as well as internally? "It's warmer here" was all I'd admit to.

"Did you get a chance to snap some photos?"

I shook my head. "There's nothing to look at. What would I photograph? My state-of-the-art paper cutter? The charming burlap delivery bag? If I had time to take a trip to the Boston facility, that would be worth a slide show."

"You might be underestimating the interest people would have in what's behind the scenes. Everyone thinks their job is dull, but a behind-the-scenes look at almost any job can be fascinating to those who know nothing about it."

"I'll give it some thought."

"Or you can get some historical photos, like the one you showed me with the early Oklahoma post office that was a converted chicken coop."

"You remember that?"

"I even remember the young boy who stood guard with a rifle."

"I'll think about it." But I was no closer to doing so.

We dropped the subject and agreed that I'd work in my newly developing home office and report for dinner in an hour.

The first thing I did was place Dennis's lighthouse snow globe on the corner of my desk. For inspiration? That would have to do for a reason. I studied the legend on the base and saw that the tiny replica was of the Annisquam Harbor Lighthouse in Gloucester, on the North Shore of Massachusetts. I'd been a South Shore person myself while I lived in Boston, heading to the cape whenever possible and very familiar with the lighthouses there. I'd taken many memorable trips to the walkable lighthouses like those at Hyannis Harbor and Chatham, and my favorite Three Sisters Lights at Nauset Beach.

I was less familiar with tourist destinations like Gloucester, Marblehead, and Rockport, on the North Shore, apparently Dennis Somerville's choice of outing. I searched for the Annisquam Harbor Lighthouse and learned a few pieces of trivia, such as: Rudyard Kipling once stayed there to work on *Captain Courageous*. A lot of help this would be in solving the murder of Dennis Somerville.

I was keenly aware that this activity shouldn't be my highest priority, given the looming of the eleventh hour before my talk. I should have been planning, outlining, and researching postal history, gathering quotes.

Instead, I pulled out my phone and texted Linda.

ready to skype?

definitely.

In three minutes we were face-to-face, in a manner of speaking. The wonders of technology.

"Hey," Linda said. "I'm glad you're checking in early. I've been thinking all day that I must have worried you this morning and, really, there's nothing big going on. You know how I get after a breakup. Like my whole world's crashed, but it's only Josh who's bit the dust." She paused and I knew she'd apologize. "Oh, Cassie, I'm sorry. I'm always doing that. There you are with a real crisis."

"It's not really my crisis. And you sounded different this time. Like the issue is more about work?"

"Yeah, well, that changed right after lunch."

It wasn't the first time Linda had swung from a very low state to a very high one, but this might have been the fastest turnaround in a while. I had a feeling it hadn't been a random pep talk, or the presence of a smiley face somewhere. "What happened after lunch?"

"My boss—Lou, the new guy you haven't met—came by. It seems a new position is opening up and I'm being tapped."

"That's great, Linda. Tell me about it."

She did, while I tuned in and out, hoping my "cools" and "oh, wows" came at the right time. Not that I didn't want to know about Linda's career path, just not while I was stewing over a murder and a talk, in alternating bouts of worry and doubt.

Linda sat as usual with her back to her window over Boston—giving me a brilliant idea. When it was my turn to talk, I presented it. "Linda, do you still have all those photos of the building that we took for the brochure a couple of years ago?"

"I'm sure I have them somewhere. Why? Are you homesick? Are you coming back?"

"Do you think you can find a few and send them to me?"

I told her about my so-called speech and Quinn's idea that I use behind-the-scenes or historically interesting photos.

"What could possibly be interesting in this building?"

"Compared to the North Ashcot PO? Everything, including the building itself."

"What you really need is pictures of the POs that are on the National Register of Historic Places, like the one in Beverly. It's absolutely gorgeous with that little steeple-thingy on the top."

"Or we could take a quick trip to Manhattan to the Farley Building." I was into this research now. "And take a picture of the only real site of what everyone thinks is our official motto."

It couldn't be helped. We recited together, accurate with respect to most of the quote. "Neither rain nor snow nor heat nor gloom of night, stays these couriers from the swift completion of their appointed rounds."

"Or you can sing 'Mr. Postman,'" Linda said. "Remember how my dad would go round singing that song? No wonder I followed him into the postal service."

Now we went into an ear-piercing imitation of the Marvelettes. "Is there a letter, a letter for me?"

If Quinn hadn't called from the kitchen; if the aroma of cashew chicken hadn't reached my nose; if I didn't have a real deadline in front of me, I'd never have signed off with my best post office friend.

I felt better than I had all day.

9

"Sounded like a good time in there," Quinn said. He was right—the phone sing-along with Linda had lifted my spirits. But I felt a certain pang of guilt now. Quinn had relieved me of kitchen duty so that I could work. Instead, I'd frittered away my time with lighthouses and Linda and the Motown of our parents' generation. I decided to wait until I'd eaten a good portion of chicken and cashew-laden sauce before owning up to my failure as a researcher.

Quinn had taken over my kitchen as he did more often than not lately, and I was only too happy to give it up. My electric mixer, which he'd miraculously located, was busy with a bowl of mashed potatoes. Next to it was a salad with fresh greens that he didn't find in any fridge I owned. The dining room table was set to perfection, like the one on display at the front of his shop, except that the Attic boasted older, finer china. There was no extra place, so I assumed my friend the chief of police was on her own this evening.

While I lived with Aunt Tess in her last days, I'd forced myself to cook so that she'd have appetizing meals to nourish her frail body. I learned all her favorite recipes—baked beans, clam chowder, New England boiled dinners, and even a halfway decent lobster bisque—eschewing the canned versions. She'd expressed great appreciation and had done her best to consume a few calories, but it hadn't worked to keep her around forever, as I would have liked.

Back on my own again, I lived on grilled cheese and tuna. I missed the endless take-out possibilities I'd had around my Fenway apartment in Boston, and the great Back Bay restaurants, though I did not miss having to hang on Adam's arm while he wined and dined his clients. Some exes were meant to be, I thought, gazing across the table at the handsome man who'd been wearing Aunt Tess's apron minutes ago.

But his return look now was challenging, and I knew he was waiting to hear the progress I'd made.

"I'm not getting anywhere on the presentation," I said, "except for collecting a few pretty pictures." I put down my fork with great determination, as if I were throwing down a gauntlet, as if Quinn had called me to task.

"I've been thinking about it," said my knight. "People don't realize how instrumental the post office was in the spread of information. You could start with something like that—how the Penny Post made the mail accessible to everyone."

"You don't think that sounds a little preachy?"

"Isn't it supposed to be?"

"You're no help," I said, though not with a great deal of sincerity.

Through the rest of the meal—dessert postponed—Quinn and I tossed ideas back and forth, eventually moving to the living room, where I took up residence on my rocker with my laptop on my knees. Quinn laughed when I removed the bust of Sir Rowland Hill, a small replica of one in Westminster Abbey, from my bookcase to the coffee table for inspiration.

"I need all the help I can get."

"Little did I know when I rescued that statue from a dusty attic."

I searched on my laptop for information on the Penny Post system, Sir Rowland's answer to the involved, expensive method of sending letters in Victorian England.

"Imagine," I said. "He thought up the idea of prepaid stamps." We both looked at the stern face of Sir Rowland. "And for that he was made a knight."

Quinn laughed, clearly pleased that I was finally drumming up enthusiasm for my talk.

"My work here is done," he said, rising from the couch to get his jacket.

I hated for him to leave, but he had an eight o'clock commitment to a boys' group in town. It had been such a nice evening, starting with my sing-along with Linda and ending with jokes that went back to Victorian England.

But Quinn was right; his work was done, for the time being. I stayed in my rocker finding more information than I'd need in a lifetime. I downloaded dozens of photos that I'd have to sift through later. I shot an e-mail to Mercedes telling her I'd like to take her up on her offer to use the great audiovisual capabilities at Mary Draper Hall. I dragged photos onto my desktop: Sir Rowland himself, Queen Victoria as she appeared on the first postage stamp with adhesive backing, a British postman wearing the red-vested uniform that inspired their being called "robins."

I couldn't stop clicking away at references. I'd never been a big fan of research, agonizing my way through term papers in college, but now I saw the addictive nature of having an endless amount of information at my fingertips. I read on, knowing that I wouldn't be able to include most of the material, but determined to mention Queen Victoria's reforms, embarrassed that I'd previously associated her only with ornate architecture and furniture.

I might not have moved from my comfortable position, except that the doorbell rang a little before nine o'clock. I left my rocker to look out the front window. On the porch, leaning over the banister, was Sunni. She waved and smiled, dancing from one leg to the other, stomping her feet from the cold.

"How come you don't use your peephole?" she asked, entering my living room.

"I've seen more than one crime show where someone was shot through the eye that way."

"Oh yes. I'm ever grateful to crime shows and B movies for educating the public on crime statistics and forensics. I hope you have food. I swear, one day soon, I'm going to take you to dinner."

"No need. I'm happy to share. Your choices are leftover chicken with cashews, or a lemon pie that hasn't been touched."

"First things first. I'll take a slice of pie while you heat the chicken."

Dessert first. No wonder we were such good friends.

I had the good sense not to bother Sunni with business—hers or mine—while she polished off a helping of chicken dinner with pie before and after. I knew that she'd probably skipped every meal since last night's dinner here, or at best emptied out the police department vending machine. Sunni lived alone while her daughter was away at college, and she saw no need to grocery-shop or cook. That was a platform I understood.

"So," she said, on her second cup of coffee. "Aren't you going to ask me for an update?"

"May I?"

Even after two years, I was never sure when to probe and when not to. I couldn't tell until it was too late sometimes whether she was in friend mode, cop mode, or a combination. I told her once that I wished she'd wear a sign like OPEN or CLOSED to let me know. She'd suggested WILL TRADE INFORMATION FOR FOOD. "Except it might be misinterpreted as bribing a cop," she'd added.

Now she nodded. I had permission to discuss police business. "Not that I have a lot to report, but we're making progress in the robbery cases."

I was disappointed but told myself there was a chance the murder and robberies were connected and progress in one might mean progress in the other. There was no proof either way whether the burglars who'd torn up the town were the same people who murdered Dennis. Just because I doubted it didn't mean the theory could be dismissed. "You've caught them?"

"Not yet, but with some results coming back on earlier cases, and a few new witnesses, and so on, it looks like there are three people involved. We'd been almost sure it wasn't a single perp. Too well organized and coordinated."

Three people. Just like my going-away party of three as I'd left the office tonight. I gulped. What a coincidence. That was what it was, right?

Sunni went on, not seeming to notice that the blood had drained from my face. "We think they're from right across the river, and we're going all out to find them. I've enlisted the help of two other departments. It looks like the incidents haven't been confined to North Ashcot." She drained her coffee mug. "We're going to get them," she said, in the manner of tough cops everywhere.

I didn't bother to tell her about the three people who had waited outside the post office earlier this evening. First of all, who said they were waiting? I asked myself. And second, I couldn't even come close to making an identification, unless Sunni could arrange a lineup that mimicked average-size human figures in the dark, and across a street.

"I didn't get anything on the letters sent to Dennis," I admitted, eager to erase the threefold image from my mind.

"I figured, since you didn't offer anything."

"I was wondering about everyone's alibi. You've probably covered all the obvious people."

"We have—all accounted for, more or less."

"More or less?"

"Some are more solid than others. Obviously, we can hardly cover every student. But he hasn't flunked anyone recently, hasn't had any actions taken against him. The overall sense is that he was well liked by everyone enrolled in his classes."

"Except for the one or ones who wrote the letters."

"Except for them."

I'd decided not to tell Sunni about meeting Joyce and Hank on campus, but now I felt I had to offer something.

"You probably know all this," I began, diffident. "I ran into two faculty members, one active and one former, that is, both part of the Ashcots. Uh, again one former member." Why hadn't I prepared this to sound halfway intelligible?

"And?"

"Well, I know that Joyce and Dennis had a disagreement over calculus."

"Sounds intense."

Sunni appeared to be enjoying my discomfort. *Some friend.*

I gave her a halfhearted summary of the dispute over scheduling.

"I'll look again at Joyce's alibi, which was shopping with her sister, but family members aren't the most reliable alibis."

I switched to my next suspect. "There's something suspicious about Hank Blackwood's behavior." I knew that sounded like a line of dialogue from one of those B movies Sunni and I often ridiculed. I told her of his lying about having a meeting in Dennis's building, and the fact that members of the Ashcots thought Dennis might have had something on Hank.

"You mean Dennis might have been blackmailing him?" She'd reached for her jacket and scarf and I knew I had only a few minutes left to make some kind of showing. "Any idea what for?"

"No, but I heard that Dennis was instrumental in forcing Hank to leave the Ashcots."

"I'll check his alibi also. If I remember he said he didn't feel well and took a nap, which is even less reliable than a family member. We'll see."

"We'll see" wasn't exactly "I'll let you know," but I was heartened. I watched Sunni's reaction carefully, amazed that she hadn't told me to cease and desist, to put things like investigating the motive in Dennis's murder out of my mind. But she hadn't, so I considered pushing my luck. I tried to think of a way to ask if there was any progress in figuring out who sent nasty words in the mail to Dennis (somehow phrasing it this way gave me a keen sense of failure in my responsibilities as postmaster) and whether the letters had anything to do with Dennis's death.

"I'm going back to campus on Thursday morning," I said, hoping the subtext was clear: another shot at trolling for information.

"For your talk in Mercedes Davis's class."

"Yes. I'm very excited about it. I've been reading about the evolution of the patch on our uniform sleeve. We had the Pony Express rider before the eagle appeared, and now, of course, we call it a sonic eagle. Even the hats—"

She opened the front door, ready to leave. "Fascinating, especially to college students, I'm sure."

"You're not helping."

"Just see what you can come up with when your standing ovation is over."

"You bet, Chief." It was hard not to salute.

Wearing my warmest pajamas, I carried my laptop and a mug of cocoa to my bedroom and settled in for an early night. I wished I could reschedule my talk for tomorrow, both to get it over with and to get to campus again. I was eager to get back there, to see and quiz Mercedes—maybe we could have lunch after my talk. I took a breath, almost a gasp. *My talk*. My presentation, as Quinn called it.

As engrossing as I'd found my research on postal history, the idea of standing in front of a classroom full of students sent shivers through my body. I was able to calm down by reminding myself that the presentation was the price of admission for gathering information at Dennis's place of business.

Place of business. Another phrase that caught me by surprise.

I took my eyes off my screen, where I'd come across a page of images of the most valuable stamps in the world. The Cape of Good Hope Stamp, the Qing Dynasty stamp, and many more, all worth tens of thousands of dollars, up to more than three million for the Treskilling Yellow. I looked up, as if to read the writing on the ceiling. The words "Dennis's business" echoed in my brain and it dawned on me—

Dennis's campus office, which I'd penetrated, was never a crime scene. It was Dennis's home that was a crime scene. My latest *duh* moment.

Why hadn't I headed right for the crime scene?

I'd been to Dennis's home only once, when he hosted the Ashcots and their guests for a holiday gathering. I knew the area well, a new development on the west side of town, where a couple of members of my quilting group lived.

I leaned back on my oversize reading pillow, snug and warm, covered by the first quilt I'd made, under the tutelage of the women in Sunni's group. The quilt had too many obvious glitches for me to give it as a present, but I couldn't bring myself to toss it. Even imperfect quilts were cuddlesome.

I told myself it would be foolish to leave this cocoon. I didn't have to search for the exact temperature to know that outside was freezing. And dark. And I was tired from the tensions of the day; tomorrow would be a full day of work and more prep for my talk. I envisioned long lines of customers wanting express delivery in time for Valentine's Day. I had mountains of paperwork; I needed a trip to the bank and one to the card shop for my own valentines. I needed my sleep.

As these thoughts ran through my head, my feet edged their way from under the blankets, into my slippers. I trekked across the room. I found myself pulling a pair of dark sweats over my pajamas, adding socks, boots, and a down vest, picking up my keys, heading out the door.

My internal debate continued as I got into my car and turned the key. *This is foolish,* said one of my voices. *But when else can I get to Dennis's home?* asked the other voice. *Why do you need to get there?* was followed by *Sunni is expecting you to help.*

Ben had agreed to take over for me on Thursday morning and part of the afternoon while I went to campus. There was only so much I could ask of a retiree, even though he did hang around a lot. I looked at the clock on my dashboard. Ten thirty-nine. Not that late. I shifted to D and drove west, telling myself I could always turn back.

Dennis's house was a gray Colonial with green trim, set back from the street, with a detached garage. A cobblestone walkway led to the front door. I could tell from the plantings that in the spring lovely peonies would line the path. Few lights were on in the development, none in Dennis's house. He'd been a widower for many years, with a son, Dyson, who was at college in Maine. I wondered how soon the young man would be able to get here and whether he had any support in town.

I knew what it was like to lose your parents at a young age, and I felt a pang of sympathy for him. How had he heard the news? I hoped he hadn't been alone. I'd been unlucky enough to have my news delivered by a seemingly inconvenienced night-duty cop who came to the door of my girlfriend's house, where a sweet sixteen party was just beginning.

Rather than sit in my car now and have a good cry, I took my mental self to another place and time—to the present, with Quinn, my job, my new friends—and reined in thoughts of the past.

I was parked at the end of Dennis's drive, bewildered that I was there. There was no crime scene tape, so at least I wasn't breaking that law. As I considered restarting my car and going home, I opened my door and stepped onto the quiet, deserted street. I couldn't remember a time I'd experienced such a disconnect between my head and my feet as there had been that evening. Otherwise, I'd have been fast asleep under an amateur quilt instead of playing amateur sleuth.

Aided by the light of a streetlamp, I walked down the path and around to the right side of the house where I knew I'd be able to peer through patio doors into Dennis's dining room. I arrived at the doors, pleased that the drapes were open. I remembered the large area rug with a pattern of gold and brown swirls, under a highly polished table.

A breath of relief came as I realized I'd been subconsciously dreading the sight of blood or the outline of a body. No matter that Sunni had told me the police hadn't done the chalk outline for years, since chalk or tape contaminated a crime scene. "It makes for good TV, though," she said. I brushed thoughts of her aside as I stood at Dennis's window, intruding on her job.

What had been a lavish buffet on the dining room table for the party I'd attended had been replaced by mountains of paper, folders, and books of all sizes. It was hard to tell whether Dennis had been using this area as his office or the burglars had disrupted the normal dining room scene.

I moved along the edge of the expansive, well-kept lawn to the back of the house. In the dim yellow light of the streetlamp, I could barely make out the short metal fence that marked the end of Dennis's property. The lawn, however, continued uninterrupted onto the next plot, where Dennis's nearest neighbor's house sat, set back a considerable distance from the fence. All the better for me to remain unobserved. And unheard as I shivered from the cold. I was aware that my face hurt, my nose was running, and sounds close to *brrr* were coming from my throat.

Farther on, a night-light in a small uncarpeted room illuminated two exercise machines, one a typical tread-mill, the other a more elaborate, shiny black machine that resembled a robot with cables drooping from the frame and arms jutting out. Maybe if I'd kept my promise to sign up at the gym, I'd have known what the second machine was for, other than a torture device. I could make out a large calendar and framed photos on all the walls.

Except for the messy dining room table, I'd seen no evidence of a crime, no trace of the possibly three men who had robbed and maybe killed Dennis. I looked up at the second-floor windows, wishing I could propel myself to them. Apparently, the damage had been done up there.

I traveled to the last set of doors that would allow me a look inside. Only a thin window covering blocked my view into the living room, dominated on one side by a brick fireplace and on the other by a large television set. Another decorative area rug lay in the center of the hardwood floor. I recognized this one as being from Ashcot's Attic, similar to one that Quinn had picked out for my living room. No telltale bloodstains, if that was what I was hoping for.

It was time for me to leave. I hoped this fruitless trip

in the freezing temperatures would cure me of making any other such journeys, without a plan, without permission, without proper clothing.

I turned to head back to my car.

And ran into a beam of light that blinded me. I jerked back, my breath catching in my throat.

"You looking for something?" A male voice, deep, and not friendly. A cop? A neighbor? Or the very burglars I'd been thinking about?

I shielded my eyes, keeping my glance downward. I doubted I could speak, but words came out eventually. "Yes . . . I mean, no. I . . ." That was it.

The man lowered his flashlight, and once my eyes recovered, I saw a young man who looked familiar in the dim light. "Dyson?" I asked, hoping I was right. Dennis's son. Not an attacker, which was good news, because he was also carrying a baseball bat.

He nodded, then squinted, studying me. "I remember you. Quinn's friend. The postmistress."

I was so relieved I suddenly felt overheated. Surely, Dyson wouldn't attack a friend of a friend of his dad's or have her arrested, especially if she was also an official government worker. I remembered that Dyson had played with the Ashcots a few times on school breaks. A large man, like his father, he also followed in his father's musical footsteps with the bass guitar.

"Cassie Miller," I said, to put a face to the woman he was not going to slam with a baseball bat. "You're home," I added, needlessly.

"A buddy drove me down on his motorcycle. We got here a couple of hours ago." He swung the flashlight up to a second-story window. "Oops, sorry," he said, when he realized he'd caught my eyes again. "My friend Noah is upstairs sleeping." He showed me the bat. "And sorry about this. I didn't know what to expect since the break-in and all."

The break-in, but not his father's murder. I suspected the word, let alone the reality, would be too much for him to handle.

"Dyson, I can't tell you how sorry I am about your dad. I . . . uh. You're probably wondering why I'm snooping around." ·

Dyson shrugged. "I figure you want to know what's up."

Exactly. "That's right. If I'd known you were home, I'd never have intruded."

"It's okay. I can't sleep anyway."

"I'm sure."

"Do you want to come in? I wouldn't mind talking for a while."

"Neither would I."

10

It had felt strange to walk into Dennis's house by the front door. Strange also to be settled now by the fireplace, legitimately, in the blue recliner I'd viewed through glass as I trudged around in the cold. Dyson, on the two-seater sofa across from me, didn't offer to light a fire and I didn't request it. I kept my jacket on and my hands around my mug of hot coffee.

Dyson was in dark gray sweatpants and a MAINE sweatshirt. I wished I'd brought some of my lemon pie, for the boys and for me. He told me about his last day and a half. Sunni's office had tried to reach him yesterday afternoon, but he'd been out of reach in the woods of Maine until this morning. I didn't envy the officers in his small town who had to break the news to him. One of his roommates, Noah, had offered to drive him here on his motorcycle, an eight-hour trip.

"By the time we got here, it was too late to go to the police station," Dyson said. I didn't tell him that when it came to Chief Sunni Smargon, there was no "too late." "And I didn't want to wake up Mrs. Larson. She comes in to clean for my dad and she's the one who found him." He took a breath, gazed at the cold, unresponding fireplace. "I don't have that many close friends around here anymore. It's been almost four years and you lose touch."

Tell me about it. "It can be hard to come back."

Dyson was more soft-spoken than his dad, with a larger quantity of light brown hair, and a music major, much to Dennis's chagrin. "I named my son after Freeman Dyson, one of the greatest theoretical physicists and mathematicians of the times, whom I met personally," Dennis had often told us. "And it didn't work. He wouldn't do the right thing and major in physics." Dennis had such affection in his voice, every one of us knew how proud he was of his only son.

"I didn't know what I was going to find, but I guess the police had come and gone and the only place that was really tossed was my dad's office upstairs. The burglars must have gone into my parents' bedroom, too, because I noticed my mom's jewelry box is missing—I know my dad still kept it in the same place on her dresser. It's been almost four years and he didn't want to change anything, like he didn't want to record over her voice on the old answering machine. Then someone who led a bereavement group told him to keep that recording, but make a new one, so that's what he did. I'm not sure how you'd do that now."

"And you say the office was upset?" I nodded toward the upper floor.

"Yeah, books and files and papers everywhere, book-cases tipped over. I guess that's where it happened. I didn't hang around to see if there was anything missing. I figured the police had been here and taken what they needed. I didn't look for any sign of . . . anything." Dyson swallowed hard, and I guessed he couldn't bring himself to use the word *blood*.

I tried to calm him with meaningless words like "It's okay, Dyson." The same kind of platitudes I'd hated when I was in a similar situation.

"And my dad's kind of a neat freak," he said, in a hoarse voice. He'll be so . . ." He choked up again, real-izing his father would no longer be angry at anything. It didn't surprise me that he'd be thinking of his father in the present tense.

"It's going to take a while, Dyson," I said. I had the feeling that without my saying so, he understood that I knew from experience what he was going through. And it wasn't the first time for him. I tried to figure how old he would have been when his mother died, but I didn't know the exact numbers. Whatever they were, they were wrong for losing a parent.

We stayed quiet until Dyson was ready to break the silence. "I guess I'll go to the police station first thing in the morning, but I was wondering if you can tell me any-thing else. Like, do they have a suspect or anything?"

My heart went out to him. Although I'd come here for information or clues, I was glad to turn the tables and give Dennis's son whatever he needed to get him through this time. I briefed him on the string of robberies that had been making headlines, such as they were in our tiny paper, and on how Sunni had a lead that there were three burglars.

"I know she's doing everything she can to track them down," I said.

I didn't mention the letters to his father, allegedly from disgruntled students, nor did I want to bring up the fact that some of us, especially me, thought Dennis's killer might have been someone he knew and not random crooks. I pushed to the back of my mind the fact that his father might have had enemies over issues as small as scheduling classes or as large as blackmail. There would be time enough for complicated theories, if they survived the investigation, once he came to grips with the basics.

Dyson seemed to want to reminisce and I was happy to listen. I heard how hard Dennis had tried to interest Dyson in physics, with frequent trips to Boston's Museum of Science, enrolling him in science programs for kids and quizzing him at dinner about what he'd learned.

Dyson smiled for the first time, remembering. "I'd have none of it, but one trip to hear the Boston Symphony Orchestra and I was hooked. Of course, I'd also heard my dad play in his little group."

I was tired, but no way was I going to call an end to this visit. That privilege went to the grieving son, an orphan at that. I hoped somewhere there was an Aunt Tess or an Uncle Someone who would take him under their wing. "Did he take you to classes, too?" I asked, just to keep things going.

"Yeah, I'd be sitting there, like ten years old, with all his physics majors. But it gave me something to talk about when it was my turn to give a presentation in class about a field trip." I wished he hadn't used the word *presentation*, but I was sure he meant no harm. "Hey, Cassie, would you consider coming with me to the police station tomorrow? It would be awkward for Noah, not knowing anyone, and he has to go back to school first thing anyway."

I remembered Dyson's upstairs guest. "I hope we haven't woken him up," I said.

"Nothing short of a SWAT team would do that. He's a great guy. I'm glad I didn't have to make the trip alone." He cleared his throat. "That brings up something else. I know you have to work and all and, like I said, Noah will be leaving at dawn. It would really be great if I didn't have to go to the police station alone." He shrugged. "I've lost touch with my classmates here."

"I'd be happy to go with you, Dyson. I'm glad you asked."

"Thanks a lot. That's a relief."

For me, too, I thought. Until Sunni sees me.

Dyson walked me to the door while we made a plan that he'd come to the post office around ten in the morning and we'd go to the police station together. I offered to pick him up, but he thought the walk would do him good. He waved me off, waited until I pulled away, until he turned toward the house.

I wondered if he saw the three figures standing under a large tree across the street. Was Dyson in danger? I thought of calling Sunni, but I was so tired by then that I wasn't sure I saw the figures myself. In the wee hours, shadows could play tricks. That was probably the case now. I looked back. I was right. All I saw was a cluster of trees that hadn't lost their leaves. It had been a long day, a long night, and in only a few hours I'd be hoisting the flag in front of my place of business. Of course I was susceptible to uneasiness and a measure of fear.

Rationality aside, I checked my rearview mirror constantly on the way home. I was never so glad to crawl under my less than perfect quilt—once I'd checked the locks on all the windows and doors.

There was no good reason for me to show up at the post office before eight in the morning on Wednesday. No reason other than to visit the group of people the late Dennis Somerville had hung out with on a regular basis, the Ashcots. His campus environment hadn't yielded much by way of insight into his life or the manner of his death; maybe his music group would provide more information or inspire a direction for me to take in my so-called investigation.

I'd finally gotten to sleep around three in the morning, after tossing and turning, trying to chase away thoughts and images of the shadowy figures that seemed to be stalking me, if not in reality, then in my mind. Only after making a list of things to do and another list of questions to ask Sunni could I nod off.

Besides trying to find out if the police had any more information on the three suspected burglars, I needed to ask Sunni to let me take a look at the letters Dennis showed me, or tried to show me. I cringed inside when I thought of how I'd brushed his mail aside when he presented the envelopes to me himself, and brushed off his request for help. Responding now would hardly make up for that behavior, but I had to keep trying.

Third on my list was to seek out details on the crime scene. All I knew from the news was that Dennis had been shot; what I knew from Dyson was that he'd most likely been shot in his second-floor home office. From the chief of police, I knew nothing extra. My information added up to very little.

Fourth, and last for now, I needed to determine what if anything the Ashcots had to do with Dennis's murder. The musicians all seemed close, their arguments trivial. But it wouldn't hurt to check them out.

Thus my entrance that morning into the community room that shared the building with the post office. The room, one large hall with a tiny kitchen, ran almost the whole length of the building, taking up most of the east side. The door that led to the inside of the post office itself was always kept locked; the other door led to the outside, opening onto Main Street. The musicians were there because their regular rehearsal venue was undergoing repairs. The acoustics weren't the best, but it was just as well they got used to the situation, since the dance itself would be there. *? Senior Center on 5th St.*

Musicians and their instruments were arriving at the same time as I did. Joyce and Shirley with their guitars, Brooke with a kazoo this time, Greg needing a couple of trips for his drums, Arthur with a bass instead of his banjo, since the bass player was no longer with us.

I lifted a chair from a stack by the window and dragged it to the front of the hall while the musicians assembled.

When Quinn came in with his dobro, he looked surprised to see me. Although I'd stopped in before to hear them rehearse, I'd seldom arrived this early.

"Burning both ends of the candle, huh?" he asked, after a publicly acceptable embrace.

"I guess so."

"I called a few times last night after my meeting, but it went to voice mail."

"I was . . . out."

"Can't wait to hear about it." My boyfriend's tone was challenging.

I pointed to the assembled band. "You'd better take your place."

Mercedes, who was even later than Quinn, interrupted us. "Cassie," she said, "just the person I wanted to see."

"I'm almost ready for tomorrow," I said.

"Terrific, but I needed you for another reason. It's about our post office box. Dennis was the only one with a key, and now . . ."

She took a deep breath and closed her eyes, tight, as if to hold back tears.

"I'll take care of it," I said. "Stop in next door when the rehearsal is over. If I'm not there, I'll make sure Ben has your key."

"Thanks." She sniffed and carried her guitar to her place at the front of the room, where there was a great deal of tuning up going on. I'd always enjoyed music but never studied it seriously. My childhood piano lessons were no more meaningful now than the ticket stubs and programs I used to paste into my scrapbooks. Maybe once

I mastered quilting, I'd take up an instrument. The kazoo seemed the easiest.

With little chatting, the group lit into the lineup of songs on its Valentine's Day list. A soft ballad with a vocal by Brooke, then a more fast-paced one, and so on for three or four numbers, mixed well together.

"So, what shall we talk about this fine Valentine's Day?" Arthur asked. I always enjoyed it when the group ad-libbed a skit in between songs, and I liked it especially on days like today when they played it to an audience of one.

"Do we really want to do that this time?" Greg asked. Everyone knew what Greg meant by "this time." *At our first concert without Dennis Somerville?* "I think we should skip it." Greg wore his gray hair in a long ponytail and usually punctuated any remarks with a corresponding beat of his drums. He ended his comment about Dennis with a few strokes of his soft brushes.

"I disagree," Mercedes said. "We either do this gig or not, but I can't see holding back. That doesn't honor anyone."

"Me, too," Shirley said. A petite, curly-haired woman with a soft voice, she was often hard to understand. Like today, when I didn't know what she was agreeing with. I found it hard to picture her with enough energy to teach high school all those years, but maybe biology was inherently interesting to teenagers.

"I'm with Mercy," Joyce said, leaving no doubt. "Let's polish up the skit we've been working on, on getting dumped, as we planned."

I thought I'd heard wrong—getting dumped? As a

Valentine's Day tribute?—but the group seemed to know what they were doing. There were a couple of mournful strains from someone and then Joyce began the narrative, with more achy-breaky music in the background.

"Here I go," Joyce said. "My most embarrassing breakup." She strummed a few low notes on her guitar, and half recited, half sang the story. "It was graduation day and while our hats went into the air"—her voice was joined by other sad notes from her guitar—"our love burned out like a flare."

First, I heard a few well-placed groans, and then a vocal chorus followed, echoing Joyce's words, "Our love burned out like a flare."

Shirley came alive when she was playing or singing. No holding back with her enthusiasm or her voice. She followed Joyce, with a story of an actual Valentine's Day breakup "many years ago." Her chorus of "A black arrow to my heart" rhymed with her last line, "My lover broke us apart." I guessed, unlike me, some people were better onstage, and maybe that was the energy she brought to her classes.

I could hardly wait until it was Quinn's turn to share.

"I'll pass," he said, earning "boos" from everyone, including me. Only Brooke stood up for him.

"Give the guy a break," she said. "His valentine is sitting right there." She flung out her arm toward me, as befitted a former cheerleader, and everyone turned. Worse, Greg pointed his drumsticks at me, then beat out a drumroll that echoed through the hall.

I felt my face grow as red as the big box of chocolates I expected from Quinn this weekend, and was sure someone had kicked up the heat in the community room.

Though the stories were sad, the deliveries were humorous. Just when I thought everyone was having a good time, Greg, possibly miffed by having his suggestion overruled, and possibly still raw from having his wife leave him for Touchstone, a clown in a theater troupe, called out to Mercedes.

"Mercy, tell us about the darkness in the lighthouse." He used his drumsticks to create a dark mood, sounding almost like a thunderstorm.

Mercedes glared at him. "Knock it off, Greg."

"Come on, be a sport. Something must rhyme with Annisquam." He kept up a low drumbeat. "Maybe my love is warm." More drumbeats. "Or not warm."

Mercedes stood and gathered her things, knocking over her music stand in the process, and stomped the length of the hall to the door.

But the damage had been done. I pictured the Annisquam Harbor Lighthouse snow globe, formerly in Dennis's campus office, now sitting on my desk at home.

Here was a new twist—Mercedes and Dennis a couple, or a former couple? But so what? Mercedes had been divorced for many years; Dennis was a widower. Could Dennis have dumped Mercedes at an outing to the North Shore? And then kept a souvenir to remember the day?

It didn't make sense. But one thing was for sure: Rehearsal was over.

"I'm just glad no one asked me for a dumping story," I said to Quinn as we grabbed a few minutes in a corner at Mahican's before my flag-hoisting time.

"They wouldn't do that to you."

"I had an alternative story ready, just in case."

"You have another dumping story? Besides Adam?"

I nodded. "Funny that I thought of it before I thought of Adam and his cruel texts. This one happened in fifth grade when our class took a field trip to the Bunker Hill Monument in Charlestown."

"Boston, right?"

"Actually, it's on Breed Hill, and the British won that battle, so don't ask me why there's that famous obelisk and June seventeenth is a holiday in some New England counties." I took a healthy swallow of coffee and continued my dumping story. "Johnny B. and I had been having lunch together, which, of course, for ten-year-olds meant we were going steady. Then, at Bunker Hill for our field trip, I was one of the few unfit kids who couldn't climb all two hundred and ninety-four steps. After that, Johnny wouldn't have lunch with me."

"That's a lot of steps. No wonder you couldn't make it," Quinn said. "I'll bet they have handicap access now."

Quinn, always on my side. How nice.

At times like this, making last-minute plans, I wished Ben used e-mail. His lovely niece, Natalie, had set him up for it, but he checked it only about once every couple of weeks. "Whether I need to or not," he was fond of saying. I decided the punishment for that would have to be an early-morning phone call, though I knew he liked to sleep in. I waited until just before opening the doors at nine.

"I know it's last minute," I said.

"Now or this afternoon?" he asked, sounding not as groggy as I'd feared.

"Ten o'clock, I'm afraid."

He grunted. "No problem. Dyson Somerville's in town, right?"

My turn to grunt. "How do you know that? You don't live anywhere near Dennis's place."

He laughed. And why not? I'd just given him two gifts: the satisfaction of being summoned to his old job, desperately needed; and the pleasure of hearing my surprise at the extent of his knowledge of everything that came or went with respect to North Ashcot.

Ben always refused to take money when he subbed for me, but this week I was going to force it on him. It was only Wednesday and I already owed him big-time for Tuesday and a promised Thursday stint. Who knew what the rest of the week would be like?

I hung up with Ben and prepared for a rush of morning customers. As I went about my routine, getting supplies ready, I went over my meeting with Dyson. It occurred to me that I was the closest he had to a mother figure at the moment. I did the math. Dyson might be twenty or twenty-one at most, which would have made me a pretty young mother, but not impossible. A sobering thought.

I'd hoped to be able to call Sunni before the morning rush. I didn't want to show up at her office, unannounced, with the murder victim's son on my arm. I had enough explaining to do as it was. But I prided myself on opening on time, and today was not going to be an exception. I'd be in her presence soon enough.

135

As it happened, my first customer, Mrs. Peters, needed help closing up a padded envelope after she inserted a gift card she'd bought from our kiosk.

"I'm so glad you carry these now," she said, waving toward the array of gift cards for coffee, clothing, dining, electronics, school supplies, and dozens more. "You know, when these cards first came out, I swore I'd never use them. I thought it was cheating, instead of buying or making a real present and wrapping it and all." Another hand wave, this one in front of her chest. "Now that's all I ever give is gift cards. Do you think I'm being callous?"

I shook my head vigorously, stapling the envelope at the top and covering the sharp pointed edges with red, white, and blue sealing tape. "Not at all. Times change," I said, "and most people would rather choose a present than receive something they can't use."

"Do you think so? Do you think my nephew will like this instead of a shirt or a sweater that I pick myself?"

I would almost guarantee it. "I'm sure he'll know that your thoughts and wishes are equally heartfelt with this specially chosen card."

"Thanks, Postmistress Miller. Have a wonderful day."

Postmistress as advice giver. Who would have thought? But Mrs. Peters left happy, and that couldn't be bad.

Soon after, I saw Ben Gentry, long legs, shiny belt buckle, and all, shuffling around the front of the lobby, straightening the Flat Rate boxes in their slots, neatening the stacks of forms—return receipt, international post, and a few seldom-used ones—picking up bits of trash. He was tall enough to reach across to the shades on the windows and adjust them to exactly the same height. I guess I'd been sloppy this morning.

He chatted with longtime customers, eventually making his way through the gate and behind the counter, earlier than requested.

"Ben, I owe you this week," I said when the line was gone.

"You sure do."

"How can I make it up to you?"

He pulled a newspaper section from his back pocket and slammed it on my desk. Our desk. I picked up the paper and read the headline. POST OFFICE CLOSING IN WEST BRANLY. "You can prevent this from happening here, is what you can do."

Not good news. West Branly housed probably twice the population as North Ashcot. "There's not much I can do about it, Ben."

"Well, there are a few things." He pointed to the kiosk of gift cards, the brand-name stores displayed in living color. "Like that."

"I thought you were against that. Something about 'preserving the purity of postal service'? Or was that some other guy who helps me out?"

Ben had been unhappy about the new merchandising trend. Besides the gift cards, we now offered gift wrap, a few trinkets with the USPS emblem, and a small number of greeting cards. One-stop shopping. I'd reminded Ben that the greeting cards especially were good for the local economy in that we sold them by arrangement with Olivia's card shop across the street. Many were handmade by local residents, some at workshops in the same store. He'd reluctantly ceded my point.

Now he grinned. "Okay, okay, I did have misgivings about those prepaid gift cards to the big stores. And maybe a few other changes you've slipped in. I hoped you'd forgotten. But this article explains why this kind of expanding is actually good for us."

Ben took off his jacket, under which was the same regulation sweater he'd worn for years. Somehow it always looked freshly laundered and I wondered how he managed that. My guess was that he'd bought a case of them years ago.

I looked at the statistics in the first lines of the article. "The volume's dropped thirty percent in West Branly. I don't think ours is that bad. And first-class mail, like bills and cards, has dropped fifty percent. That's huge."

"There's online bill paying to blame," Ben said. "Online everything. Like those electronic cards people send. How can you compete against an animated card that jumps off the screen at you and practically serves you cake? And they're cheaper than what we're selling." He shook his head as if there was no hope.

I thought of Mrs. Peters and her nephew's gift card, certainly less expensive to mail than a bulky sweater. I hated to think in those terms rather than what was good for customers, but that was the reality. When every customer was choosing less expensive options, the retailer's bottom line suffered.

I'd continued to scan the article. The writer had presented startling numbers of closings and consolidations across the country. Many of the facilities were part of the legacy of historic properties, beautiful buildings of architectural significance and beauty.

"Customers are joining workers in the protests," I pointed out to Ben. "I guess you saw the photos about the sorting plant closing in the south." One of the photographs showed a fleet of enormous semitrucks with the postal logo, a graveyard of abandoned vehicles.

"Yeah, people complain about us, but when the chips are down, they want their local post office to stay open."

"But it's out of their hands, isn't it?"

"Sure is. You can't count on anything."

"Thanks for the reminder," I said, and gave the incoming customer my best smile.

11

At ten o'clock sharp, Dyson arrived in the lobby. He looked as though he hadn't gotten much sleep, or the long walk had been too much for him. The way I looked. Hard as I'd tried, I couldn't get the image of the three shadowy figures out of my mind. I went back and forth in my mind between *It's my imagination* and *I'm being stalked*. I didn't dare ask Dyson if he'd noticed the figures last night when I left his house. He had enough to worry about. Now he had his hands in his pockets, his posture that of an old man. I recognized the signs. It was astonishing how much a person could age in a day when personal tragedy struck.

He gave me a nod and a half smile and said, "Hey," a word that seemed to have established itself as a full-on greeting. He looked around the neat (thanks to Ben) lobby. "Wow, I remember this place. Hey, Mr. G."

Ben pushed through the gate and took Dyson in a half-hug, half-handshake embrace.

"We're going to find the sons a' guns who did this," Ben said. "And make them pay." His voice was soothing, his meaning sharp.

"Cassie is coming with me to the police station," Dyson said. "I don't think I want to face it alone."

"She's a good one to have with you." Ben crossed his index and middle fingers. "Cassie and the chief are thick."

I wasn't sure why Ben thought that mattered but didn't ask. Instead, I remembered something I should have asked last night. "When was the last time you talked to your dad?" I asked Dyson.

"Over the weekend. He was upset as usual about faculty meetings, thought the administrators didn't know what they were doing. He was always saying that, though. But I know he loves teaching and would never leave it."

Ben seemed to notice the slip also, the assumption that Dennis was still with us. He opened the gate and ushered Dyson through to where my desk was. A first for Ben, who usually treated that simple wooden gate as if it were guarding Fort Knox.

We took seats, Ben hoisting himself on a nearby table, a popular perch for him.

"Did he have any particular problem with any one person?" I asked.

"See what I mean?" Ben said. "When she gets going, you know she's going to get to the bottom of things. Count on it."

I'd never heard such an endorsement from Ben. He was spare with his praise, and I saw that it took a young man in pain to bring out his full measure of compassion.

"What Ben means is that I sometimes help our chief of police when she needs a layperson's take on things."

"Well, thanks, whatever you call it." Dyson scratched his head. "I'd have to think about the details of that call on Saturday. I know he said he was going to duke it out with some lady over the curriculum. Someone who's in the Ashcots, too, I think."

Joyce Blake, I thought. Not earthshaking, unless they had more to argue about than a curriculum issue.

"And there was a guy he was always preaching about. I guess this teacher did some awful thing, like take money from a student for a good grade." Dyson's eyes opened wide. "Like I would ever try to do something like that. That would have been enough to send my dad over the edge. He was, like, a straight arrow that way."

"He was trying to set a good example for you," Ben said.

"Totally. He was even thinking of turning in some faculty member he'd seen pulled over by a cop on the turnpike. Can you believe it? I told him, what if the guy just had a busted taillight?"

I hoped I remembered all these tidbits. I was too intimidated by Ben's presence to take out a notebook.

We'd started to dress for the walk to the police station when Mercedes rushed in. She was wearing another of her dramatic winter capes, this one in a mottled pattern of yellows and gold, matching highlights in her hair and reminiscent of a Turner seascape. I stepped to the counter to help her.

"Dyson," she said, flustered, opening her arms to embrace him. "Oh, Dy, I didn't expect to find you here so soon."

While they connected, I pulled out the paperwork and

retrieved the key to the Ashcots' post office box and had it ready to hand over to Mercedes.

I looked at her with a new eye, now that I knew she and Dennis had been an item. More than that, their breakup was apparently memorable. I thought again of one of Aunt Tess's keen observations, borrowed no doubt from someone more famous than she was: There's not much to see in a small town, but what you hear makes up for it.

The question, as always, was how much of it was true?

Mercedes left, apologizing for being in a rush, promising Dyson she'd see him again, assuring him of her best wishes. There was nothing more personal in her remarks than there was in mine.

"You taking some time off?" Ben asked Dyson.

"I'm not sure what I'm going to do. It's funny how when you come home it's not really home anymore, except for my dad, and now . . ." Dyson struggled to keep his composure. "We probably should get going. I told them at the station that I'd be there around ten thirty." He turned to me. "Is that okay, Cassie? Maybe I should have asked you first, about the time."

"It's not a problem."

I wondered if Dyson was always so diffident or if the loss of his only family had set his growth and self-confidence back a few years.

I could see that Ben was already rearranging the desk in the configuration most convenient for him as he took over the duties that had been his alone for so many years. Was this how I was going to be in about thirty years?

I supposed I could do worse.

* * *

Dyson was quiet on our short walk from the post office to the police station on a cold-but-not-bone-chilling morning. I wanted to allow him space but felt compelled to offer advice. I groaned inside, realizing I was already behaving like Ben, whose rule seemed to be: When speaking to someone younger than you, make as many suggestions as you can.

"You know, the chief of police is going to ask you some questions. Don't take it as anything like a personal affront, and don't be afraid to say you don't know, or that you'll have to think about it."

"Didn't Mr. Gentry say she was your friend?"

"She is, but she's also an excellent detective and she can be intimidating when she's in the middle of a case."

"When I told her that you were coming with me, she seemed happy."

"She did?" I hadn't meant to sound so shocked.

It crossed my mind that I had some nerve warning an innocent person about Sunni, as if she would be insensitive to the family of a murder victim. The only defense I could think of was that Dyson's situation brought out memories of the most traumatic days of my life. The chief at the time was an old (to me) man who thought being a cop meant you never smiled and you treated everyone like a past or present criminal or a potential criminal.

I'd been summoned to the station more than once in the weeks following the wreck that killed my parents.

Each time, the top cop made me feel as though (at best) I might be withholding information regarding the crash, or (at worse) I might have had something to do with it. His voice and my thoughts at the time echoed in my head, as clear as if they were not more than half my lifetime ago.

"Were your parents getting along all right in the last week or so?" I was asked.

They've been getting along for the last twenty years. They loved each other.

"Do you have any reason to think there was alcohol involved in the crash?"

The driver of the other car, the two-ton SUV, was drunk, not my parents, who never *drank anything stronger than espresso.*

"Did any of your friends have a reason to wish harm on your parents?"

Are you crazy? A drunk stranger ran into my parents.

"Did you have any kind of argument with your parents this evening or within the past few days? Maybe before you left for your party?"

No, no, and no. And it wasn't *my* party; it was my friend's sweet sixteen celebration, which turned out to be a wake.

As if I didn't feel guilty enough that I hadn't accompanied them on their shopping trip and, therefore, hadn't died with them.

I looked at Dyson, walking with his head down, like someone with a walker, careful of each step. There was a difference between death by car crash and death by gunshot, but they both said "murder" to me, and in the end, the emotional toll was the same. Enormous.

"Is there anyone you can stay with for a while? An aunt or uncle?" I asked.

"I might just hang out at the house for a while. I really don't know."

I took that as a no. No Aunt Tess in Dyson's life. How much harder this was going to be for him.

"Of course you don't know yet. And I don't mean to pry. I just want you to know that I'm here for you if you need anything."

Other than having your family back.

Sunni was ready for us with a brunch of fruit, pastry, and a platter of cheeses spread out on the conference table in a side office. Maybe not college student food, but that was a good thing. She welcomed Dyson with a warm embrace. "I figured you hadn't bothered to get breakfast this morning," she said to him.

Things had changed for the better in the North Ashcot PD. Dyson showed his appreciation by making sure there were no leftovers.

It turned out that Dyson and Sunni's daughter knew each other from high school. Dyson was a year or two ahead of Avery, but they'd been on a couple of the same teams and in a club or two together. Sunni and Dyson reminisced about some famous wins and losses on the soccer field, taking Dyson back to a time when this was his home.

Seeing her in action in this situation, I had the feeling Sunni would have responded this way even if she'd been meeting Dyson for the first time.

I wished I'd called ahead and gotten some tips from Sunni about what she expected from me during this interview, which seemed more like a reunion for the two of them. Was I supposed to be quiet, seen and not heard? Maybe even leave the room once I finished my third cup of coffee. Probably the one thing she did not want was me asking questions of my own. Did Dyson know about his father's hate mail? Did he know about Dennis's relationship to Mercedes?

I had an answer to at least one of my questions when Sunni turned to me and looked at her watch and then, not too subtly, at the door. "We should be done here in an hour or so, Cassie," she said.

I smiled and put on my jacket. "I'll see you then," I said. *Bummer.*

The only reason I could think of that Sunni would invite me back was that she assumed I'd picked up Dyson and would drive him home. But she had officers who could do that, so maybe I was to be part of the end of their interview. Either way, the morning hadn't worked out as I'd hoped.

I decided to leave Ben at my job for the morning, as he'd originally planned, and do something useful on my own. Granted, I was headed toward a week when I was off more than I was on at work, but it wasn't as if I were getting a mani-pedi or a haircut, the last of which was obvious. My shoulder-length style would be a midback style, more suitable to the young Officer Greta Bauer if I didn't take care of it soon.

There was one more thing I could do before I left the police building. I stopped at the reception area where the blond Greta sat behind a government-issue desk not unlike my own, her long hair tied back in a ponytail. I guessed her age at early twenties, not much older than Dyson. She was tall and fair and, I hoped, naive.

"I'm going to need some coffee before I face that wind," I said as I approached the credenza, with its minimal supplies for really bad coffee. Sunni kept her upscale, state-of-the-art machine away from the casual visitor or arrestee.

"That's not like the coffee"—she tilted her head toward the room where Sunni and Dyson were most likely carrying on a meaningful interview that I was not invited to—"back there."

"I know, but I had to leave to go back to work. I'm so glad there's finally progress on"—I drew quotes in the air—"the three bad guys." Winging it.

Greta chuckled and drew her own quotes. "You mean the two bad guys and a bad girl."

I laughed, because she did, and to cover my surprise. "Guilty of gender stereotyping, I guess," I said.

"Yeah, nothing's going to change until we give female crooks their due." Greta chuckled. "I'm surprised you know about it already. We just brought them in early this morning."

I thought about the shadowy figures outside the Somerville residence. Had I just missed an arrest? "Oh, I thought they'd been arraigned earlier." Still winging it.

She shook her head. "Sunni's just beginning to break them." She lowered her voice. "Apparently, they're being stubborn about the murder."

"You mean they admit to the robberies but not to the murder?" I stirred sugar and yellowish powder into the very bad coffee. Why not? I had no intention of drinking it.

"Yeah, I'm just sending out the notice for the newspaper and other folks." She indicated a stack of pages on the corner of her desk. "You want a copy?"

I pretended to think it over, then said, "Sure," with as unexcited a voice as I could manage. "Something to read on my break."

Greta's phone rang. I jumped. I imagined Sunni watching a video of her reception area, calling Greta with orders to toss me onto Main Street. Or have me arrested and ushered down to the unpleasant cells in the basement.

I waved to Greta and left while I had the chance.

Safely (I hoped) out on the street, I rushed toward Mahican's coffee shop, tossing the nasty coffee in the nearest trash. I stuffed the paper in my pocket; I didn't think it would be wise for me to read the memo as I walked. More cameras, probably.

I made it to Mahican's before eleven thirty, ordered a cup of real coffee, and took a corner seat. Mahican's wasn't the most popular place for dining at this hour, serving only packaged sandwiches and boxed salads, so I had no trouble finding a table in the corner.

I finally unfolded the paper Greta had forced on me (such was my story) and read the report on the suspects in the string of robberies.

Chief Smargon of the North Ashcot PD is pleased to report progress in the investigation into multiple home burglaries. Three suspects, ranging in age from twenty-two to twenty-five, have been taken into custody. The suspects are being held for questioning in several burglaries in the last two months. "We've had useful tips from the public," the chief said, "and our lines are still open to new information."

I read a couple more lines with the exact dates and addresses of the burglaries, apparently not privileged information. The report read like the general notices that usually appeared in police briefs.

No names of the suspects, of course, even though they were adults, and no mention of the gender representation. Also, no mention of progress in the more important investigation, Dennis's murder. How disappointing. And it was all I had. How was I supposed to help Sunni if all I was getting was what the general newspaper-reading public was told?

A major sticking point was that I'd assumed that if the robbers were following me, that meant they were also responsible for Dennis's murder, and therefore wanted to keep tabs on my progress. Not that I had any, but I had to acknowledge that I was developing a reputation for assisting the NAPD. It would mean that we—the NAPD and I—didn't have to look further into Dennis's friends and coworkers. A stranger, or three, looking for money—that was who did it.

Wouldn't it be interesting if I didn't see my shadowy tails while the two-boys-and-a-girl group were in custody? Through some perverse working of my mind, I was almost disappointed that they'd been grabbed up—my working theory was that they were following me because I was investigating and getting close. Grandiose? There were many who would think so, especially since *close* was not a word I would use to characterize my progress.

I was grateful to Greta for the one specific tidbit—two boys, one girl—and thought about cultivating a closer friendship with her.

I skimmed through the rest of the Police Briefs section. It was hard to tell one day from another in this catalogue of crimes. Motor vehicle accidents, disorderly conduct and malicious disorderly conduct (the difference being?), disturbing the peace, shoplifting.

The most interesting report was of an unannounced raid in a particularly questionable neighborhood by tow companies, allegedly contracted by the town to remove cars that were in violation of parking rules by even an inch, and tow them away. Some residents said they were ordered to pay as much as four or five hundred dollars to reclaim their vehicles. Residents claimed the city was essentially bailing out a failing towing business at the expense of its citizens. Whether in a small town like North Ashcot or a big city like Boston, politics seemed the same, inscrutable to a layperson.

I'd almost folded the paper when I caught a glimpse of one more item, this one rare: assault and battery of a police officer. I wondered who'd been involved and remembered that the bulletins covered South Ashcot as well as North Ashcot, and often a neighboring town if it had been slow that week in the Ashcots.

The term Ashcots rang a bell, so to speak, reminding me of the not-quite-famous musicians. As usual, my mind made a leap and I remembered Sunni's request of me when we met on the community college campus.

"See if you can find out, without being too obvious, who else has seen the letters Dennis showed you at the post office." Or something close to that, with an emphasis on trying to determine which students might have been involved. I guessed it would be hard for a faculty member to snitch on a student if it came down to cooperating with "townies" over "the gowns," the term reserved for campus folks. I'd never worked on a campus and could only guess.

Wouldn't it be great, I thought, to pull this morning out of the "useless" category and be able to tell Sunni I had a lead? Or a clue. Or anything. Something that might help her "break them," as Greta called Sunni's interviews.

I had an idea.

I called Ben first, to make sure he and everyone else knew I still considered myself Cassie Miller, North Ashcot postmaster, and would be back at my duties in the afternoon.

"No problem. It's not like I'm going fishing in this weather," dear Ben said. "You be careful, now."

"Careful? I'm just going to meet someone for coffee."

"Yup."

So that was that for Ben.

I called Quinn, the next step in my data-gathering plan.

"What's up?" I asked, though I was more eager to get

on with my agenda, which he seemed to have figured out halfway through his opening.

"I'm working on that table I showed you. I decided a good cleaning wasn't going to do it. I'm going to have to remove the old finish. That means . . ." He paused. "But I'm betting that's not why you're calling."

"It is partly. I'm interested in what you're doing."

"Yup," he said. *Yup?* What was happening to North Ashcot men? Was there a memo I didn't get about watching old cowboy movies? "I know you're out there. Not at your counter dispensing service and goodwill. Fred just came back from the post office and told me Ben was asleep on the chair. He had to wake him up by ringing that little bell on the counter."

"Oh dear. I guess that's why Ben brings that old bell out every time he takes over. I didn't realize he was overdoing it. He seems to like being back there."

"I didn't mean to make you worry. We all fall asleep on the job once in a while, and I don't think anyone would take advantage of him."

Not since the robbers have been caught, I thought.

"Now, what can I help you with?"

"Okay, you got me. I need to call Mercedes and I don't have her number."

"Well, that sounds harmless."

I waited while he dug out his phone, or perhaps an early twentieth-century notebook, and read it off to me. I tried not to rush off now that I had what I wanted, but a call waiting came in from Greta. I think Quinn believed me when I told him and signed off.

"Oh, Cassie," she said in a muffled voice. "You know

that paper I gave you? It turns out I probably shouldn't have done that."

"What paper?" I asked.

"Um. Oh. Thank you," Greta said, letting out a *whew* of a sigh.

"Thank *you*," I said.

12

The longer I sat with my coffee, the better Mahican's boxed salads looked. I picked out a Greek salad, just for the feta cheese and olives, as well as a caramel brownie, just for the sugar. I'd been much too nervous to eat at the police department brunch. Besides, I wasn't sure I was supposed to partake. Although Dyson had told me Sunni seemed happy that I was accompanying him, he was not much more than a kid, and I questioned his ability to psych out a chief of police with a wide array of super-powers.

I was due back at the station in an hour or so. If I took "or so" to mean twenty minutes, then I had until twelve thirty before picking up Dyson. Close to an hour on my own. Time for a little useful interaction with the key players in this week's drama. Where had they all been on Monday afternoon, for example, when Dennis Somerville's

home was supposedly being invaded? According to
Sunni, she'd checked all their alibis, but what if she
missed something? You couldn't always depend on su-
perpowers being foolproof.

I wished Sunni had shared the alibis and whatever forensics she had. Had she found the gun, for example? How
about perfect fingerprints all over Dennis's office from
someone who shouldn't have been there? Too soon for that
feedback, I realized, recalling Sunni's lectures on how
much backlog there was in understaffed crime labs.

I took my salad to the table and dialed Mercedes, who
picked up right away. Coming through my phone was background noise that seemed to match exactly the noise in
Mahican's. No wonder. Mercedes marched toward me with
her usual swagger, today's cape a deep green. We had a
good laugh when we realized that she'd been entering the
coffee shop when I called.

"When I saw Ben behind the counter at the post office,
I thought you might be sick."

"No, no, just some personal business."

She smiled. "Oh, good," she said, and headed for the
barista. I suspected she was relieved as much that I
wouldn't be cancelling my presentation to her class as
that my health was good. She came back with her lunch,
a packaged sandwich and chips, and joined me at my
table.

We chatted about how accommodating Ben was. Mercedes had lived in town all her life; her ex-husband and
Ben had been good friends until Cyrus passed away a
couple of years ago.

"Fishing buddies, I'll bet," I said.

We pried our packages open and tried to look as refined as possible unwrapping primitive plastic utensils, tearing apart impossibly sealed dressing packets, and arranging tiny napkins on our laps. "I almost forgot," Mercedes said, taking a small pill container from her purse and placing it next to her picnic-style box. "You called me?"

"Right. I thought we could verify some details for tomorrow." Face-to-face with someone I was considering, however dubiously, a murder suspect, I became tongue-tied. It would have been much easier to interrogate her by phone. Or so I told myself. "Shall I meet you at the same place?"

Mercedes chewed on a cracker and nodded. "Mary Draper Hall."

"Also, I realize I don't know exactly how long the classes run these days."

"Fifty minutes. You can plan on talking for about a half hour and then take questions. Does that sound okay?"

"Yes, and I'll have enough material in case everyone falls asleep and there are no questions."

Mercedes laughed. "If they do, it won't be the first time." She picked a tiny pink pill from her box and swallowed it with a swig of water.

"I thought I'd start with Sir Rowland Hill and how the valentine tradition took off in Victorian England once he instituted penny postage."

"Now, see, that's the kind of thing I find fascinating," she said.

It was hard to tell whether Mercedes was sincere or doing her best to encourage the slow kid in the room.

"How come I wasn't invited to the party?" a throaty voice came from over my shoulder.

Joyce Blake had the same idea for dining today. I hadn't noticed her arrival, but she joined us now with yet a different variety of Mahican salad, hers being spinach based. Had I lost my chance to query Mercedes? I wasn't sure whether the addition of Joyce at the table would work for or against my little plot to play interrogator, but I had to make use of the little time I had left. Neither was it lost on me that with the capture of the three burglars, the murder case might also have been solved, and I could hang up my nonexistent badge. My curiosity won out as usual—I reasoned that Sunni might need more information, if only for completeness in her report.

I allowed a little more small talk about the postal service, sharing a tidbit about the young "post boys" of Victorian England who wore scarlet jackets and delivered the mail by horseback, and who often stopped to play together, leaving their horses and their precious cargo untended and the object of a great many robberies.

"Cassie was giving me a peek into her lecture tomorrow," Mercedes said. "You should drop in if you're free."

"A lecture on the post office. How fascinating," Joyce said, and this time the insincerity was blatant.

"Seriously, how often do you think about it?" Mercedes asked. "Having a postal service accessible to the masses was a significant step in free information exchange."

"You're right," Joyce said. "I usually dwell on the negatives. Bills and endless junk mail, plus solicitations, and even hate mail."

Hate mail. I was nearly overcome thinking of the mail

that had caused Dennis Somerville such consternation. It bothered me to cut short a discussion of the postal service, but I was aware of my mission of the moment. If I was going to do this, it had to be soon.

"You know, I'm still a little upset that my last interaction with Dennis was unpleasant," I said. Both women became intensely interested in their salads. I plowed on. "He came into the post office on Monday morning, very unhappy with some letters he'd received, ostensibly from students." When this little poke drew no response, I went further. "Mercedes, weren't you in the lobby at that same time?"

Mercedes covered her mouth, indicating she was chewing and unavailable to answer. Joyce took over.

"If you ask me, Dennis made much too big a deal about those letters," Joyce said. She caught herself quickly, covering her mouth, also. "Oh, I'm so sorry. I shouldn't be speaking that way. It's just that I wish he hadn't gotten all worked up about them. It's not the first time a C student tried to make our lives miserable. These days, he's lucky it didn't go viral."

Mercedes nodded, in sweeping vertical motions of her head. "They're getting ruder and ruder," she said. "The other day, I made a note on one guy's paper, that he was using too many words that were foreign to the general reader. Do you know what he did? He sent me an e-mail saying 'look them up.'"

"One of my complex variables students said I should put all the assignments online. He said, 'It's not rocket science.'"

"Hey," Joyce said. "We ought to do a skit on this."

"Most insulting moments. It doesn't have to be all

students, though I've certainly had enough of them." Mercedes seemed to come to life at the idea, then became aware that she might be scaring me off. "But they'll love you, Cassie. Really, they love any speaker who isn't me. For a break, I mean. Trust me."

"I'm trying to," I said.

Possibly to lure me away from thoughts of mean students, Joyce cited a rude taxi driver she'd met at a conference in Albany.

I realized they were talking about a skit for the Ashcots, like the one I'd heard at this morning's rehearsal, on being dumped.

"I love this idea, Mercy," Joyce said, and came up with a chorus of "we get no respect."

"We don't get paid enough," Mercedes sang in response.

Mercifully, they kept their voices low and well below the volume of Mahican's patrons.

I was tempted to add a few stories of my own, of customers who'd been rude to me over the years—complaining when I asked for an ID, blaming me for damaged or soiled mail, wondering why I didn't have on hand every single commemorative ever produced. As entertaining and therapeutic as this interlude was, I needed to get back on topic.

"I didn't realize you knew about the letters," I said, addressing both women. "Did the police ask you about them? Whether you had an idea who might have sent them?"

Joyce rolled her eyes. "The police." Mercedes took another mouthful of spinach, seeming happy to let Joyce be the spokesperson. "You know, they come on campus as if they're so important. I know you're friends with the chief, Cassie, but this time they sent this rookie who's probably not even old enough to attend the college."

Greta. I pictured her with her bouncy ponytail. But Greta was a police academy graduate, if nothing else, and deserved our respect. On the other hand, I'd seen Sunni on campus and wondered why she didn't do the interviews herself.

"You mean Officer Bauer?" I asked. "Is she the one who asked you about the letters?"

"The letters and Dennis's murder. What is she? Eighteen?"

"She's a sworn officer, Joyce. Maybe Sunni thought Greta would relate better to the students." I spoke before realizing that I'd be seen as predictably defending my friend.

Joyce grunted. "Maybe. And it is certainly more and more a youth culture. I wonder if the killer is a youth. Getting even with an old person."

It surprised me that a teacher of youth would speak the word so harshly.

Mercedes gasped. Joyce put her hand on that of her friend. "I'm sorry, Mercy. Sometimes I forget that you two . . ."

She trailed off, much to my dismay. "You two what?" I wanted to know but didn't ask. Some interrogator. Afraid of offending the interrogatees. Mercedes had been off the hook for these questions, and was now breaking into her brownie.

"How about you, Mercedes?" I asked, before the first piece of chocolate made it to her mouth. "Am I right that you and Dennis were at the post office at the same time on Monday?"

"Yes, I was there that day, but way in the back of the line. I noticed that Dennis stormed out, that's all. I didn't know why."

"He wanted me to investigate where the letters were coming from. It's such a funny feeling," I said, "when the last thing I remember about Dennis is going to be that unpleasant interaction."

"Tell me about it," Joyce said. "I thought we'd settled all that fuss about the curriculum, but that morning it all came back."

"Catalogue time," Mercedes said.

"What time?"

"We're getting next fall's catalogue of courses ready."

"So soon?"

Mercedes and Joyce both chuckled. At the blissfully ignorant postmistress, I guessed. "We have to get all the courses and requirements squared away, and, not that we have to, but we always end up rethinking every decision, rearguing every outcome."

"Like that calculus course you mentioned?" Lucky I remembered the term. "I don't see why the stakes are so high about what gets offered when."

Joyce took a breath and let it out with a loud sound. Not loud enough to drown out the mix of music coming through Mahican's speakers, but loud enough to tell me she was heavily invested in the issue. The issue that was no longer a problem with Dennis Somerville out of the way.

"What one department requires from another department at the college is at the heart of ninety percent of our meetings."

"She's right," Mercedes said. "For example, if I'm going to teach Locke's theory of government in the Enlightenment period, it would be nice if the English department offered a class in the literature of the era, perhaps some of the early feminists."

"There's another dimension in the case of math and science," Joyce said. "If you're teaching a topic in science that depends on a certain course in mathematics, as physics does, then you assume the mathematics department is going to offer the necessary courses before the student takes physics."

"That makes sense," I said, venturing into areas where I had no business.

Joyce let out another tense breath and I thought her face reddened slightly. Who knew science and math were hot topics fraught with such intense emotion? Joyce had been much more low-key when talking about the same disagreement yesterday. Today her ire seemed to have bubbled to the surface. I wondered if it had bubbled on Monday afternoon, with dire consequences for Dennis.

"It does not make sense," Joyce blurted out. "Let me explain something to you, Cassie. Some people, like you, think that all mathematics is is a service to physics and other sciences." She threw up her hands and brought them down again, nearly knocking over her box of salad.

"I didn't realize—"

Mercedes rolled her eyes and gave me a sympathetic look. I guessed she'd heard all this before.

"As if it's not a legitimate field of study for its own

sake, with no applications to anything else. As if it shouldn't be taught in an order that coincides with its own development."

I was stumped. "Oh," I said.

"There are studies in complex analysis, abstract algebra, and many other classes that never mention the physical world."

"Oh," I said again.

I would have thought it was a good thing to be of service to science and studies of the physical world. But apparently not. I had a lot to learn, and Joyce still wasn't finished.

"It's arrogant physicists, like Dennis and others in his department, who can't see that. But you see those students over there?" She pointed to a table along the street side of the shop. "They're my math majors. They're not taking linear algebra to be able to find the trajectory of a bullet or to find out how fast a ball falls from the roof of a building. They're studying it for its own sake, because it's beautiful and elegant."

I felt another "Oh" coming on, and took a bite of cracker to stifle it. I wanted to ask why her students had traveled a half hour for an expensive cup of coffee, but then remembered what campus cafeteria coffee was like. Besides, I knew that any off-topic remark would only annoy Joyce more.

I'd started out on Joyce's side, but now I began to wonder if the math department deliberately scheduled courses so they would not be useful to science majors. Strange. Wasn't a college campus—the Gown—supposed to be a model of higher learning, unfettered by the pettiness of the politics that ran the Town?

Joyce's tone took an abrupt turn as she apologized for being "callous," as she called it. "It's probably a good idea if I leave," she said. "It's not a great day for any of us." She looked at me. "Maybe I'll see you tomorrow, Cassie. Good luck with your lecture." She hoisted her rainbow-colored knitted purse over her shoulder, grabbed her trash, and headed out.

"Me, too," Mercedes said, following close on her heels.

It wasn't clear what she was referring to. Was it something I said that drove the women to cut short their lunch hour?

I knew what I hadn't said: I'd forgotten to sneak in a question about Joyce's or Mercedes's alibis for Monday afternoon. I'd stopped counting how many chances I'd blown, and I still had a half hour before I was due at the station. If I tried, I might be able to fit in a few more failures.

Now that the table had quieted down—that is, no one but me was left—I had an opportunity to look around the café, now fairly crowded. I checked each table as best I could to see if I knew anyone else in the shop. I wasn't looking for company; I was looking for suspects.

The room had grown more crowded, noisy with chatter and background music, mixed with the occasional sound of the coffee grinder. I seemed to be the only one dining alone. When my gaze landed on the table Joyce had pointed out along the Main Street side of the shop, I saw a group of what looked like five female students crowded around a card table—the one designated for handicapped customers, I noted—with cell phones and tablets or laptops.

What were the chances the students would talk to a stranger? But I wasn't really a stranger, I told myself. I ran the post office, which they must use at least once in a while, if only as part of an office job. Maybe to send valentine cards through Romance, Arizona, or Loving, Oklahoma. They might have been in Mercedes's classroom on the day I visited. I wished I'd paid more attention. Finally, I could claim that I was practically BFFs with their math teacher, whom I'd recently annoyed.

An idea formed. I summoned my courage. I was glad I'd decided to stuff my tablet and stylus into my shoulder bag at the last minute, and pulled it out now. I called up a greeting card site I subscribed to, one I'd kept from Ben's view, lest he blame me for the fall in USPS revenue. I searched for an appropriate sympathy card and selected one for my "project," as the menu options called it. I carried the tablet over to where the young women were keyboarding, texting, and sliding their fingers across screens. Not a pen or piece of paper in sight.

"Hey," I said, to indicate how cool I was. "I'm Cassie Miller. I was having lunch with Dr. Blake just now and she pointed you out to me." So far, no blatant lie. They (more or less) granted me the favor of their attention. I opened my tablet and showed them the screen. "I'm helping to collect thoughts and signatures for a card in Dr. Somerville's honor." Not entirely false. I could conceivably send a card like this to Dennis's son. I was sure Dyson would appreciate the tribute.

The girls came alive with sounds of sympathy mixed with dubious looks. Should they or should they not trust me? I was glad no one challenged me openly. *Exactly whom are you helping? What do you mean "in his honor"? What's going to happen to these signatures? Aren't you just the post office lady?*

"It was terrible, what happened," said a chubby girl sitting behind a laptop, to my right.

"I guess it would hit physics majors even harder," I said.

Chubby Girl nodded. "One of my roommates was supposed to have class with him on Monday afternoon. Now she still doesn't know if the class is going to continue." She looked up at me and appeared to accept my cover story. "What would you like us to do?"

I handed her my tablet and stylus. "If you could write a few words of condolence, or whatever comes to you, and sign your name, that would be great."

"Sure," she said, then, "Wow, cool tablet. Is this an N-trig stylus? I need to upgrade."

Young woman number four gave her a look. "Now's not the time, Amanda."

I said a silent "Thank you" to Number Four for sparing me. I had no idea what kind of stylus I'd been toting. One of these days, I'd read the literature that had come with the set.

"I know. Sorry," said Amanda, formerly Chubby Girl.

The screen showed a somber image of a bouquet of white lilies on one side and a large, empty text box on the other. Amanda trapped long strands of dull brown hair behind her ears and wrote a few lines.

"I had Dr. Somerville for an intro course," said young woman number two. She was dressed in a purple ski outfit from head to toe, except for a sliver of black or white here and there. She took the handoff from Amanda and started writing. She looked at me and added, "Everyone liked him."

"That's what I hear," I said.

"You didn't hear everything," said young woman number three, whose face was mostly hidden by her laptop screen.

My ears perked up.

"Don't say that, Morgan," Amanda said.

"Well, it's true. He hated math majors," Morgan said.

"Morgan's a transfer student," Amanda said to me, though I wasn't sure why. If it meant that her opinion didn't matter as much, it wasn't obvious from her attitude.

Morgan handed the tablet to Number Four, without adding a sentiment or her name to the digital card. I didn't realize college women could be so cold. But then, I'd been cold enough to plan and execute this charade. I shivered in my jacket, telling myself it was because it was chillier near the door.

"Come on, Morgan, just because you didn't do well on the pop quiz?" Number Four said, writing for a few seconds while I marveled at how she could hold the stylus properly, given her extremely long fuchsia nails, each sporting a decorative icon in glittery colors. I could make out a heart, an angel, and a rainbow. I couldn't guess at what the other seven might be.

"Stuff it," Morgan, the transfer student, said. She stood out with her black jeans and expensive-looking sweater, compared to her friends' worn blue jeans (which, I realized, might have been more costly) and logo sweatshirts—an out-of-season Red Sox shirt on Amanda, an in-season Bruins shirt on Number Five, and Boston College Eagles on two others.

"I'm not a math major," Number Five said, and giggled. A typical self-conscious reaction, from a girl with typically long, straight hair. "I just hang out with them."

"You shouldn't sign," Morgan said to the non–math major."

After a little teasing and chuckling that I didn't understand, Number Five said, "I flunked out of math the first week. I'm an English major now. I guess I can sign the card anyway?"

"You shouldn't," Morgan said, blowing out an exasperated breath.

"Of course you can sign," I said, and was pleased that she did.

The tablet and stylus came back around to me. I smiled. I had what I wanted. One student in five was upset enough with Dennis Somerville not to sign a sympathy card on his death. Who said statistics was hard?

I returned to my table, where I'd left my scarf and a paper notebook to mark my place, a practice usually honored at Mahican's. Was Morgan upset enough with her physics teacher to have sent him a nasty letter? Upset enough to go to his home and shoot him? I saved the card as SomervilleProject and sat back as far as Mahican's rickety, short-backed chairs would allow.

I allowed myself a few seconds to bask in the idea that I'd solved Dennis's murder. When reality hit, I had more questions than answers. How seriously would Sunni take the story? I was lucky enough to be in the coffee shop when the killer was there. I happened to think of introducing myself as the person in charge of arranging a gesture of sympathy for Dennis's son. And, even more luck, the killer revealed herself by being unwilling to sign the card. All the chief of police had to do was go to campus and ask for a math major named Morgan.

I could hear Sunni's laughter bounce around the room, mixing with the conversational sounds of satisfied coffee drinkers. But regardless of the far-fetched nature of my story, I had something I hadn't had at any time this week. A lead. I stuffed my tablet into my shoulder bag and headed for the police station.

I zigzagged through the crowded tables, skirting a couple of strollers on the way to the exit, paying more attention to the other patrons than I usually would. Were there any other groups of students who might have known Dennis, or disliked him enough to act on their feelings?

I also wondered if the mostly math table occupants would figure out that theirs was the only klatch I approached in my alleged quest for messages of sympathy for the Somerville family. Finally, there was the question of whether Joyce would find out that I'd used her name to gain entry into the student body. If she did, I supposed, I could rule out an invitation to lecture in one of her math classes.

I recognized several patrons as post office customers and exchanged quick greetings. I saw one or two other gatherings that might have been study groups or cliques of college students, but couldn't think of a way to approach them without arousing suspicion and possibly being ushered out as a public nuisance. I left the shop, memories of my own school days flitting through my head, days when tablet meant a paper notebook and none of my professors had been murdered.

On my walk to the police station, two freezing blocks away, I tried to rebuild my case against Morgan, ignoring the taunts of reality. Morgan had an arrogant air about her, as if she were used to being pampered. What if Dennis had been the first person in her life not to give in to her sense of entitlement? She'd refused to sign a simple sympathy note, in public.

My case fell apart before I passed Mike's Bike Shop, on the opposite corner from the police building. As Joyce had reminded us, what college student hadn't "hated" a professor at least once in her life? What professor hadn't experienced the ire of a student who got a grade less than she expected or an unappreciated criticism in red ink? If those feelings always led to murder, no school would survive more than one semester. Similarly, no postmistress would survive if every complaint about misdelivered mail led to homicide.

As I crossed Second Street, I saw one of Sunni's small fleet of black-and-white patrol cars with blue trim pull out of the lot. Greta was in the driver's seat, and, if I wasn't mistaken, it was Dyson Somerville who was slumped down in the passenger seat.

Had I overrun my time? I checked my watch. Five

minutes before the early end of the range I was given, to report back "in an hour or so." It was clearly Sunni's intent to have Dyson on his way before I returned. Then why ask me to return? To deputize me, perhaps? I thought of turning that phrase into a skit for the Ashcots: *Deputy Cassie Miller, never going to happen.*

I'd missed my chance to spend more time and talk further with Dyson. I'd planned to drive him home and perhaps invite him to dinner. I could still do that, but it would have been much smoother if I didn't have to make a separate call, as if I were tailing him. Not that I would admit it, but I'd hoped to be seen as part of the police department. I'd hoped to get a briefing on what Sunni and Dyson had covered, as if I were a member of her force.

At every step along the broken concrete sidewalk, I had a different guess as to what Sunni had in mind, letting Dyson go before I returned. I walked onto police department property, past the wooden bannerlike sign with a white background and NORTH ASHCOT POLICE in large black letters. I was about to find out.

In the warmth of the small police building reception area, I felt better. Even though I came face-to-face with Sunni, who was at Greta's desk, on the phone.

"You bet, Mr. Carson." Pause. "Yes, sir." Pause. "Consider it done."

She hung up and gave me a look that said I should be glad I didn't have her job.

"Am I late?" I asked.

"Not at all. Come on back." Sunni motioned for a

subordinate to take over the phone while we walked back to her office.

"Well?" she asked, indicating that I should take the chair in front of her desk. She sat back in her vintage office chair, a mismatch to her new desk, crossed her arms.

As usual, I was to go first in our information sharing confabs.

I started with my morning visit to the Ashcots' rehearsal, and the news, to me, that Mercedes and Dennis had at one time been an item.

"I don't have any idea which one of them called it off," I said, but, since I hadn't asked a question, Sunni's face remained impassive. I believed it was called a poker face. Maybe this was not news to her. I thought of stirring her to a response by mentioning that Dennis had kept a little souvenir by way of a snow globe lighthouse that I now had in my possession.

Instead, I moved on to my indoor picnic lunch with Mercedes and Joyce at Mahican's. All I could report was that Joyce still hadn't gotten over the faculty meeting skirmishes. I explained as best I could how Dennis apparently ignored her right to schedule math courses for the educational benefit of her own math students and not for the convenience of his physics students. If she already knew more than I did about this issue, she didn't mention it.

Sunni took a note now and then but didn't respond to me directly. Unnerving. For all I knew, she was writing out her valentines list.

I moved on to my interaction with the students, playing

down my method of introduction, emphasizing the signing of the tablet and my suspicion about the one student, Morgan, who refused to sign.

Sunni sat up, her old chair clicking into the upright position. I'd finally got her attention.

"You say you have signatures from a group of math majors?"

"I have four signatures, three from math majors, one from an English major who dropped out of math."

"Let's take a look," she said.

While I dug out my tablet and called up the greeting card app and the screen for SomervilleProject, Sunni opened a box on the floor near her desk and pulled out a stack of plastic bags containing letters and envelopes. I had no doubt they were the letters I'd shunned when Dennis tried to foist them on me, on Monday.

The letters looked different now, each one spread open in its own plastic bag, each envelope also in its own bag, all six of the bags marked with a number I took to be related to evidence cataloging.

I placed my tablet on the desk and turned it so we could both look at the screen. "I didn't realize this was really evidence," I said.

"It is until it isn't," Sunni said.

"Of course."

"Tell me what we have here."

Once again I skipped over the preliminaries of my cover story and began with describing the young women. I'd been watching while they entered their text and noticed that they wrote one underneath the other. Handy for me—I'd be able to tell which message went with which student. I pictured them as they'd sat in front of me, standing at one o'clock. Seated counterclockwise from me were Amanda (formerly Chubby Girl, with apologies), Purple Outfit, Morgan, Fancy Fingernails, and English Major.

Sunni smoothed out the first letter, keeping it in its sleeve. I hadn't realized how exciting it would be when the signatures on my tablet would be compared with the letters. The initial delight faded soon, when I felt I had to warn her.

"These were written with a stylus, so even if the same person wrote the letter and tablet message, they're not going to be an exact match."

"I realize that, but these signatures are finer than any I've ever seen on a computer screen, or whatever you call this thing. We've already had an analyst go through them and tell us the same person wrote all of them, so that's a start. Now let's see if that person is on this list."

How nice that my friend was sharing. "Also, remember, Morgan, the student who was so angry with Dennis, didn't write anything," I said.

"True, but let's see how the others compare. She might not have been the only one with a grudge. At the moment it's the only lead we have on where these letters might have come from."

"Does this mean you think the letter writer or writers are connected to the murder?"

Sunni took out a magnifier and moved it back and forth from the letters to the signatures on the screen, several times. By now, I was used to having my questions go unanswered. Still, I marveled every time at how effort-lessly she could ignore someone who was asking a question in her face, so to speak.

"Well, by golly. Look at this." She turned the screen slightly and showed me what caught her interest. "I'm no expert, and I will definitely get an expert back in here, but check this out. The letters on the paper notes and the computer notes all slant to the right, and there are wide spaces between the words. Also note the correspondence between the upper case *S* in Somerville and the upper case *S* in Sampson."

Sunni indicated the message written by the English major, Norah Sampson, and then showed me the letters. It was the first time I'd seen the texts of the letters. I'd missed my chance when Dennis brought them to the post office and I sent him and them away. Since that time they'd been in police custody.

I read the three anonymous letters first.

Dr. Somerville,

You will be remembered as the worst teacher this school has ever had. You should be fired and I'm going to see that that happens. I know people on the committee.

Dr. Somerville,

The handbook says the school should be a force for good in the lives of all our students. You will be remembered as a force for evil.

Dr. Somerville,

It is those unfair (unethical) quizzes that will be remembered long after you're gone.

They were all short and to the point. Could these sentiments have been the start of the real, physical attack on Dennis that had cost him his life? They certainly were nothing that should have been forwarded to a postal inspector. Or maybe they were? Was *long after you're gone* a warning? My stomach acted up, reminding me of the feta cheese I'd consumed for lunch.

Even I could tell that the same person had written the notes Dennis had received in the mail. The uppercase letters all had a certain flourish, and the three messages all had the same tone, though I couldn't put my finger on it.

I looked again at the condolence messages on my tablet and scrolled to the one by the last student to sign, the English major.

Dr. Somerville will be remembered fondly by all.
Norah Sampson.

Sunni had been waiting until I finished my inspection. "Besides the close match to the uppercase *S*, notice how the same phrase comes up in all of them. Some form of 'Will be remembered.' We all have certain words that we use more often than others, especially when we're expressing something laced with emotion. In the notes to Dennis, the tone indicates a certain superiority, knowing someone on a committee, for example, and in the sympathy note, it's passive, meaning she herself will not necessarily remember him fondly."

"How do you know all this?" I asked.

Sunni shrugged. "Strictly amateur. From one of those obligatory training sessions in forensics. I thought it was going to be one of those woo-woo courses."

"Woo-woo?"

"You know, like astrology. If you were born under a certain sign, you're likely to be a caring and supportive person. If your handwriting is upright, it means you're independent; if it's slanted to the right, you're open to new ideas. Et cetera, et cetera."

"Intriguing."

"Yes, and there is more to it than I thought, as long as you don't give it more credit than it's due." She tapped the six envelopes, now piled on her desk. "In this case, I'm not trying to use it to determine personality or trustworthiness or anything like that. I'm just comparing handwriting styles to see if they match."

I thought back over the time I'd known Sunni. Had I ever handwritten a note to her? I hoped not.

"Are you going to question Norah Sampson?"

"Who's cooking tonight?" she asked.

As non sequiturs went, that one ranked high on the creativity scale. I didn't try to fight it. Instead, I answered her question. I put my finger to my head. "Let's see, Wednesday night? Quinn."

"Like every night. Can you get rid of him for one night?"

"Absolutely."

"Cefalu's at seven? I'm buying."

I nodded, because I didn't trust my voice to respond to this unexpected invitation. In fact, I thought I'd dreamed it.

Somewhere in the distance a bell tolled. One o'clock. I gathered my tablet and woolens. "I'd better get back to work."

My walk back to the post office was uncomfortably cold. My cheeks burned; my eyes watered; my fingers and toes felt numb. I managed to take my hand out of my pocket once or twice to wave at another pedestrian across the street, but most people were smart enough to use their cars. I distracted myself from the pain by considering reasons Sunni might be taking me to dinner. One thought was that she was ready to deputize me. A smile was nearly impossible with my stiff cheeks, or I would have produced one of my widest. More likely, she was gearing up to warn me off and alert me to the fact that I was finished as a helper.

It could go either way. Like all interesting relationships.

I opened the side door to the post office and, despite the delicious warm air, stamped my feet as if I'd walked through a foot of snow. I still had ten minutes before I'd unlock the front doors to customers at one thirty.

I realized I had a lot to do before tomorrow morning's lecture. I'd pushed it to the back of my mind, considering it part of the investigation—to hang around Dennis Somerville's environment—not giving equal weight to the fact that I was expected to deliver a lecture. A presentation.

A talk. No matter how I labeled it, I needed to prepare it, instead of thinking up ways that I could "accidently" run into Norah Sampson, the English major with incriminating handwriting.

Another visit to the physics and math building, Patrick Henry Hall, might be possible, but it would be hard to come up with a convincing excuse for Gail, the gate-keeper extraordinaire, the second time around. I felt I'd made it out of there the first time with little room for error.

As one thirty struck, so did a realization: Norah Samp-son would likely have English classes tomorrow. I should drop in on that building. If the college was anything like mine, there were no special English department quarters. It was a good bet that their classes were held in the same building with history and other lab-free courses in Mary Draper Hall, where I'd be lecturing (in the loose sense) tomorrow. Could I be so lucky?

I opened the front doors of the post office to the cold and the wind, but to no immediate customers. I had time to sneak in a call to the college. As I made my way through the empty lobby, back to my desk, I used my cell phone to look up the main number and hit DIAL.

Once I got past a menu of number preferences and a couple of minutes of crackly music, I was able to ask my question.

"I need to pick up my daughter after her English class this morning," I said, trying to insert a sense of urgency. "I've forgotten the name of the class. Is there a special building for English classes?"

"One moment please."

My "Sure" was followed by another minute or so of

14

Luckily, it was a slow day. Not that I would ever use the words *lucky* and *slow* in the same sentence in front of Ben. I checked the small stack of to-do items and other notes he'd left me. Order more international forms. Destroy outdated registered mail forms. Check on new advanced shipping notice forms. And my favorite, a peek into Ben's sense of humor: Look into the form for ordering forms.

He'd also left me a couple of books on post office history that he'd picked up on his last trip to the postal museum in Washington, D.C. I'd visited that museum a number of times, as well as many other regional museums. In keeping with today's merchandising practices, most had gift shops. I considered wearing a red and gray baseball T-shirt I'd bought in D.C. or the I DELIVER cap I'd bought in Boston instead of my uniform at tomorrow's presentation, but I figured I needed all the help I could get from wearing something less frivolous.

Ordinarily, I used downtime during the day for picking up around the office. I had a cleaning staff of one, a loyal and efficient retired letter carrier from Springfield, Massachusetts, Brenda Mallory, who came only once every two weeks for a couple of hours. A lot of dust, grime, and litter accumulated between her visits, and it fell to me to make sure the building was always neat and welcoming. Today, while I made a token attempt to dust the shelves and racks in the lobby and ran a hand vacuum in the corners of the expansive floor on both sides of the retail counter, my mind was cluttered with memories of Dennis Somerville on his last visit.

I switched my attention to the stack of postal employee memos and bulletins Ben had left me. I wouldn't want to miss an urgent news flash on an increase in first-class rates or changes in the budgets for supplies. The bulletin was online, but Ben liked the smell of the ink and the sound of paper crackling, he said, making us probably the only PO in the country with a paper version.

I perused the newsletter, parts of which read like a tabloid newspaper. A worker had used her government credit card to put gas in her personal car. Among the thousands of extra postal workers hired for Valentine's Day, one of them had driven onto a homeowner's yard and was the subject of a damaged-landscape lawsuit. A dog running loose in a neighborhood put its mail carriers at risk; thus home delivery within a three-street radius would be cancelled until the problem was resolved by the dog's owner.

When I came to an article on yet another post office closing in a small town, this one in Pennsylvania, I took a break and began an outline of my talk in a notebook—the old-fashioned paper kind that Ben would favor—and browsed through the reference books he'd left me.

When my cell phone rang, I could hardly tear myself away from a staged photograph of "Santa" and two armed guards loading sacks of mail into a postal vehicle. Apparently, the children in a small Kentucky town in the early twentieth century were close to having their Christmas wishes fulfilled.

"Busy?" Quinn asked. When I admitted I wasn't, he added, "I'm not, either. Where is everybody?"

"Keeping warm."

"Good point. It's supposed to snow later. I'm snuggled up to a sixty-year-old space heater."

"Did they have those things back then?"

"They did and this one has a cord that appears to be the original, in mint condition. It actually looks more like a fan. The base is vintage green that a lot of appliances came in in the fifties and sixties. I picked it up at the estate sale last week, along with some cast-iron skillets."

Not a minute too soon, I remembered my plans for dinner with Sunni. I told Quinn about the surprise invitation. "I was hoping to invite Dyson Somerville to my house. Actually to your cooking, but it's not going to work out now."

"Maybe it can still happen," he said. "I know Dyson from when he played with us."

Of course. Quinn had been in North Ashcot a year before I returned. Dyson would have been in high school and would have had more time to join the Ashcots for their gigs. "I forgot. You've known Dyson longer than I have."

"Uh-huh. I've been meaning to give him a call and express my sympathy. Can I use your kitchen?"

"Consider it yours."

I put my thumb over the mic in my phone and gasped. I hadn't meant to imply anything by the uncensored reaction. Quinn and I had never talked about the future and whether we wanted to share a kitchen, and all that implied for people dating in their thirties.

"No problem," Quinn said, and I let out the breath that had been stuck. Either my comment went over his head or he chose to let me off the hook.

"I'll see you later, then."

"Right," Quinn said, suddenly also at a loss for words.

My first engagement hadn't worked out so well, but I knew I'd be forever grateful that whatever had caused the breakup between Adam and me, it was better before than after a wedding. Did I want to be engaged again? I liked things as they were with Quinn, recognizing that they probably couldn't stay that way forever. But they could at least for this week.

I had only easy customers all afternoon. Stamp sales, small packages, domestic mail prevailed. No money orders demanding more cash than I had on hand; no complaints about the lack of Wi-Fi or the poor selection of greeting cards. I had plenty of time to flip through the postal history books and the Internet for my talk.

I'd decided to take a chronological approach—

probably the deadliest as far as level of boredom was concerned, but I didn't feel confident enough to mix it up. I'd start with Sir Rowland Hill, about whom I had so much information already. Who doesn't love a knight?

In his day, Victorian England, the recipient paid the postage for a letter, often a large sum, since the charge was by the mile traveled and the number of sheets being sent. One story had young Rowland as an eight-year-old boy being dispatched to town to sell some of his clothes so his family could afford to receive a letter. Boring? Fascinating? I wished I could tell. I thought of the high school girls giggling over the valentine-related postmarks and was glad my audience would be more mature. Wouldn't they? Was I at that age?

If there was a way to share the excitement over the first prepaid stamp, I didn't know what it was. With all the advances in communications that especially young people had at their fingertips, how could an adhesive-backed picture of Queen Victoria almost two centuries ago hold their interest?

I found myself learning a lot, but not necessarily preparing a talk. Panic, in the form of regurgitation of my lunch, surfaced.

I needed support. Taking advantage of the next-to-zero traffic in the lobby—a couple of people not needing assistance, dropping in for free Priority Mail envelopes and boxes—I slipped in a call to Linda.

"Busy?" I asked.

"Yes, thankfully. I have so much to learn in this new position."

"So I guess you don't want to substitute-teach for me tomorrow." Silence. As if she thought I was being serious.

"It's okay, Linda. I'm just kidding. I'm all prepared." Why pass my anxiety on to someone one hundred and fifty miles away?

Linda talked on about her new job. Not for the first time since I knew her had she gone from a low of two days ago to a high of today. I knew it would do no good to suggest that she try to hit the middle. But who was I to give advice? I was happy to hear her so upbeat about her new duties. She was not in the mood to hear about a murder investigation. I could live with that.

"Nothing's out of bounds for this job," she said. "We're looking at everything from sorting procedures, to migrating over to electronic stamps, to employees who accept bribes in exchange for expedited services."

"Surely, no one offered—"

"Oh yes. Someone," Linda said. "But I'd better not say any more."

"Any good stories for my class tomorrow?"

"Let's see. I think Jeannie got this off the Internet. A poet comes into the post office to mail a copy of his poetry somewhere and says he wants insurance.

"'How much do you want to insure it for?' the clerk asks.

"'Well, it's my heart and soul in that package,' the guy says.

"'Okay, let's go with one hundred dollars,' the clerk says."

At which point Linda dissolved into laughter and I had to deal with a customer walking in with a package that might be a book of poems. We said a quick good-bye and I took care of business. Maybe on our next call, Linda would be open to hearing how the investigation was going. We hung up with a promise to talk later.

Another break came around three thirty and I called Quinn this time. We usually texted through the day, but this called for phone contact.

"We're all set for tonight," he said. "Dyson is going to come to your place around seven and we'll have a little male bonding over dinner."

"You're wonderful," I said, and didn't hear a denial.

My last customer was a surprise. Not that she didn't use our services on a regular basis, but this time Mercedes Davis showed up without a package to mail or stamps to buy. She walked through the lobby to my counter like a woman on a mission, her gray wool cape furling behind her, her white hair minus its highlights. She leaned on the counter as far as her short body would take her, lips tight, eyes wide.

"Where's the lighthouse?" she said.

I stepped back, glad that I towered over her and could probably withstand an attack. As long as it was weaponless. "The . . . uh," I stuttered, as if I didn't know which lighthouse she meant. The miniature Annisquam Harbor, sitting on a bed of fake snow on the corner of my desk at home, seemed to be swinging its intense beam my way, settling on me, blinding me.

"Gail Chambers told me you paid a visit to Patrick Henry and wormed your way into Dennis's office."

Ah, I knew the hefty lady with the fifties pumps and a jeweled eyeglass chain was a serious gatekeeper. No surprise there. "I'm sorry, Mercedes. I didn't realize it was yours," I said, my voice sounding shaky and weak.

"So what? Why would you take it in the first place? From someone's office." Her voice rose with each word, so that "office" was loud and an octave higher than "so what?" "Just because he's . . ." Her voice was nearly back to normal now, ending with a deep sigh.

I had no answer for her. What could I say? That I thought it would bring me inspiration, luck—something— as I tried to help with the Dennis Somerville murder investigation? I'd probably come across as more credible if I said I'd been a closet shoplifter since I was a kid. Or that I had a collection of lighthouse snow globes and the Annisquam Harbor site had been the only gap.

But Mercedes didn't need any response from me. Her body seemed to lose its stiff purpose and relax into another state. I broke a rule and invited her behind the counter, where not even Quinn was allowed, hoping Ben didn't decide to make a surprise visit. She didn't seem to notice but let me guide her through the STAFF ONLY half gate onto a chair near my desk.

"I don't know why I took the lighthouse, Mercedes. Maybe I just wanted a souvenir of Dennis."

"I want it back," she said softly.

"Of course. I'll take it to campus tomorrow."

Her eyes teared up. She seemed to be focused on a framed print of a Civil War stamp that hung on my wall. "We had broken up," she said, nearly choking. "And it wasn't even about us. It was over some dumb issue he had at school. He wouldn't talk to me about it. But we loved each other, and that weekend we drove to Gloucester, where there was this perfect view of the lighthouse. We decided we'd work it out." Mercedes's words came haltingly, threaded through with sniffles. "And then . . ."

"I'm so sorry, Mercedes."

"We stopped at this shop. We both loved the globes."
She looked at me, where I was perched on my desk. "They
were just the right amount of schlock, you know." The
corners of her mouth entertained a tiny smile. "We decided
we had to have them. Matching lighthouses. The symbol
of light in the darkness. The beacon. Strength, guidance,
safe harbor. We would always be that for each other."

It wouldn't have taken much for me to run to my car, drive
to my house, and bring the lighthouse back to its rightful
owner. Fortunately, Mercedes made that unnecessary.

"But I'm being selfish," she said. She gave me a sad
look, pushing her wiry gray hair in place. "Maybe you need
to remember him, too. I'm glad you have the lighthouse."

What a roller-coaster day. Or was it a pendulum? First,
Linda going from a low to a high, and now Mercedes
making it from one end of the swing to the other within
minutes. I waited until she was ready to get up, indicating
the restroom behind us. She shook her head and walked
out to the lobby.

"I'll see you tomorrow," she said, as if she hadn't done
a one-eighty with regard to the Annisquam Harbor Lighthouse snow globe.

After she left, I sat at my desk for a time, thinking over
Mercedes's reaction.

My first thought when she'd made her dramatic, ac-
cusatory entrance was that there was something about
the globe that Mercedes didn't want me to notice. A clue
or a hidden message from Dennis that would reveal her
as his killer. She was, after all, the closest thing Dennis
had to a spouse, and wasn't it the spouse who always "did
it"? My expert opinion, formed from years of reading

crime fiction, wasn't worth the paper it might be printed on, as my dad would say.

But Mercedes had changed her mind and suggested I could keep the globe. To lull me into thinking she was innocent? And what about the "issue" Dennis had at school? Was Mercedes trying to direct my attention to the nasty student letters and away from her?

My final thought on Mercedes Davis, prime suspect, was that it was crazy to think that a highly educated professor could murder someone she'd played music with, and loved. A final final thought crept in as I recalled reading that anyone is capable of murder, given the right, or wrong, conditions.

I wondered how my friend the chief of police ever slept with all these aspects to consider. Of course, she had facts. That probably helped.

On the way home, I stopped to pick up some special add-ons to what I knew would be a delicious pot roast dinner, cooked by Quinn, eaten by him and Dyson, with leftovers for me. I doubted Dyson had much of an appetite at this time, but I suspected that food other than a meal prepared for hundreds of college students would be enticing enough for him to accept it.

I called ahead and cleared my list with Quinn. Bread, ice cream, and an appetizer of my choice.

"What do college guys like for an appetizer?" I asked.

"Pizza bites, of course," Quinn said. "And maybe some barbecue chips."

"I'll do my best."

With help from a clerk, I found and bought frozen "bites" of pizza, which, along with the barbecue-flavored chips, took a lot of the thrill out of the otherwise classic New England dinner. But it had been a long time since I dated a college boy.

Quinn had stopped in during the day to start the roast in my Crock-Pot. The smell of the thawing pizza bites I'd brought in now lost out against the overwhelming aromas coming from my kitchen. Chuck roast, potatoes, carrots, unidentifiable but pungent spices. It seemed unfair that I had to breathe them in and not serve up a heaping plate for myself. The nutritional effects of Mahican's boxed salad were long gone.

Dyson was due to arrive at my house in about a half hour. Quinn took pity on me and threw together a small caprese appetizer plate. Fresh grape tomatoes from some-where warm, I assumed, chunky mozzarella, and basil leaves. Enough to get my stomach to stop growling.

As we sat close together in the living room, I noted that the mere presence of Quinn calmed me. Maybe his was the typical antiques dealer temperament. He entered the past every day, a place where restoration was possible, but nothing could really be changed.

I debated whether to draw Quinn into the investigation by asking him to do more than enjoy Dyson's company and offer support. I had no idea what Sunni had offered Dyson, or what she'd gotten from him by way of clues to what might have precipitated the end of his father's life.

I let Quinn talk for a change and heard about the pluses

and minuses of estate sales versus auctions. Quinn and his boss were often in a position to advise executors how to handle sometimes vast amounts of property, the disposal of which has been left to their discretion.

"This case today was a prime example," Quinn said. "This guy is the executor for one of those mansionlike homes on the west side. He thought sales and auctions were the same thing." He chuckled at the idea.

"Imagine that," I said.

If he expected me to join him in the laughter, he was disappointed. Not only had I missed the joke, but my eyes had glazed over as I struggled to maintain interest. I was sure my voice conveyed my attitude. Quinn caught on. He pulled his long arm from around my shoulder and faced me.

"Is there something you want to talk about, Cassie? Maybe something about Dyson's visit?" His smile helped relieve me of the burden of pretending I wanted a lecture on tag sales or no tag sales.

"What might that be?" I asked.

"Oh, I don't know. Like, will I ask him if he has any idea why his dad was murdered?"

"Only if it comes up," I said.

The doorbell rang, putting an end to our charade. We both stood to answer.

15

I left for Trattoria Cefalu around seven thirty, with no trio of shadowy figures plaguing me on my street or along the road to the restaurant. I recalled that the three burglars who had defeated North Ashcot's home locks and alarm systems were themselves locked up. Coincidence? I thought not. But that did nothing to explain why they would have been tailing me in the first place. I reconsidered the theory that they thought I was closing in on them as Dennis's killer, but that was far-fetched in more ways than one.

I'd stayed home with Quinn and Dyson only long enough to help set the table for two. The three of us had a brief conversation to determine if Dyson had friends coming to stay with him (maybe later, for the service), if there was enough food in his house (frozen pizza and frozen dinners his dad had), and whether he had all our

phone numbers, and vice versa, in case he needed anything (we took out our cell phones and filled in the gaps).
Quinn asked if he'd like to stay at his place for a few days
(no, but thanks for the offer).

I approached Cefalu's large gravelly parking lot and
saw Sunni's personal SUV. I was surprised and disappointed that she'd beat me there. I'd hoped for a few minutes with a good cup of coffee to prepare my agenda. Too
bad I hadn't thought to extend the invitation first, and
therefore treat Sunni. A certain amount of power was lost
when your companion was paying for your dinner.

Cefalu's looked like every suburban Italian restaurant I'd
ever been to, an elaborate attempt to evoke an atmosphere
that was part ancient Rome and part modern Italy, with vary-
ing degrees of success. I walked past hanging ferns,
"chipped" white columns that served no construction-related
purpose, and window boxes on faux-brick interior walls, to
where Sunni sat looking at an oversize menu. The music
was an eclectic mix of Dean Martin, whom my parents had
listened to, and Luciano Pavarotti, whom my ex-fiancé had
listened to. I thought of the restaurants and festivals in Boston's North End, where many of the culinary and cultural
traditions of Italian immigrants had been preserved without
the questionable benefit of modern influence and marketing
techniques.

I pulled out a chair across from Sunni and sat down.
"This is nice," I said, as if we were on a first date.

"Thanks for not reminding me of how it's about time,
after all the meals I've mooched," she said. She'd changed
from her uniform into corduroys, her casual clothing of

choice most of the time. I was in my choice, somewhat dressy jeans with a heavy Irish knit sweater.

"I don't look at it that way," I said. "It's not mooching when you're invited."

"I hope you're not expecting more from me than this dinner," she said.

I smiled and shook my head. This really was like a first date, except the agenda concerned murder talk as opposed to sweet nothings.

Over enough food for six, we chatted about a series of unrelated topics, her daughter first.

"Avery sweats over a B-plus," Sunni said, obvious pride in her voice. "Also, she might be in love. She mentioned one guy's name twice in connection with a study group."

"Sounds serious."

We moved on to what was going on in our quilting group, another three-minute topic.

"How do you like the new round-robin pattern that Fran suggested?" I asked.

She wrinkled her nose and shrugged. "Too much red, white, and blue, if you ask me." She paused and smiled at me. "No offense."

"None taken."

I contributed the next topic, this one five minutes in length, updating her on Linda's new job responsibilities, and repeating the lame joke about the value of a book of poetry that had been forced on me at the end of our phone conversation.

"I'll bet you're really busy with valentine mail," Sunni said. Before I could do much more than nod, she interrupted herself. She put her fork down and sighed. I thought I detected a slight reddening in her fair cheeks. "Is this how it's going to be?" she asked.

Could it be that best-ish friends that we were, we were stuck for conversation unless we were discussing a murder investigation? I looked around at the other tables, almost fully populated, mostly with couples, and wondered if their conversations were as bumpy as ours was.

"Have you read any good books lately?" I asked.

She dipped a hunk of bread in olive oil, then had a bright thought apparently, because she smiled and wagged her free finger at me. "Aha. I see where you're going. Books equals literature equals English majors. I knew you'd bring up something related to the Somerville case eventually."

I raised my napkin to my face, the better to finish a mouthful of pasta and laugh at the same time. It was tricky. Like trying to be best friends with the chief of police.

Sunni had no such trouble and continued without prompting from me. "Even though I warned you, since you brought us Norah Sampson, I guess you deserve a little briefing."

I didn't remind her that I'd agreed to "nothing but dinner" earlier. I was too delighted with this turn in the conversation. And Sunni seemed to be having a great time teasing me. "You've already talked to Norah?"

"You think we're a bunch of slugs in the NAPD?"

"No, no offense." I was on the edge of my seat at the prospect of a briefing. And I hadn't had to bring it up, except by inadvertently playing into her little game. "How did it go?"

"We talked to her right after you left. It's amazing how

quickly kids respond to an invitation from the police. They'll do anything to keep their parents from finding out. Like we're going to report on their cutting a class or lying about their grades. I'm guessing the kids are afraid of cutting off the money flow, or that they genuinely don't want to upset their parents."

"Did Norah admit to writing the notes?" Not that I was impatient. I was anxious to be able to tell Dyson that his father's murderer was off the streets. The fact that the murderer might be a giggling young girl wearing a college sweatshirt took away a lot of the satisfaction, however. I tried to picture Norah, her long dark hair cascading over her shoulders, training a gun on one of her professors. Even if he'd flunked her.

It seemed Sunni was having an equally hard time with the vision. She shook her head. "I can't believe Norah had sufficient reason to write the notes or to commit murder. And two friends confirmed that she was in her room taking a nap on Monday afternoon." Sunni thoughtfully dropped her voice a few decibels. "Not that roommates are that reliable as alibis, but I can't break them yet."

"So that was it? You let her go?"

"I had no reason to hold her except for a completely inexpert opinion on her handwriting. But Norah's definitely hiding something. I told her I'm not finished with her. That was enough to rattle her."

"I have no doubt."

"By now she's told all her friends and maybe something will shake out." She raised her hand to signal the waiter. I wondered whether he knew Sunni or if he rushed to everyone's call as quickly as he did now. When she asked for more bread, he all but bowed. "Then there are the burglars. The feds want to step in tomorrow to claim the case. Apparently, the group all live in Vermont, and hadn't confined their sprees to Massachusetts."

I felt better knowing that the thieves were not from among the citizens of North Ashcot. In my job, especially since we didn't offer home delivery, probably every one of the three thousand or so citizens walked through my doors, even if only once or twice a year. I met representatives of all groups, from grandparents sending off birthday presents to grade-school kids who came in, sometimes three or four at a time, to access their families' post office boxes. People trusted me with their packages and their letters and their bill payments; I trusted them not to burglarize my home. Or murder one of my friends.

"How does that work?" I asked Sunni. "If you want them for murder and the FBI wants them for burglaries, who gets them?"

"Murder will trump most of the time, and I'm doing my best to keep them until I'm sure, but, honestly, I don't see this clique shooting someone."

I almost asked whether she thought they were capable of stalking someone, but I was reluctant to report to Sunni on my shadowy visitors. I knew she'd either think I was losing it or lock me out of any more investigating. Neither response appealed to me.

"I'm almost completely convinced it's not in their wheelhouse," Sunni continued. "I have another half day to sweat them. I don't have forensics yet on prints at the scene. That might be ammunition for me, but I doubt I'll get results that soon."

There were times, and this was one of them, when Sunni sounded like all the television cops I loved to follow. Danno Williams, Olivia Benson, Danny Reagan, Kate Beckett. As much as our chief of police claimed to shun them, as much as their forensics was "outlandishly wrong," television cops had had a great influence on Sunni's vocabulary.

"What are the chances that you'll find a gun or good prints? Wouldn't that be stupid? Leaving the weapon?"

"If the bad guys weren't stupid . . ."

"The jails would be empty," I said, waiting for a "dumb criminal joke."

I wasn't disappointed. Sunni smiled and I knew she had a story.

"Two guys broke into a fast food store and stole the whole cash register, plus a huge bowl of coleslaw."

"It's already funny," I said.

"Apparently, they took turns eating it as they made their getaway along a nearby trail. Cops followed pieces of cabbage and carrots to where they were camped out. It might have been the fastest collar in years."

"Better to be lucky than good," I said, before I could catch myself. I switched immediately to the noncomic aspects of law enforcement. "How about Dyson? Does he have any clue about how this happened to his dad?"

"He told me his dad was having a hard time with some issue or someone at school, but he didn't know any details. Of course, now he's suffering from guilt pangs that he didn't pay more attention to his dad's moods."

"That's the same thing Mercedes told me," I said. *And aren't we all?* I recalled Dyson's litany of issues his father had, involving a teacher who'd accepted a bribe and another one who'd been pulled over by the troopers.

"Maybe it's your turn to report."

I worried that Sunni was trying to trap me into confessing unauthorized snooping. I thought twice about telling her that, as we spoke, Dyson was at my house eating dinner with my boyfriend and settled on "no" the second time. I took a chance and gave her a summary of my interaction with Mercedes a few hours ago, spilling all, emphasizing the breakup and the makeup, hand waving over the part where I snuck around and stole Dennis's lighthouse.

"Why was it that you took the snow globe?" she asked. I bit my lip and did a quick eye roll, combined with a pleading look. The facial gymnastics worked: "Never mind," she said.

"I think she really loved him," I said. "Mercedes, I mean."

Sunni pointed her fork at me and wagged it up and down. "Now you've just stated the world's strongest motive."

"Not what I meant."

"I know. And all the musicians have alibis, but none of them are ironclad. Mostly spouses vouching for them. Although Brooke was definitely at her desk at the bank. They have the most decent security footage of any facility. Including ours."

That was a relief. Who wanted to think a former Miss Berkshire County could be a killer? "It's interesting that both Mercedes and Dyson mentioned a problem Dennis was having at school. Do you think Dennis was referring to the student letters?" I asked.

"Could be."

"Or maybe the issue had something to do with Hank Blackwood." I flashed back to Gatekeeper Gail's comment that it was Dennis who was responsible for Hank's having to leave the weekly discussion group held in Patrick Henry Hall. Then the flash faded and I wasn't at all sure that had been the scenario. I thought I might have been confusing it with Hank's leaving the Ashcots on account of something Dennis did. Or said. Or didn't say.

"I know Hank. What's he have to do with this?" Sunni asked.

"Probably nothing," I said, wondering how cops kept straight who said what, when.

"Anything else?"

I sighed, straining to remember another thought that was nagging at me. "Yes," I said, with more glee than the thought warranted. It was just nice to remember something. "Joyce Blake. She and Dennis had an issue over course scheduling." I explained how the mere fact of whether one course should come before or after another could spawn a battle of considerable magnitude.

"It wouldn't hurt to recheck her alibi. I'll do that."

Sunni took no notes during our discussion, made no to-do list except maybe in her head. Here she departed from television cops who had an endless supply of notepads handy, pulling them out of their pockets no matter where they were, or from a desktop in the station house. They never had to fumble for a pen, either. I wished I felt comfortable taking out my own notebook or using my cell phone Notes app. I was getting a headache trying to keep everything, organized and complete, in my head.

I closed my eyes for a moment and made a mental chart of suspects and motives. Three thieves because Dennis had interrupted their burglary; Norah Sampson because he'd flunked her; Mercedes Davis because she loved him; Hank Blackwood because Dennis had ousted him from this or that group; Joyce Blake because he was dissing her department and her students.

It would have been helpful if I could come up with a mnemonic. Which would attract more attention—pulling out a notepad and pen or singing a ditty using suspects' names and motives as lyrics?

I chose a third option and finished my gnocchi.

"Affogatos for dessert?" Sunni asked.

I began to regret the caprese appetizers and the extra bread and olive oil, but I nodded yes to gelato and espresso.

"My talk in Mercedes's class is tomorrow morning," I told Sunni as we prepared to leave the trattoria.

"You mean, is there anything I want you to search out on campus?"

"Psychic—that's what you are."

"Keep your eyes and ears open," she said as she buttoned up, the biggest, brightest green light she'd ever given me.

I couldn't wait to hear how dinner had gone with Quinn and Dyson. Maybe Dyson had come up with something by way of a lead to his dad's killer. A word remembered, a casual comment that might have been heavy with meaning, a person's name that none of us had heard before.

I drove home reciting the acronym TNMHJ, the letters of the first names of the suspects on my list. I wondered how many of them I'd be able to watch and listen to on campus tomorrow. Possibly all but the band of thieves.

Dyson had left, but Quinn was there to greet me when I arrived home. I'd heard the sounds of his dobro as I climbed my steps and approached the door.

"Don't stop playing," I said, removing my layers of accessories.

"That's okay. I was wrapping up."

"Please? I'd love to have a private concert."

Quinn took a seat on a straight-backed chair and placed his rich mahogany-colored dobro across his knees.

When he played with the Ashcots, his dobro hanging on a long strap in front of him, the tunes were mostly country or bluegrass, many of them foot-stomping, but tonight he picked and strummed away at a mellow Irish tune that a friend of his in San Francisco had written.

I sat in an easy chair, closed my eyes, and let the notes float over me.

After a stressful couple of days, with way too much food under my belt, there was nothing I needed more than soft dobro music. I gave up the idea of querying Quinn about his dinner with Dennis's son, and running my TNMHJ mnemonic by him. I felt myself drifting, unencumbered by the details of reality.

When I woke up at one o'clock, Quinn was gone, having draped an afghan over me and placed a sweet pre-valentine note next to me.

The new day was off to a good start.

Then I remembered it was the day of my presentation.

The image of dozens of students in front of me, expecting words of substance, nearly woke me fully, but I staggered to my bed and followed Scarlett O'Hara's "another day" rule of survival, even though technically it was already tomorrow.

16

My phone rang just before I was ready to crawl out of bed on Thursday morning. If I hadn't seen Linda's name on the screen, I might not have answered. I clicked on and barely squeaked out a "Hey."

"Hey, it's your turn," she said, in much too cheery a voice for the hour.

"Excuse me?" I struggled into my robe, holding the phone under my neck.

"You know, you called me yesterday. Then I talked and talked and we hung up. So now it's your turn."

I laughed. "Don't worry about it. I'm thrilled about your new job."

"Yeah, yesterday was awesome. We actually had some action items for the new leadership and incentives programs. I have an intern who's . . ." She paused and I heard a soft gasp. "There I go again. You. Cassie. Talk. Talk."

I took her at her word and brought her up to date on the investigation. She was fascinated (or seemed so) by the handwriting analysis Sunni had carried out on the letters sent to Dennis and my role in ferreting out the student who might have written them.

"You still feel guilty, don't you?" Linda said. "Because you didn't send those notes off for inspection."

"A little, I guess."

"Cassie, don't you remember how we scribbled notes to Dr. Rafferty when he moved up the exam date to the day after the homecoming game?"

"That was different. We didn't threaten to have him fired."

"We might have. I know we said uncool things about what he could do with the exam."

I chuckled. "We were pretty bad, weren't we?"

"Yes, but it didn't mean we were about to murder him. Even if it turns out to be one of those students who's your friend's killer, there was no way to predict that and it doesn't mean anyone in the inspector's office would have been able to help him in time. Wasn't it only a few hours later that the murder occurred?"

I admitted that she had a point. "Thanks, Linda. I'm okay, really. We now have a few possibilities for suspects."

"Those burglars?"

"As well as a couple of others on campus."

"Where you're going today, right?"

"Uh-huh. Thanks for the reminder. Now I'm nervous again."

"You're going to be great. Oh, and here's something

else for your talk. Did you know that George Washington has been on more stamps than anyone else?"

"Wow," I said.

Linda laughed. "I know what that 'wow' means. G'bye."

"Skype you later," I said.

Since I was up and nearly awake, there was nothing left to do but get ready for school.

Possibly because I needed a transition from my stressful day yesterday to my long-awaited (or so it seemed) class day today, I attended the morning rehearsal of the Ashcots. The community room was cold, so I stayed huddled in my jacket in the first row of chairs.

The selections matched the soft tones of last night during Quinn's solo concert for my ears only. But the mood patterns of the musicians were different from those of yesterday. This morning, the players were somber, their movements gentle. Whereas yesterday humorous skits had arisen, today they could have been preparing for a memorial service rather than a Valentine's Day dance.

Because Dennis had been shot, and his shooter was still unknown, his body was being held by the coroner. There was no telling when it would be released. Why couldn't I get rid of the feeling that it was partly my responsibility to find the shooter and give Dyson Somerville control over his father's remains?

Mercedes, of more moods than I could count, was quiet today, as were Joyce and Shirley, the ones who knew Dennis best. I hadn't decided how to handle the Annisquam

Harbor Lighthouse globe. I was inclined to return it to Mercedes, but I didn't want to start another riot. Maybe I'd wait a few months, or until she brought it up herself.

I heard a slight commotion at the back of the hall and turned to see Hank Blackwood tromping down the aisle, lugging his guitar. He'd timed his entrance during a slight lull between numbers. I figured he'd been waiting at the back for the right moment.

"I guess you changed your venue this week," he said. "I went over to the school. That's why I'm late."

The Ashcots fell silent while Hank made his clumsy way to what would have been a pit if there'd been a barrier of any kind, but really was an invisible line on the floor to separate the performers from the audience.

I was surprised when Quinn stepped up. He'd been wearing his dobro, its wide black leather strap hanging around his neck. He removed the instrument and placed it on the chair he'd been using.

"We're in the middle of things here, Hank, on a tight course for Saturday night's dance," Quinn said. He kept his voice low, but there was no doubt what he meant. Hank was not welcome. I thought it unusual that Quinn would take on the role of spokesperson, but it might have been because he was the closest to the oncoming, heavy-set Hank.

"You know me," Hank said, a shaky laugh coming from his mouth. "I'm a quick study." He moved to Quinn's left, heading for an empty chair behind the one Quinn had abandoned.

It took Quinn only one long-legged step to block his path. "Maybe we can revisit the situation after the weekend," he said, not moving now, but clearly ready to intercept Hank whichever way he dared to go.

I held my breath. This was a new side of my boyfriend. I admired his self-control but wondered what was next. A foot taller than Hank, and certainly more fit, Quinn was clearly in charge and would win any contest. I had no idea how far he might go. At the moment it was a stalemate, neither man moving.

Hank leaned his body so he could address the musicians behind Quinn. "Do you mind telling me why I'm being harassed here, by the new boy, no less?"

Hank was correct that Quinn was the "new boy," and the youngest, with less than two years in a group that had started decades ago.

"We mind a lot," said Greg, his voice booming as only a drama coach's could. "Now, why don't you turn around and march out of here before things get nasty?" He punctuated his message with a drumroll.

Quinn stood in front of Hank, unthreatening, unless being taller and more muscular could be deemed a threat in itself, and waited for Hank's next move.

Hank's face reddened to the point of my concern for his well-being. His already beady eyes became narrower. He glared at me, as if I were Quinn's accomplice, and stormed out of the hall, his guitar case bouncing two or three times on the way.

Someone—it might have been Arthur Chaplin, at the bass guitar, since Dennis was gone—struck a note and the Ashcots continued their rehearsal without further interruption. I didn't dare smile until every one of the other musicians did.

I thought back to my TNMHJ list of suspects and in my mind made the *H* bold, wondering how long it would be before he'd be bumped to the first slot. I knew that Sunni had only this morning to sweat, as she'd put it, the *T* in the list, the trio of thieves before they'd be turned over to the feds.

One thing for sure was that I had a *Q* on my mind for a coffee before I left for campus. I hung around until Quinn had packed up and had no trouble talking him into a chat before he went to work. When he put his dobro down to give me a hug, I didn't feel threatened in the least.

We walked across the street to Mahican's together. Not quite nine o'clock and the flag was up at the post office end of the building. Ben had already clocked in. I tried not to feel guilty.

"I wish I could come and hear your presentation," Quinn said as we crossed Main Street. "But Fred is determined to wrap things up with the Carey estate before the weekend. I can't justifiably leave him with all the paperwork."

How nice of him not to mention kitchen duty at my house several times that he might have been at work.

I'd had mixed feelings when Quinn told me he'd asked Mercedes if he could attend my talk. On the one hand, his presence might bolster me; on the other, if I failed I wanted as few people as possible to know. The relief I felt now, knowing he couldn't make it, was a good indication of what my true preference was.

"You already know most of it," I said.

"What's your opening line?" he asked.

I froze, and not because the wind had blown my scarf aside, away from my neck. If it weren't for Quinn's hand on my elbow, I might have stopped in the middle of Main Street.

"I forgot."

Quinn propelled me to the sidewalk in front of Mahican's and in through the door. "I wasn't trying to put you on the spot. Have a seat and I'll get our coffees."

He took his place in a long line while I scouted a table, as embarrassed about my panic attack as I was about the pettiness of the cause. What would I do if I were faced with a real fight-or-flight situation? A threat to my survival that was more worthy than a roomful of twenty-year-olds?

Most of Mahican's customers at this hour were there for takeout, so it wasn't hard to find a table in a long row against the wall. I removed my scarf and took a breath. Somewhere deep in the haphazard notes I'd made this week was my opening line. I just had to find it.

By the time Quinn returned with our coffees and the Berkshires' best scones, I was somewhat calmed down. He took a seat and started what I knew would be a pep talk.

"You know, I still remember the first time I played music in front of an audience. I was in college, and I was terrified."

"Is that so?"

If Quinn noticed my disbelief, he didn't let on. "I'd been playing with this group for a couple years, just for ourselves. We were all friends and we'd let off steam by getting together and riffing off each other, making it up as we went along. Then one day the girlfriend of one of the guys suggested we play at the coffee shop on campus. It was a small place, an alternative to the cafeteria, and we'd sometimes hang out there on a weekend night. She thought it would be cool to have live music."

"Don't tell me: You were nervous."

"I told you. I was terrified. That first night I kept trying to hide in the back. There were only four or five of us, not like the Ashcots, no drummer or anything like that, so it wasn't easy to disappear."

"Thanks for sharing, Quinn," I said. "I'm not nervous anymore."

We exchanged playful nudges and moved on to a burning question I had. "I didn't hear much about your dinner with Dyson," I said.

"Let's see. The chicken could have been a little moister; Dyson likes his asparagus cooked until it's limp, which defeats the purpose of veggies; but the mashed potatoes passed muster." Still not through playing, maybe needing another nudge. I gave him one and he got serious. "Okay, well, it was pretty low-key. We talked music mostly. He loves his classes but doesn't have a chance to play very much, like with a group."

"Like with the Ashcots," I said.

"Yeah, I suggested he do what we did back in the Dark Ages and just offer some music to the coffee house or a club on campus. He might look into it." Quinn gave me a sheepish look, as if he'd failed me in some way. "I didn't think it was the time to grill him about, you know, the murder."

"I think you did just the right thing." I meant it but couldn't help slipping in a question. "Do you think Dyson knew about his dad and Mercedes? Either the breakup or the makeup?"

"As far as his father's having a girlfriend goes—it didn't come up, though he mentioned a girl in his own music theory class, Chrissy, a couple of times, without actually calling her his girlfriend. But I'm not surprised that kids and dads wouldn't be discussing their love lives. And Dyson has been away a couple of years, so he might not even know that Mercedes and his dad were together."

I thought back to the greeting when Dyson and Mercedes met in the post office and decided there was something special there, that Dyson was probably aware of the relationship between Mercedes and his dad. There was no reason to hide it in the first place, except that lives were complicated.

Once Quinn left for work, I had no excuse to stay in the coffee shop. I stayed on anyway, my mind going in many directions at once, dealing with questions as if I were taking the quiz of a lifetime. How was Dyson doing this morning? Where was his father's killer at this moment? Would I fall on my face on campus? Would Linda still be on an upward swing when I talked to her next?

It was past nine o'clock and I could see out the window across the street to the flag Ben had raised. The first customers were making their way out the doors of the post office, clutching packages, opening letters. One young woman, whose name I couldn't remember, walked across

Main toward Mahican's, oblivious to traffic, reading a letter. Her expression was one of joy. The image struck a chord with me and I pulled a quote out of my freshman English class.

More than kisses, letters mingle souls. Why a John Donne poem came to me at that moment was as mysterious as the rest of the workings of my mind. I couldn't remember any other line except the one following. *For thus, friends absent speak.* I hoped the rest of the poem wasn't nasty or offensive.

I had the first line of my talk. I left Mahican's finally convinced that the other two hundred or so would fall into place.

17

Instead of parking in the same lot on the north side of campus, closest to Mary Draper Hall, today I chose the south lot, purposely giving myself a long walk to the classroom building. I thought the journey might increase my sense of where Dennis Somerville spent his time when he wasn't strumming his guitar with the Ashcots. I had little hope of meeting the math majors I'd conned into signing the card in Mahican's coffee shop and be able to follow up with a few questions. But I couldn't risk another visit to the math department in Patrick Henry Hall where Norah Sampson and her friends were more likely to be gathered. The specter of Gatekeeper Gail put an end to that idea.

The college campus, situated on a small rise, seemed to be consistently cold and windy, no matter the season. I remembered taking an AP history class there one summer when I was in high school and wanting to linger on campus to keep cool.

Today I didn't appreciate the drop in temperature from the lowlands. My head down, my mouth and nose buried in my scarf as far as possible without cutting off my breathing, I nearly bumped into oncoming foot traffic several times. Thursday was apparently a popular day for classes. I hoped only a few of the students rushing around me were headed for my presentation in Mary Draper.

At one point, I sensed a roadblock ahead of me. A student unwilling to yield the right of way on a narrow section of the path. I wriggled out of my cocoon and looked up to see Norah Sampson, just the young woman I wanted to run into. I wondered if real police work relied as much on random strokes of luck as mine did.

Either she was from Minnesota and had braved sub-zero temperatures all her life, or she was simply used to the climate at the college on the hill. She wore a down jacket, but barely zipped up, and a scarf that was more a fashion statement than a neck or chest warmer. Maybe I needed to look into vitamin supplements.

Norah stood before me, in a hands-on-hips posture, though her hands were stuffed in her pockets. She had such an unpleasant countenance I thought she might be fondling a weapon. I also had the sense that this was not the same kind of serendipitous meeting as the one I'd had in my mind with John Donne.

"That was some kind of trick," she said, then let out a "Bravo" with a sneer.

"Excuse me?"

"I was called into the police station, to see Chief

Smargon, no less, moments after we talked to you in Mahican's. A coincidence? I think not."

"Moments?" I asked, knowing it had to have been at least an hour. Norah glared at me. I thought I saw finger movement in her jacket pocket. "I think she's talking to as many of Dr. Somerville's students as she can," I said.

"Don't give me that. You set us up. How did you know I wrote those letters?"

I thought back as I often did when on a campus or in the company of a young student. I was no longer startled by their extreme self-confidence and their willingness to take on anyone who challenged them. Even the chief of police, I guessed, though I'd never fear for Sunni's ability to maintain her authority.

"You must have felt very strongly about your ex-professor to write those letters."

"A lot you know," she said.

"You didn't write them?"

"I didn't write them for me. They were for somebody else."

Was Norah using the standard alibi of petty criminals who claimed they were holding the gun or the drugs for a friend? My expression seemed to have given away my disbelief. "But you did write them and send them to Professor Somerville?"

"Do you know how it will look if my parents find out I was summoned to the police station?" she asked.

We'd both been hopping slightly from one foot to the other, to prevent frostbite. People passed us by, walking around us on the grass on both sides of the path. Several gave us strange looks, but we'd kept our voices normal and most were too focused on keeping their blood circulating and spending as little time as possible in the outdoors. But I wasn't aware of the cold so much as the strong feelings Norah's selfish attitude was calling forth from my entire body.

"Is there something you'd like me to do for you?" I asked, since she wasn't answering any of my other questions.

"Yes, mind your own business. No wonder the post office is going out of business."

That did it. I'd had about enough of this cheeky girl, barely out of her teens. I took a step toward her, forcing her to move back.

"Even if you don't care enough about who killed a faculty member at your school, aren't you at least interested in finding out if there's a murderer on your campus?" I raised my voice, enough to grab her attention. *Or do you have one of those foolproof apps on your phone that will protect you from harm?* I wanted to add. "If you know something about those letters, Norah, I suggest you report it now. This is not a classroom where everything is theoretical, or a video game. It's real life."

"I'm . . . I'm just saying—"

"A killer has struck down a man who was a father and a teacher on this campus. A young man the same age as you has lost his dad. Don't you feel any responsibility to help find out who did this horrible thing?"

It might have been the longest reprimand I'd ever uttered, but it seemed to have had some effect on the brazen young woman. She'd gasped, pouted, stuttered, and hunched her shoulders, in turn, and repeated the cycle during my extended speech. "I guess I didn't think of it that way."

"Of course you didn't, but you'd better start."

She nodded in a way that I understood to be sincere.

I took a long breath and led Norah into the close-by Student Union Building, where we took seats on a bench in the lobby.

"Whenever you're ready," I said.

I couldn't imagine better preparation for delivering a presentation to Norah's peers.

What Norah poured out made sense in a college-kid kind of way. Morgan, the alpha girl of the math majors, brought up to think she was a real princess, was so put out by her physics teacher's treatment of her that she wanted to retaliate in some way.

"She wanted to make him sweat," Norah said, summing up the letter project. "But she was afraid he'd recognize her handwriting." She took a deep breath and fell silent.

"So you volunteered to write it for her?" I prompted.

"More like won the lottery. Or lost it, I guess."

"All the math majors knew about the letters?"

"Most of us," she said, by which I assumed she meant the cool kids.

I wondered how they thought Dennis would recognize anyone's handwriting. Didn't those science and math classes use only symbols and numbers and keyboards? I couldn't imagine homework or quizzes requiring long handwritten essays, but that was irrelevant at the moment.

"You know what you have to do next," I said.

"Do my parents have to know all this?"

"I'm not sure. But I do know that the chief of police is more than fair, and if you tell her the truth, you'll have nothing to worry about."

"Can I tell her you sent me?"

I nodded, suppressing a laugh.

We went our separate ways after about a half hour, ending our talk with an unexpected hug. I walked away wondering whether invoking my name with Sunni would work for or against Norah.

Less than a half hour until my talk. I wondered how many other unscheduled meetings I might have to fit in.

The news had reported a low of thirty-five degrees today. Whoever gave information for their "feels like" poll submitted thirty-one degrees; I would have said twenty-one, with a slight chance of freezing even a cup of coffee.

I arrived at Mary Draper Hall, my cheeks dried out, nose aching, tears streaming down my face from the cold. A small buffer zone right inside the doors was overheated, as was standard for New England buildings in the winter, but the lobby was well-balanced for temperature. I loosened my scarf, removed my outer jacket, and took a seat to catch my breath. And to pull my thoughts together.

I sat in front of a portrait I'd missed the last time I was there. In a large framed painting, Mary Draper sat wrapped in a black shawl over a black dress. Her face was somber, and her lace cap lay on black hair that was pulled back tightly, making me wonder if her forehead hurt. A white lace collar at her neck was the only relief on the dark canvas.

I didn't have much time to myself. I'd hardly pulled out my sheaf of notes and photos when Mercedes bounded in, a blue paisley cape flapping behind her. I could have sworn the highlights in her hair today were blue also. Did she really take the time to match her hair with her outfit?

"I saw you ahead of me on the path," she said. "I'm glad you're early. I want to apologize for my behavior yesterday. Completely uncalled for."

"Everyone is on edge," I said.

"Thanks for not rubbing my nose in it." She removed her gloves and stuffed them in her leather tote, then blew her breath into her hands. "And about the lighthouse itself," she continued.

"I'm happy to give it to you. I have it in my briefcase." I'd packed it this morning, in case Mercedes did another one-eighty, demanding I return it to her.

Mercedes shook her head. "It was silly of me to want both. But I was thinking. You know, it was a favorite spot for Dyson and his parents when Charlene was alive."

I got the message. "That's a great idea—for you to give it to him," I said.

Mercedes blew out a great breath. "Yes," she said. "That would be lovely. But it doesn't have to be me. You can give it to him." She took a seat next to me and leaned in. "Who do you think did it, Cassie?"

I couldn't very well tell her about TNMHJ, where the middle letter represented Mercedes herself. "Me?" I asked, as if it were an outlandish thought to assume I had a clue or an opinion about Dennis's murder, let alone an inside track with the police investigation.

"Come on, Cassie, it's not a secret that you're the eyes and ears of the chief of police and that she talks to you."

"We're friends," I said. "We have dinner together sometimes."

"Oh, of course. It's not that she'd be sharing anything more than fat quarters with you." When I gave her a curious look, she reminded me, "I used to be part of the quilting group, until . . . until I got too busy."

My devious mind went straight to Dennis Somerville. Had they started dating at the time Mercedes dropped out of the quilt group? Had she then harbored bad feelings about the man who interrupted her life and then broke up with her? Or did she break up with him? Not a question I could easily ask.

Mercedes stayed put on the bench and made another appeal. "You'll let me know, won't you, if you hear anything at all?" She apparently knew better than to wait for an answer and made a final pitch. "The sooner they find who did this to all of us, the sooner we'll be able to move on."

I couldn't have agreed more.

I sent Mercedes on ahead of me while I wrote a quick text to Sunni.

Norah on her way to you.

Norah wrote for Morgan.

I wished I knew what the nasty notes and their true author had to do with Dennis's murder. At the least, I had to reconsider my acronym, TNMHJ. The *N* for Norah might have to be eliminated, the *M* for Mercedes might turn into *M* for Morgan. That left TMHJ—*T* for the three thieves, *M* for Morgan, *H* for Hank, and *J* for Joyce. I tried not to let the other twenty-two possibilities in the alphabet cloud my thinking.

Like most things I wasted energy fretting over, my presentation went better than I'd expected. The John Donne quote, *More than kisses, letters mingle souls*, drew smiles and murmurs of pleasure from the crowd of students— about fifty, I estimated—giving me a boost of confidence. I gave due credit to Sir Rowland Hill and made swift work of the positive effect of fast, inexpensive postal communication on the masses in Victorian England. I hoped I didn't sound too preachy. My goal was to provide background that would give the layperson an understanding of the importance of the postal system in social reform. "A power engine of civilization," as Hill had called it.

Why did it seem like a century ago that I'd sat in a similar classroom, thinking I already had most of the answers to life's big questions, giving half an ear to what a professor was saying in most courses? Behind me now was a fancy whiteboard, but somehow I could have sworn I smelled chalk, as if this lecture hall carried with it the odors of each preceding year.

At some point, I abandoned my notes and relied on my own experience of an exciting profession. I gave a shout-out to one of the many postal museums, in Washington, D.C., and reported on a special exhibit Linda and

I had seen that included an anthrax-laced letter addressed to a congressman. The examination and decontamination processes carried out by postal inspectors had rendered the letter and envelope nearly illegible, but it had been fascinating to see nonetheless.

The same was true for the handcuffs on display, which had bound the wrists of one of the nation's most wanted criminals, the Unabomber. The cuffs had been snapped on the perpetrator as he was brought out of his Montana hideout in the late nineties, and later given to a postal inspector in recognition of his work on the case.

My gaze landed on Mercedes and I had to push back thoughts of the letters Dennis Somerville had brought to my small post office. Why hadn't I been able to help him with his tainted mail? It was not a headliner case like an anthrax-laced letter or a manifesto, but a postal situation that was worthy of help, and I'd refused it.

The fact that my friends let me off the hook for the refusal, and that the letters still hadn't proven to be connected to his murder, did little to ease my conscience. I wouldn't be able to rest until I knew for sure. I chided myself for not asking Norah the last name of Morgan, the instigator of the mailing. Surely, Sunni would have uncovered it, and a lot more about the young woman, by now.

I returned my attention to the student body and talked a little more about the role that postal workers played in investigations such as the conviction of white-collar criminals in illegal financial schemes.

"So these inspectors are, like, cops?" asked a young woman in the front row, without raising her hand.

I was glad for an excuse to extol the impressive forensics capabilities of the USPS and wondered why it remained such a secret, when they were involved in mail-screening for high-profile national political and sporting events.

When attention started to wane, as evidenced by cell phones being accessed surreptitiously, I threw it open to Q and A.

Q—from a tiny woman with a pixie haircut: "What's the weirdest thing you were ever asked to mail?"

A—from me: "A box of bees."

I followed up the surprised laughter with a summary of the packaging requirements for shipping bees, highlighting queen honey bees, which may be shipped by air transportation, accompanied by up to eight attendant honeybees.

I wondered what the students would think of the pages of regulations for shipping poultry and live scorpions.

Q—from the young man next to the tiny woman: "What's the biggest thing you ever mailed?"

A—from me: "Bricks, up to two hundred pounds by one person."

The students seemed a little too interested in the practice of sending bricks as a form of protest to junk mailers. The restriction on weight had been instituted after a builder in Utah overwhelmed the post office by sending a bank—an entire building's worth of bricks, fifty pounds at a time, for a total of forty tons.

I glanced now and then at Mercedes, sitting in the front row, and was bolstered also by her smiles of approval. In spite of what I deemed a successful presentation, I was happy when Mercedes stood and announced, "We have time for only one more question, ladies and gentlemen."

A young woman with a laptop in the center of a cluster of students raised her hand. "This is a history question," she began.

I heard Mercedes whisper, "Finally."

"Who was the first female postmaster?" the woman asked.

"A very good question, and not as easy as it sounds to answer, but I'll give it a try. At first there were no records of women in the postal service."

An outburst of comments from several female students followed.

"Of course, there were no records."

"It figures."

"All the work and no credit."

I let them go on a few minutes before I added a few facts to what was becoming a feminist rally.

"Women would pinch-hit for a male worker—a father or a husband. Benjamin Franklin's sister-in-law Elizabeth worked in a general store that also held a post office, but she wasn't officially called a postmistress. I can give you references to a few well-known women in the early days: Lydia Hill—no relation to Sir Rowland—Mary Katherine Goddard, Adeline Evans—"

Mercedes stood up again and interrupted. "I'll have Postmistress Miller give me a list of references for you. Let's thank her for giving her time today with a round of applause." She joined the clapping, leaning over to me. "You went ten minutes over and no one left," she said. "A minor miracle."

"But I'm just getting started," I said.

"You have to leave them wanting more."

I wished there were a way to thank John Donne for giving me the push I needed. Or maybe it was my live friends, like Linda, Ben, Sunni, and Quinn, who'd done it.

18

Mercedes flew out the door to keep an appointment in town. She fell short of giving me a high five or a fist bump but uttered complimentary words about my presentation and smiled an *I owe you* as she left. Several students stopped to thank me personally on their way out of the classroom. All in all, it was such a pleasant experience I wanted to do it again.

A small seating area near a window outside the classroom looked inviting as a place to unwind before braving the cold. I settled on an extra-wide chair and turned my cell phone on. I scrolled through texts from Quinn (I'll bet you were terrific) (I wished I hadn't discouraged him from attending), Linda (I can hear the applause from here) (She would have done better), Ben (I'm sure you did us proud), and Sunni (Lunch 12:30 here) (Uh-oh, more like a summons than an invitation).

I checked in with Ben and was promised no unpleasant surprises when I returned in the afternoon.

"Did you do good?" he asked.

"I think so," I said. "I'll tell you some of the questions when I see you."

He filled me in on his shift, noting that there were still a lot of valentines coming in and informing me that he'd issued warnings about the late arrivals. I regretted that I missed a visit from the postmaster at South Ashcot with a request for a larger post office box for mislabeled mail. There was long-standing animosity between him and Ben, for a reason I wasn't privy to, and I hoped Ben hadn't set him off. Only a small creek divided the towns, and I felt it was important to be neighborly.

"Don't worry," Ben said. "I told him we had no more large boxes and got him to rent two of the regular size."

"Nice work," I said, not really sure.

Though I didn't know what Ben's attitude had been during the negotiation, I had no right to complain, no matter what. He was making it possible for me to indulge in a couple of what college kids called extracurricular activities, the kind that got you a cool yearbook entry but weren't necessarily a plus in one's professional life.

"I'm glad your talk came off well."

"Thanks. I'll see you after lunch," I said, thinking I really had to get him a present, more than a box of his favorite donuts this time.

I packed my things and walked down the long hallway, my only disappointment being that I hadn't come through for Sunni as far as discovering anything useful for the murder case went. Unless you counted bullying a student into turning herself in for facilitating a written attack on a professor. Hours spent on campus and all I had was a snow globe and a couple of interactions with faculty and former faculty. I looked out the windows onto the campus pathways as I passed empty or partially full classrooms, but not even Hank Blackwood was there to hassle me this time.

When I arrived at the exit, I reconsidered making my way to Patrick Henry Hall, the math and sciences building. I was relieved to realize I didn't have time for that round-trip and still make a twelve thirty lunch with Sunni. I couldn't face another one-on-one with Gatekeeper Gail, and I didn't see how it would do me any good. I expected she'd give me some kind of reprimand, as Norah did, claiming I'd set her up or tricked her into giving me in-formation, which, of course, was true in both cases.

The final vote came in the form of the freezing tem-perature and biting wind that I knew awaited me as soon as I stepped outside. I bundled up and left Mary Draper, heading away from the central campus buildings to where my car was parked. I told myself that Sunni's text invita-tion was a good sign—she was eager to share progress in finding Dennis Somerville's killer. Or not.

I passed Greta's desk at the front of the police building. An intern, a lunchtime sub I'd met briefly, greeted me and waved me on to the chief's office. I smelled Sunni's special brew of coffee, a good sign: She wasn't going to punish me by forcing me to drink the caffeinated bever-age in the lobby.

Our custom was that when we ate in my office, Sunni brought lunch, and vice versa. I'd stopped at the market and picked up her favorite mixed cold-cuts sandwich and a few sides. I also picked up a gift card for Ben, to a sporting goods store, a card our post office did not carry. I didn't have time to look, but I hoped the shop sold fishing supplies.

With her usual lack of ceremony, and before I could remove my gloves, Sunni handed me three sheets of paper, stapled together. The heading read RAP SHEET.

"That's an official name? A rap sheet?" I asked.

Sunni shrugged. "Some people think RAP is an acronym for Record of Arrests and Prosecutions, but while you can find this in police manuals and forms, it's really a 'backronym' and not the origin of the term." She motioned for me to read it. I got it: no more questions.

The sheets contained more numbers than letters—dates, case numbers, police codes. I identified several standard abbreviations, like DOB, HGT, WHT. Many lines contained information, such as DISPO: CONVT, which I took to mean that the person was convicted, since that line was followed by the notation 12 MONTHS PROB, 3 DAYS JAIL, all for the CRM of OCCUPY PROP W/O CONSENT.

I mumbled past many more acronyms and abbreviations and another DISPO: CONVT with regard to BKG/ENT THEFT OF PROP. Not until I noticed the list of names, buried under more identifying alphanumerics, did I understand why Sunni had given it to me. Five names appeared at the top of the sheet, MORGAN HAMMOND being the first and, I guessed, most current. Other names listed were variations, all with the same initials. MAR-IAN HARRISON, MORGAN HOOPER, and more. I supposed that meant she didn't have to change her mono-grams every time she took on a new name.

"Get it?" Sunni asked.

"She's the girl in the ring of three?"

"No, that girl has been in custody. We're not sure of Morgan's full story yet, but it appears she acts alone. We did a quick check while Norah was here, and found a warrant for her in New Hampshire. I'm sure she's worked in other states as well."

"I knew she was a transfer student, but . . ."

"A lot of transfers, apparently," Sunni said.

"She makes a career of this?"

Sunni nodded. "It's not that uncommon. Recently they caught a guy in New York, posing as a student, stealing identities as well as property. And there was another couple in Florida, did the same thing. I think they were even prom king and queen, and they were packed to move on the day after, except they were caught."

"Talk about an exciting life. But is it worth it? I mean, I don't think of students as wealthy targets."

"Doesn't matter, if you have access to everything they own, including their identities and all their portable de-vices. And it's a great cover. Anyway, it's the FBI's prob-lem when they take their business across state lines. We're working on getting them to hold off on taking Morgan, plus that ring of three, as you call them, to see if there's any connection that we're missing with the Somerville murder."

Was this a good time to tell Sunni about my own ring

of three, the shadowy figures that had been following me? I wasn't sure of the timing. I'd seen them outside Dyson's house on Tuesday night. Sunni had said she had a lead on the three burglars on Tuesday afternoon; Greta said they'd been taken in yesterday morning. The timing could be right. The threat, if there ever was one, might be over. There was enough to deal with now, with Morgan's status.

Less than five minutes in Sunni's presence, and there were no answers, just more questions and more confusion in an already complicated case. I took a seat at the small table she'd cleared for lunch and wrapped my hands around my mug, trying to keep from embarrassing myself by shivering. "Is Morgan even a student at the college?" I asked.

"She is enrolled. A cover."

"Math is a tough major for a cover."

"No one is saying she's dumb. And I have you to thank for pursuing that line. Norah came in and eventually gave us her name. She did try to hold out for a few seconds."

Poor Norah, in a face-off with the NAPD chief. "Did Norah know that Morgan is—a little more experienced than the average math major?"

"She seemed genuinely surprised when I put it to her. I don't think she's involved more than she's admitting. She was just the hired hand, so to speak."

Once I recalled how Morgan tried to convince Norah not to sign the card on my tablet, that made sense. Morgan didn't want Norah's handwriting on record any more than she wanted her own.

Sunni unwrapped her sandwich and uttered an approving sound as a garlicky aroma was released from the cold cuts. "Tell me about your presentation." This was Sunni, keeping me on my toes, making an abrupt switch to friend mode. I could only imagine what her tricks were when she was with a suspect, constantly knocking her off-kilter.

I took the cue and unwrapped my own sandwich. "The presentation went pretty well. I was amazed that they actually asked questions and listened to my answers."

"I guess everyone thinks their particular place of employment is not as interesting as someone else's."

"Except for yours," I said.

She smiled. "It's the opposite with mine. Everyone thinks it's glamorous, but it isn't. They think there are exciting adventures every day, triumphant music when the bad guy is brought in."

"The perp walk," I said.

"Exactly. If they only knew how much time was spent on phone calls and using the Yellow Pages—now the Internet, but it's the same grunt work. And the paperwork itself—before, during, and after a case—is overwhelming. Writing reports in triplicate, making sure they're filed properly. It's endless."

"Not what you expected when you signed up?"

"Oh no. I was thinking more like kicking down doors and pushing bad guys against a wall."

"Well, thank you for your service," I said, glad she didn't demonstrate any moves on me.

"Smart aleck. By the way, here's a little cross talk between your job and mine. Apparently, there was an attack on a mail carrier in Springfield the other day."

"Wow. Was he hurt?" I asked.

"The article said the mailman is okay, and that all the attacker made off with were the keys to the mail truck."

I nodded. "That happens a lot, especially close to tax season."

"That's what I didn't get. What good does it do to have the keys to the mail truck? It's not like the guy can drive it very far before being picked up."

"He probably didn't drive it at all. He was really after the arrow key."

"Let me guess." Sunni nodded as if a light dawned. "The arrow key is like a master key for all the mailboxes that have locks."

"You got it in one. But what the bad guys don't know is that the carriers don't usually put the arrow keys on the ring with the truck keys. They're carefully guarded at the post office and the carrier has to sign it out of a vault or a safe. Every carrier has a different way of keeping it protected. And as it gets close to the first of the month, there are checks in jeopardy, or in tax season, even worse, and the carriers are on high alert."

"Except for this one in Springfield."

"Except for him. But I'll bet the arrow key was still safe somewhere. Sometimes we're smarter than they are."

Sunni's desk phone beeped. She pressed a button and answered. When the call was over, she announced, "She's ready to talk."

"Morgan? Or whatever her name is?"

Sunni nodded and handed me my gloves, which I'd placed on her desk. A not-so-subtle clue.

"Do you think I could have a word with—"

"Maybe later," she said, handing me my half-finished sandwich.

It was time for me to leave, with no clue as to how much later it would be before I'd be welcomed back.

I was at loose ends. My talk was over, and all the tension from anticipating it was gone. A new tension, or an expanded older one, took its place: Dennis's killer was still at large and there was nothing I could do without more information. If I had my way, there'd be a rule that citizens could interview suspects in murder investigations. After all, we were expected to serve on juries. Didn't we deserve to be part of the whole process?

I wished I could talk to all of my TMHJ crowd. T and M—all four of them—were beyond my reach, in Sunni's care; H, who had been a pest immediately after Dennis's murder, had disappeared after being ousted from the Ashcots' rehearsal. Had that confrontation with Quinn been only this morning? I couldn't remember whether I'd seen Joyce after the rehearsal, either.

Other than drum up an excuse to find and talk to Joyce or Hank, I was stuck. I couldn't very well offer to give a math class for Joyce or establish a new group of musicians that would accept Hank.

There was one other possible source of information. I called Dyson Somerville's cell. He answered immediately. I figured he was at loose ends, also, for a different reason.

"Have you had lunch yet?" I asked him.

His "No" seemed enthusiastic, for company if not for food.

"Would you like me to bring you a sandwich?"

"Sweet."

I made another stop at the deli, for a sandwich fit for a college boy, like the hefty one I'd brought Sunni.

I was touched that Dyson had set the kitchen table with plates and silverware. Did that make it more or less reprehensible that I was here for information? The fact that Sunni didn't give me details of her talk with him didn't mean that they were state secrets.

"This is great," Dyson said, adding serving spoons to the slaw and array of salads I'd picked up.

I poured myself a cup of coffee and dipped into the salads. I paid attention to all the small talk Dyson brought up. He chattered on about his classes (He loved chromatic harmony but was having trouble with his counterpoint professor), a female friend of his who would be coming for the service (Did I have any idea when he might be able to make those arrangements? I didn't), the changes around town (He hadn't heard that the library had moved to a bigger location), repairs around the house (His dad had been asking for help fixing the heater and he finally went out and bought a new filter for it this morning).

I felt so sorry for Dyson, guessing at what must have been in his mind as he made a trip to the hardware store three days after his father was murdered. Why hadn't he done the chore when his father would have appreciated it? *Why hadn't I stayed longer at the dinner table every night that my parents were alive? Why? Why?*

Dyson managed to do most of the talking around

school topics especially, and still put away a large roast beef sandwich, a few Kalamata olives with feta cheese crumbles, and a scoop of pasta salad.

I wished I could find an opening to ask what Sunni had shared with him, but finally decided to make the move myself. I walked back to the entryway, where I'd left my briefcase. "I have something to give you," I said.

I returned to the table with a package in bubble wrap. I'd packed it for Mercedes, who'd decided in the end that I should present it to Dyson. Now was as good a time as any.

Dyson took the package and seemed to know what it was. His eyes teared and I felt worse than ever. What kind of friend, surrogate mother, anything, was I? He gave me a questioning look and I hoped he wouldn't demand to know how I'd come by a piece from his dad's collection.

"A lighthouse," he said, before unwrapping. He removed the bubble wrap and took a deep breath. He turned it over in his hands, bringing about a flurry of snow. He ran his fingers over the surface and said only "Annisquam."

"I understand you visited there often."

He nodded. "As a kid." He smiled, the way we do at a happy memory, and I took a relieved breath. "His collection goes way back. Lighthouses in snow globes, from all over the world, from places we'd never been. Even one someone brought him back from China. When I was really little, we'd play this game. He'd hold one up for me to look at, and then shake it and make me laugh. At one point I started to pretend to be surprised, just so he'd think he'd fooled me."

"What a wonderful memory."

"Would you like to see the collection? It's in his office, upstairs."

I gulped, tried to act natural. Dyson was inviting me to the crime scene, and it had been all his idea. "Sure," I said, not too excited, just enthusiastic enough so he wouldn't withdraw the invitation.

I followed Dyson up the carpeted steps to the second floor, taking in and trying to memorize the surroundings. Only a few days ago, a killer had climbed these steps. As I put each foot down, I heard no squeaking, no noise at all. The carpet extended smoothly along the hallway that we trod to the first door on the right.

Dennis would have had no warning that an intruder was on his way. Either that or the killer was someone he knew and led up the stairs himself. Another possibility was that three people, all thieves, had climbed these stairs when the house was empty. They might have broken in, run up the staircase, and then been caught by Dennis later, midrobbery. So many possible scenarios. And more that I couldn't even imagine.

"I straightened it up," Dyson said when we reached the office. "I kept hearing my dad, all upset that things were out of place." He set Annisquam down, giving it one last shake, completing a long line of globes on a shelf.

I knew there was no chance that I could look through Dennis's files without appearing rude and uncaring. I doubted the police would have left behind anything vaguely interesting to the investigation anyway.

My gaze went to the line of lighthouse globes on the bookcases, placed much the same way as the Annisquam model had adorned Dennis's campus office bookcase.

Some replicas were large enough to include houses on the property; other lighthouses sat at the ends of piers; still others were completely isolated and inaccessible except by air or sea. A realistic assembly of lighthouse venues.

I looked at each globe in turn, with Dyson behind me, listing a few of the names. Cana Island in Wisconsin, Saint Augustine in Florida, Cape Hatteras in North Carolina. He picked up a medium-size globe from the Oregon coast and turned it upside down. Not only did he create a "snowfall," but a compartment was revealed.

"My dad would try to take the bases apart and make little hiding places. Then he'd tell me to go visit the Barnegat on the Jersey Shore, say, and see what I found. And there would be a small toy or a special marble or, like, a tiny action figure or some coins, depending on the size. He was always trying to turn me into an investigator, like a scientist."

I barely heard Dyson's last words. The idea of a secret compartment had captured my mind. What if one of those snow globes held a clue to Dennis's murder? I laughed at the idea as soon as it was formed, especially as I pictured a miniature gun as the weapon. Was I that desperate?

But when Dyson's phone rang and he excused himself to take the call, I couldn't resist. I looked for the largest globe, not big enough for a gun, but perhaps for a letter (occupational hazard) or a photo or an incriminating document.

I lifted the heavy globe with a replica of the Boston Harbor Lighthouse and saw no sign of a compartment. Neither did Oswego, New York, nor San Pedro Harbor, California, yield results. Maybe Dyson made up the endearing story as he journeyed back to his childhood, when he had two parents.

In the hallway, Dyson was still talking. I made one last try. I picked up the Yerba Buena Island globe and read the label. San Francisco, where Quinn was from. Maybe this would be the lucky one. I slid my finger along the base and pushed open a tiny trapdoor. A shiver ran up my spine. I froze, listening for Dyson's voice, and swallowed hard when I heard him, in the hallway, his voice somber but not choking. Did I dare risk getting caught messing with his father's prized collection and lose all the connection I'd built with him? Apparently so. The greater good, I told myself. How satisfying it would be, especially to Dyson, if a killer were exposed.

I continued my probing and was able to insert two fingers into the cranny at the base of the globe. I extracted a piece of paper, probably eight-and-a-half-by-eleven, folded five or six times, forming a thick cube. I stuffed the treasure (or so I hoped) in my pocket and placed Yerba Buena back on the shelf in front of a biography of Albert Einstein. Just in time for Dyson's return.

"That was my, like, girlfriend, I guess. She wanted to know everything. I'm sorry I left you by yourself."

"No problem," I said. "No problem at all."

19

I was amazed that my key still worked in the side door to the post office. I wouldn't have been surprised if Ben had changed the lock and withdrawn his resignation, pending the hiring of a more responsible postmaster.

I hadn't made it back to the building in time to beat the first customers of the afternoon. Fortunately, they were friends—two women from my quilting group and the daughter of one of them.

"Don't worry, we won't tell Ben," Fran said.

But it was too late. I was sure the blinking message light on the answering machine was the notice that Ben had called, making sure that the citizens of North Ashcot would have the services of the USPS this afternoon.

"I'm back," I said when the phone rang again. I cradled the phone in my neck while I opened the cash drawer.

"Heard it went very well."

"How could you possibly know that?"

"Friend of a friend," he said.

I didn't doubt it. "Thanks for everything this week, Ben," I said. "Stop by and pick up a little something I have for you."

"No need. I'm glad to help."

"Well, this is something only you can use."

"One of them sporting goods gift cards?"

My mouth dropped open. "You're scaring me."

I should have known there'd be a last-minute rush of afternoon customers with valentines for Express Mail. At least, no one wanted cards rerouted to towns with romantic names. But it would be a while before I could take a break and open the folded piece of paper shouting at me from my pants pocket.

In between a priority package to Michigan and a stack of flyers for the Albany area, I took some wild guesses about the content of the paper. The sheet of paper might concern a possible romantic issue with regard to Mercedes. A Dear John letter either to or from Mercedes. I had no clear idea about which of the two instigated the breakup.

Maybe Dennis had a new love and secreted a letter from her to keep it from Mercedes. Or vice versa. I considered the blackmail angle—something Dennis held over Hank Blackwood's head, as Sunni and I had discussed. Dennis might have uncovered proof of a misdeed. I couldn't eliminate the students, either. It was possible that Norah penned more than just the three letters I'd seen, and Dennis was holding back a more serious threat with the intent of following through with the police. Or the USPS, I thought, with chagrin.

It wasn't until three o'clock that I had a break in the line. I poured myself a cup of coffee—better than the weak liquid in the college cafeteria, but not as good as Sunni's—and sat in the chair behind my desk.

I pulled the folded sheet from my pocket with the care a surgeon might use to remove an organ, if they ever did that. I could tell that it was new paper, not some rare specimen that had been trapped in the base of a snow globe for a century, or even decades. Nothing Quinn would be interested in for Ashcot's Attic. Still, I opened the folds carefully.

No handwriting analysis would be required for this project. It seemed that four separate notes, each a couple of inches long, had been placed on a photocopier and copied onto one sheet. The lines were not all square with the edges of the machine's glass platform, and the quality of the copy was poor, as if the operator was in a rush. I read the slightly angled messages.

Professor—1 K is steep. LJ.

Prof. One week to finals How much? B.

Professor ~ Merci! Such a bargain. C.

Prof.—You can't stop now. A. Mc.

How to interpret the set? Were the notes to or from Dennis? Or did Dennis happen upon notes that he neither authored nor received? The fact that they were in Dennis's snow globe didn't clarify who sent them, who received them, who copied them, and most important, why.

I could only speculate, something I'd been doing too much of lately. But I had no other choice. High on the list was that either Dennis had been involved in an illegal operation or he had uncovered one. The sale of stolen merchandise, perhaps. The designation "1K" had to be one thousand dollars. Didn't it? Never mind that "LJ" might have been talking about scaling a one-thousand-foot slope. Or that "1K" was the answer to a math problem. *What's five hundred times two?* Something more sophisticated, of course.

Then why hide the paper? Dennis's lighthouse games with Dyson were over now that his son was an adult, though I probably should check that with Dyson. It was possible that Dennis suspected an unfortunate end, and had been counting on Dyson to alert the police to a possible clue to his murderer. He wouldn't have been counting on my supercurious, interfering nature.

Since Dennis had been murdered, it seemed more likely that he discovered evidence against his killer and was protecting it until he could go to the police. Maybe the student mail he'd brought to me was related, or maybe it was sent as a distraction from his mission to expose the criminal activities revealed in the copied notes from LJ, B, C, A McC. If there were any criminal activities. If, if, if.

This case was one of initials, it seemed, from my TMHJ to LJ and the others.

I couldn't rule out the three thieves as murderers after all, in league with a professor to get rid of the merchandise they stole? I had to ask Sunni if any of the three people in her custody had initials LJ and so on.

A customer with a bin of mail came into the lobby with the usual sigh of relief as she hit the warm air. I knew the young woman as part of the clerical staff in the real estate office downtown. I smiled to myself—the nerve of her, expecting service, interrupting important police work.

Before I greeted her, I read a quick text from Sunni.

Meeting 5-ish?

Sure, I wrote.

I took care of the hundreds of flyers in the bin while we chatted about the upcoming dance, whether there would be many from South Ashcot or other surrounding towns, what the predominant fashion would be. Long and elegant or short and chic? It occurred to me that I'd better pay attention to my own fashion statement that evening. I knew I'd never buy a short dress with one long zipper up the back and hoped it would go out of style soon. It was a good thing Linda would be around to help. In fact, why didn't I delegate the whole project to her? Like in the old days of clubbing in Boston.

I completed the transaction for the flyers, wondering why the real estate office, and so many other businesses, bothered to send full-color brochures through the mail. Most of them also had Web sites and sent regular e-mail ads. If my personal in-box was any example, there was a constant, daily barrage of merchandising. Not that I was complaining—I told an absent Ben—about a practice, like sending out physical flyers, that kept us in business.

Another break, and back to the notes. There was no end to the possible interpretations of the hidden notes. This time I focused on Dennis's behavior toward Hank Blackwood—the *H* in my TMHF—which seemed common knowledge. He'd been responsible for Hank's banishment from the Ashcots, and allegedly had something to do with Hank's early retirement from the community college math department. It wasn't a leap to think that Dennis had found out something damning and that Hank Blackwood killed him to protect whatever the something was. How much better it would have been if the pseudo signatures had included *HB* or the greeting had been to *Professor HB*.

I thought back to Dyson's report on the last conversation he'd had with his father, over the weekend. I recalled something about a teacher who accepted bribes for good grades. Hank? Joyce? Mercedes? Another dead, or multiple, end.

No other break came until closing. The last customer out the door took the prize for bringing me the most unusual shipment of the month: a set of four tires. No box, just a tag with a mailing label.

"I don't trust anyone else with these," the burly man said.

"I appreciate your confidence," I said, wondering how my pickup manager was going to react tomorrow morning.

Once the tires were safely locked in the delivery room, I dressed for the outdoors, first to lower the flag, then to head to the police station.

Each time I raised or lowered the Stars and Stripes, I

felt a renewed sense of patriotism and responsibility toward the citizens I served.

Today, however, with the chief of police waiting for
me, I felt my real work was just beginning.

I decided to walk to the police building. It wouldn't hurt
to clear my head, plan my approach to informing (or not)
Sunni about the notes I'd found in Dennis's lighthouse
globe. I tried to make some sense of the texts from, and
perhaps to, LJ, et alia, but came up with nothing new. Just
as well that I simply let Sunni talk.

I wished I knew if the gun that killed Dennis had been
found, or if ballistics information on it had come back. I
wished I knew Hank's alibi, and whether the thieves had
come through with a confession or a lead.

I pulled my scarf, a present from Linda and therefore
very fashionable, up over my nose and increased my pace.
How could I have forgotten how much colder it would get
once the sun was down? Once again my cold-weather
head-down stance caused me to nearly run into an oncoming pedestrian. This time: Joyce Blake.

We both apologized and then chuckled. "Women,"
Joyce said.

"Huh?"

"I read somewhere that women always say 'Sorry'
when they bump into someone. Men say 'Watch out.'"
Joyce repositioned a red scarf that clashed mercilessly
with her burgundy down coat. I thought Sunni and my
newfound quilt group must be rubbing off on me as they
taught me the elements of design and color.

I couldn't believe that Joyce's observation was true for every guy. I'd have been willing to bet that Quinn would apologize in such a situation. I wasn't so sure about Hank Blackwood. As for my former fiancé, I was sure his response would depend on how high up on the ladder the other person was. "Well, I wasn't watching where I was going," I said, "so it couldn't have been all your fault."

"I'm just coming from the police station," Joyce said. "I'm a little flustered."

"Oh?" Even though Joyce was the *J* in my TMHJ, her potential as a suspect in Dennis's murder had faded as that of the thieves and Hank had risen. Petty squabbles about course schedules paled in comparison to fighting over the loot from a possible gang of thieves or some underhanded operation Hank might be running.

"I'm not sure why, but the chief needed to question me again. She said it was routine, but it was intimidating anyway."

I almost shared how Sunni could be intimidating when in her building, but I held back in favor of defending a friend.

"She has a tough job," I said. "Did this have to do with some of your majors?"

"As a matter of fact, yes." A light seemed to dawn in Joyce's mind. "Wait a minute. Did you do this? Hassle those students I pointed out to you in Mahican's? Is that where the chief is getting her information?"

It was good to know that Sunni kept her sources to herself as much as possible. It wasn't her fault that I wasn't as good at maintaining anonymity.

"I'm not sure what you mean."

Joyce stiffened. "I think you are. You're something else. Maybe you should just leave the post office and go to the police academy. At least then we'd know to watch out for you."

Her reprimand reminded me of Norah's, except at least Joyce didn't blame me for the possible demise of the USPS. Joyce stomped away, her red scarf drooping over her shoulder. I was losing friends faster than an overnight delivery service. Hank, Norah, now Joyce. I hoped I still had one in the office of the chief of police.

I was deposited in Sunni's office by an intern while Sunni and Greta were busy in a back room. I did my best to sit still, holding a mug of delicious coffee. This was not a campus office or a home office. It was a place unique unto itself and I resolved not to so much as look with curiosity at anything in it that was remotely official.

That left a few photos and odd knickknacks. To keep my eyes from wandering, I studied a formal picture of Sunni's daughter, Avery, in her high school photo. She had her mother's coloring, with auburn highlights in long, straight hair. And her mother's eyes, which in life alternated between a soft green and a hard gray, depending on circumstances. Next to Avery's photo was one of her and Sunni at a mother-daughter event at Avery's sorority, and a clunky ceramic frog that held pencils in its wide mouth. I suspected this was also thanks to Avery a few years ago, since Sunni had no grandchildren that I knew of.

I did my best to assume a relaxed posture in the chair, though the back was too short to support my neck. My goal was to close my eyes so I wouldn't be distracted by the files in Sunni's in-box, the stack of papers at the corner of her desk, and handwritten notes on yellow paper, the sign of suspects' statements everywhere. Surely, Sunni wouldn't have left such important matter out. Since I couldn't rest it, the only option for my neck was to strain it and try to read the sheets of paper. No luck.

I took out my phone, always a good time filler. I thought of giving Dyson a call but didn't want to be engaged when Sunni returned. I texted him instead.

Nice to have lunch with u.

I was surprised to get a phone call in reply.

"Thanks, Cassie. I appreciate all your help."

"Are you keeping busy?"

"I guess. There's not much I can do until . . ."

I knew that the medical examiner hadn't released Dennis's body yet. I rushed to change the subject. "Do you want to come by for dinner tonight?"

"Sure. That'd be great."

I remembered too late that Quinn and I had planned to go out this evening. I knew he'd be okay with the change, for a good cause. "I'll let you know the time later."

"Okay. I had some company today after you left, which was nice."

"Some of your old friends?"

"Nah, more like my dad's friends. A couple of teachers, and his friend Mercedes. Well, she's a teacher, too, I guess, but I know they were, like, more than colleagues."

One question answered: Dennis hadn't kept his relationship with Mercedes a secret from his son. It made sense. It also made sense for Dennis's colleagues to visit their friend's son to offer special condolences. But that didn't mean that my investigative ears didn't go up. I wanted more. "Oh, which teachers came by besides Mercedes?" I asked.

"The math teachers, Dr. Blake and Dr. Blackwood." That would be Joyce and Hank. "Not together, though. They just all stopped in and brought me food."

"Very nice of them," I said, meaning *What did they want from you?*

"They're all very concerned about finding out who did this. I told them I don't know anything that isn't already on the news."

"I'm sure it's frustrating, Dyson, but Chief Smargon is working very hard on this."

"And you are, too, right? That's what they said."

"They said?"

"Yeah, all of them. Mercedes, Dr. Blake, Dr. Blackwood. And I remember Ben at the post office said that, too. They all said you know more than anyone because you're investigating on your own."

"They said that?" I was aware I was parroting but couldn't seem to break the rhythm.

"Yeah, I forget who said what, like, you were on campus searching my dad's office or you've been to the police department a lot and the chief visits you. It sounded like they wanted me to ask you what you've come up with and then let them know. But I probably have that wrong. I think they just wanted to show they're interested and they think whoever did this should be caught as soon as possible."

"Your father was very well liked, Dyson, and many people are eager to see his killer in jail." Though I didn't believe for a minute that Dennis's "friends" didn't have an ulterior motive for their questions. One of them might very well have been worried that the police were closing in. Or that I was, which would have been great if it were true.

"You'd tell me if you really know any more, right?" Dyson asked.

"Of course." I paused while I phrased a key follow-up question. "Dyson, did you by any chance get the feeling that one of the teachers knew something about the case? You know, maybe Mercedes or Professor Blake or Professor Blackwood has been doing some investigating also?"

"Huh. I didn't think about that. You mean, maybe they wanted to help, too?"

"Yes. I'm just wondering. It would certainly be wise for all of us to share."

"I don't know. The only thing I can think of is that they wanted to check out my dad's office. Like, Professor Blackwood asked if my dad left anything for him, something with his name on it."

What? Hank was using the same ploy I'd used to get into Dennis's campus office? "Did you take them up there?"

"Not Professor Blackwood because then actually Professor Blake came by and we got interrupted. But Mercedes wanted to go up, too, when she came by later, and I did take her. She just looked around and got kind of weepy and left pretty quick. Maybe I should have asked them if they needed me to do anything else for them."

"Dyson, don't think about that. You just need to take care of yourself right now. Make sure you're resting and eating and even doing classwork if you can. I think that's what your dad would want you to do."

I nearly screamed out loud at the memory of hearing those words when my parents died. What had I been thinking at the time? Nothing rational. What made me repeat them to Dyson?

"I guess," Dyson said, in a squeak.

"Dyson, I'm sorry. I must sound like I'm preaching, and that's not what I mean to do." The noisy appearance of Greta in the doorway prompted a rushed ending to the call. "Just promise you'll let me know if you need anything."

"Okay. And please promise you'll tell me if you find out anything, you know?" Dyson asked.

I managed to sound as if I were promising without actually doing so. No mean feat.

"She's on her way," Greta told me. I wondered if Greta deliberately made her announcement as a warning to me, in case I was doing or saying something neither of us would want Sunni to know about. Greta had, after all, nearly blown her job earlier when she supplied me with an advance copy of a news bulletin. I liked that we could cover each other's backs. I knew it would come in handy in the future.

By the time Sunni arrived a few minutes later, I'd taken out my e-reader and, I hoped, looked so engrossed in a thriller that I had no interest in what might be in my surroundings.

"I ran into Joyce on the way here," I said.

"Morgan is about to get herself a deal," Sunni said, taking a seat behind her desk. "Which could break the case." I guessed we'd come back to Joyce later. "Thanks to you," she muttered.

I gave her my best nonthreatening, quizzical look. "I didn't think that sympathy card trick got us very much."

"That wasn't the first time she'd interacted with you. She'd seen you with me a number of times, and then saw you on campus near Dennis's building. She passed the info on to our trifecta of thieves, warning them that you might be onto them and their route."

"And they're the ones who've been following me."

Oops. Did I really say that out loud? I guessed I'd held it in too long. I hadn't seen the three shadowy figures since they were in custody and figured there was no sense telling Sunni if the threat was contained.

"Yes, nice of you to let me know about the tail."

"They never approached me. I was going to. If they spoke to me, or anything, I would have said something." Throwing everything out there. "So Morgan knows the thieves?" Digressing now.

"Correct. I guess they all know each other." Sunni smiled. "Like all chiefs of police everywhere know each other."

And all postmistresses, I thought. "But you don't think she was in on the robberies around town?"

"That's how it looks right now. The feds are giving us another day to work the murder angle with all four of them, but I honestly doubt that any of them have branched out into violence. Morgan has had her own gig going for a while—she's really in her twenties, fakes her way into colleges as a base. When she landed in North Ashcot, she saw that she had competition. They decided they'd all cooperate, separate but equal marks."

"Wow. She's been doing her own break-ins and following the crew's jobs? How does she ever get her math homework done?"

"Apparently, she has a very high IQ, one of these little geniuses, and she can pass for much younger than she is. In the end, it's her pride that was her downfall. Dennis Somerville gave her something less than an A and she fell apart and engineered that ridiculous letter campaign against him. Which you followed up on. As I told you, I'm not sure we would have caught up with her otherwise."

"So you think they're all innocent of Dennis's murder—Morgan and the group of three—but you're still holding them all?"

"The longer we can keep them, the better the chance they'll give us something. Remember these creeps know the towns they work. They're onto people and places better than we are. That's all they have to do, day and night, is figure out where homeowners are and what are the easiest places to break into. And there are a lot more of them than us."

I was newly impressed by Sunni's reasoning. It must take a while, I figured, not only to track criminals, but to think like them. "I get it. They're out there, watching everyone, casing potential sites for opportunities to commit crime. They're like your auxiliary force."

Sunni laughed. "That's a strange way to put it. But right on. I get the sense that Morgan in particular saw something outside Dennis's house around the time of his murder. She's holding out for a deal."

I thought I did well, containing my excitement that my charade with Joyce's math majors had panned out even better than I thought. So what if Joyce wasn't happy? Once Dennis's killer was brought to justice, she'd be fine. I figured it was safe to bring her up now. "I met Joyce on the way in here today."

"So you said."

I waited. No matter how much help I was to my friend, she'd always have a hard time including me fully in her investigation. I knew it was her way of trying to keep me safe. "I guess she's in the clear. Didn't you say she'd been with her sister at the critical time?"

"Good memory. Yes, her alibi is solid. She and her sister took her nieces shopping for clothes for some junior high Valentine's Day dance. I guess it hits all ages." I sensed a cynicism in Sunni's remark. It occurred to me that I didn't know very much about Avery's father, except that they'd divorced years ago. "Anyway, no one is going to make their little kids lie for them."

"She's upset with me for cornering her majors," I said.

"She's probably embarrassed at being tricked into defending and protecting a career criminal, working out of her department."

"That department has had its problems," I said, thinking of Hank's ignominious departure.

Greta came to the door and alerted Sunni that "We're ready for you."

Sunni moved from her position behind her desk. "That's it for now, Cassie," she said.

"Where are we going?" I asked.

She laughed, handed me my jacket, and pointed to the exit. "You're going that way. *I'm* going downstairs."

"Okay, maybe later," I said, but she'd already left the room.

It wasn't my fault, then, that I didn't get to tell her about the snow globe notes.

20

Walking back to my car in the post office parking lot, I checked my phone for messages. I had to accept the fact that I'd become one of those walk-and-talk people I often criticized, oblivious of their surroundings. I liked to think at least I'd never use my phone while crossing the street. That was some concession.

I had messages from the usual array of people—if the FBI or NSA ever dumped my phone records, they'd be bored to death, seeing the same list every day. Except for the recent addition of Dyson Somerville, now an orphan, I realized.

I called Dyson back on his landline, where his call had originated. I stopped short when I heard Dennis's voice asking me to leave my name and number. I hung up without doing so. Too upsetting to respond to a dead person.

I'd follow up later, when I was sitting in my living room, able to check my contacts for Dyson's cell number.

My mind was turning over what Dyson's faculty visitors had told him about my activities relating to his father's murder. Even stranger was their request that Dyson report back to them. And strangest of all was Hank's request to visit his nemesis's office. I thought I had it right that only Joyce didn't make that request. I felt that Mercedes had more of a sentimental reason, but why not ask to see the bedroom or the exercise room, too? The probing would seem most reasonable coming from Dennis's killer, but they couldn't all have killed him.

I wondered how the word got out that I'd been to Dennis's campus office. I doubted Gail would have told Hank, since she'd expressed displeasure even referring to him as part of the faculty. I imagined that Dyson, in his naïveté, would have let it be known that I'd also visited Dennis's home office. For now, I thought it was just as well that I couldn't reach Dyson. It wouldn't be very sensitive of me to keep querying him about the faculty visits.

Too bad all the fuss over what I knew was wasted. If anything, I had more questions than anyone.

Dinner was also on my mind. Quinn and I had made tentative plans for a celebratory dinner out. I smiled as I thought how, thanks to my nervousness, everyone was making such a big deal out of a single talk—something real teachers did every day without fanfare. But I'd also invited Dyson for dinner and now thought it would be better to have it at home.

It took only a couple of quick texts with Quinn to

straighten it out. He'd cook in my kitchen for all of us. I couldn't have wished for anything better.

I had a flashback to many similar situations with my ex-fiancé. Adam Robinson could turn a simple change of plans into a major incident. What if the important councilman he'd planned to meet got upset and crossed Adam off his list? What if he lost time at the office because the timing had to be changed by thirty minutes? Even worse, what if the only tie that went with the Tuesday evening suit had not been cleaned properly? I felt relieved and lucky that Quinn offered no such drama over small things.

My timing was good. I reached my car as I wrapped up a text to Linda, confirming her arrival tomorrow evening. I'd also had an e-mail from Linda, who must have been especially bored today. She'd attached a clip from the police brief in a suburban Boston paper. I scanned it to learn that an angry resident in West Milton, Massachusetts, punched out his mail carrier when a package he was expecting didn't arrive. The unnamed attacker, twenty-five, was charged with aggravated assault, with possible federal charges pending. The mailman was injured but drove himself to the hospital. Was Linda trying to send me a message?

Out of habit, I looked at the darkened windows of the post office. A small night-light in the lobby and another behind the counter cast odd shadows around the space. I resolved that next week I'd put in five full days behind that counter and would cook dinner for Quinn every night. I felt secure making the second promise, since I knew Quinn would never allow it as long as he was upright.

I checked the corner across the street, where I'd first seen the trio of stalkers. All was quiet. I wondered if Morgan or any of the other three crooks in custody had given up useful information in the murder case. I imagined Sunni, arms folded across her chest, waiting them out.

I drove home, conscious of the notes in my pocket. I might have shown the page to Sunni, if I hadn't been summarily ushered from her office. Now I thought it better to wait until I had more of an idea, or any idea at all, what they could mean. I had the startling thought that the notes might even be left over from a silly game Dennis had been playing with his son years ago. Maybe I should ask Dyson if there was ever a game that went unfinished. Of course that would mean explaining to him where I'd found the paper in the first place. Another dead end.

No wonder I needed a nap.

Quinn had his own key to my house, like any trusted home helper, but he never used it if he thought I was home. I woke, therefore, to a persistent ringing of my doorbell.

I'd fallen asleep on my easy chair, fully clothed except for my jacket, the one with the eagle patch, which had inspired such confidence in my listeners during my classroom presentation.

I staggered to the door, noticing the time on the way. Close to eight o'clock. "I can't believe I slept this long. What about Dyson?" I asked Quinn. "I was expecting him to come for dinner."

"He called me earlier and said some old high school

friends were luring him away with the promise of pizza at their old haunt. I told him I knew you wouldn't mind. I texted you, but . . ."

"I fell asleep."

"It's just as well he reconnected with his buddies. He couldn't hang around with us, uh, folks forever."

"Were you about to say 'with us old folks'?"

He smiled. "Possibly. You realize we're almost a generation older than Dyson. He's barely twenty, and we're—"

"Ouch. No wonder I fell asleep."

"And now I have to tell you that I'm going to be leaving soon. But I can throw together something for you from leftovers before I go, if you want."

My face reddened at the thought that Quinn felt he was responsible for my every dinner. "No, please don't. I'm not even that hungry."

"Okay, if you're sure."

"Where are you going? It's not the boys' club night, is it?"

Quinn shook his head and explained that he had an emergency, which was how he and Fred labeled a prime business opportunity. An estate lawyer had requested their presence as the family made their decision about who would be trusted to manage their auction. Fred was out of town, so it fell to Quinn to meet and woo the potential lucrative client.

"It sounds like a shoo-in," he said. "They're not even considering other options, like a tag sale. The bad news is it's all the way down in Northampton, at least sixty or seventy minutes, even at this hour."

"Do you want some company?"

He pushed the hair from my eyes and stared at my face. I knew what he was seeing. Fatigue, among other signs of stress. "I couldn't put you through that."

As much as I would have liked time to talk to Quinn about all the loose ends of the Dennis Somerville case, I thought I'd only be a distraction. Or asleep in the passenger seat.

"I'll see you in the morning," I said. "Another rehearsal, right?"

"Unless we cram on Saturday before the gig."

We hugged at the door and I waved Quinn off. I found myself suddenly wide-awake with no one to talk to. And full responsibility for getting my own dinner.

I solved the first problem with a Skype call to Linda. I caught her up on the developments—how the crooks might turn out to be a help in finding Dennis's killer, how some old notes might also be useful, and how all my suspects were lining up.

"I wish I could get you to stop," she said.

"Stop what?" As if I didn't know.

"I know you're good at this investigating stuff. But I worry about your safety."

"I appreciate your concern."

Linda laughed. "Don't treat me like one of your customers."

"That's how you sound."

Linda was in her Fenway apartment, completely color-coordinated in black and chrome, with dashes of red. Nothing Quinn would have bought or sold. "Maybe you should apply for a position in the Inspection Office. I'll check to see what the dates are for applying. You know they have all these special windows of operation."

"I don't think so, Linda."

"Why not? You'd at least have a bulletproof vest and gun training."

"I'll pass."

"Well, be careful, Cassie."

"What time do you think you'll get here tomorrow evening?" I asked.

"I leave right after work, so probably around eight. What are you going to wear?"

"Didn't you threaten to take me shopping on Saturday?"

"Yes, yes. The timing's perfect, by the way," Linda said. "I like this new guy, but not enough for a Valentine's Day date, you know."

"Too soon for big expectations," I offered, having been there.

"Yeah, so I have the perfect excuse. My old friend in the boonies needs some company."

"Whatever you need," I said. "I'm all yours."

My so-called dinner was particularly uninspiring. I'd tried to make a soup out of old veggies and new pasta, but the broccoli was soggy and the pasta tough. Nothing like the wonton soup I could have in Boston at the touch of a button, or the sushi offerings I used to have on speed dial. I settled for toasted cheese and tomatoes.

Done with food for a while, I cleared a spot at the kitchen table for my laptop, paper notebook (a low-tech backup plan I couldn't shake), and the sheet of copied notes I'd found hidden in Dennis's snow globe.

I smoothed out the paper and studied the words.

Professor—1 K is steep. LJ.

Prof. One week to finals How much? B.

Professor ~ Merci! Such a bargain. C.

Prof.—You can't stop now. A. Mc.

I ran through all the scenarios I'd already concocted and got nowhere all over again.

I was ready to give up and call it a night when I had a flash of insight. I'd been struggling to figure out the wording on the notes. One thousand what? What did final exams have to do with anything? Who'd use French? Don't stop what? Did the *A*, *B*, and *C* signatures represent grades and not the senders' initials? Then what did LJ represent?

I'd been intent on examining the message, parsing the phrases, when I should have been considering the medium. The paper they were written on, the original notes, in the shape of standard sticky notes, except that these notes had a border on each edge. It was hard to make it out because the copy process had smudged the letters. On closer inspection, they weren't actually letters. They looked like Mrs. Wyman's algebra class, with symbols and Greek letters. I was proud that I recognized the letter *pi*. Or was that from geometry class? Finally, I realized I'd seen the characters more recently—on the office door of Hank Blackwood.

Did that mean the notes had been sent to Hank? If so,

how did they end up in Dennis's snow globe? With no real proof, I made a leap. If I couldn't be a cop, then why not take leaps that cops couldn't legally take? What if the speculation about a professor taking bribes was true, and Hank was the professor? If Dennis found out, he would have a great deal of leverage against Hank, forcing him into early retirement at the college and out of the Ashcots.

I considered that Dennis was blackmailing Hank but ruled against it (why not be a judge also?), since I liked him and his son.

After those leaps, it was all clear. LJ didn't want to pay Hank a thousand dollars for a good grade; B was still negotiating; C was very happy with the outcome; and A Mc was unhappy that Hank either was closing down his little side business, or simply wouldn't accommodate A Mc.

I picked up the phone to call Sunni at the same time that my doorbell rang. It was almost ten o'clock and I wasn't expecting anyone. Quinn would still be in Northampton. And anyone else would call first at this hour, even Sunni.

My dining room and living room combo space was dark. I decided to go to the window onto the porch and get a look at my guest. It was impossible, however, to do this with complete privacy, since the window was at the same level as the door. As soon as I moved the curtain, the person would see me.

But it was too late to hide, since I'd already made too much noise, so I pulled the curtain aside and looked out. And into the face of Hank Blackwood.

21

I dropped the curtain and jumped back as if a bolt of lightning were about to strike me.

"Hey, Cassie," Hank said, his voice cheery. "It's freezing out here. My car is stalled and my phone is dead. Can you open up?"

Hank's car was stalled in front of my house? What were the chances? On the other hand, what were the chances that Hank knew within seconds of my figuring out that he was the likely killer of his colleague and musical cohort, and had come to make me his next victim? Pretty low all around. But statistics were no help in my deciding whether to open my door.

"I'm ready for bed, Hank," I said, striving to keep my voice steady, and counting on the fact that he couldn't see through the curtain that I was in perfectly presentable jeans and a sweatshirt, not a filmy negligee or even pj's. "I'll call a tow company for you."

"Come on. Can't I get a cup of coffee while I wait? Nothing's open downtown."

I knew he was right about that, but it didn't matter to me.

"Just throw on a robe," he said. Still more pleading than threatening, but I wasn't buying it.

"Hank, the best I can do is to call Bud's Towing. You know he'll come at any hour."

Hank banged on the window. I flinched again and stepped back.

"You know what? Never mind. I should have known you'd be a"—and here I lost him, since the word he uttered was not in my regular vocabulary. "I'll go next door. Maybe someone on this block is neighborly. Don't expect any more business from me."

With that, and a few more choice words that I did recognize, he stomped off.

I blew out a deep breath and moved away from the window, straining to hear his footsteps, descending my steps. When I was satisfied that he'd left, I sat in an easy chair in the dark living room. My heartbeat was still elevated, but I grabbed my cell phone and punched in Sunni's number.

Voice mail.

Not what I wanted to hear. I tried her office number, and the recorded message told me that if I had an emergency, I should call 911. Was this an emergency? It all depended on whether I was right about Hank. What if I had just shown myself to be a poor neighbor in a friendly small town, perhaps jaded by big-city living for so many years? Not willing to help out a guy who was stranded on a cold winter night. I told myself that Hank wasn't a well-loved citizen and probably wouldn't be successful in ruining my reputation as well as that of the USPS.

I clicked my phone off and tapped it on my thigh. Where was Sunni? Why wasn't she in her office working on the case as I'd been? I had a thought. I'd check my contacts for a direct line to the front desk. Someone had to be on duty all night.

I was so stressed that I didn't immediately recognize Greta's voice and thought I'd reached another recording.

"Is this Cassie?" she asked, apparently seeing my caller ID.

"Yes," I stammered. "This may be nothing, but . . ." I stopped. What to tell her? That Hank Blackwood had rung my doorbell and frightened me? That I knew Hank killed Dennis and might now be after me? Too paranoid.

I opted out of that approach. I took a huge breath and told her that *someone* had come to my door and wouldn't leave. "Can you possibly send a car around?"

"Are you okay, Cassie?"

"Yeah, I think he's gone. I'd just like someone to check my property."

"Sure thing. All the cars are out right now, called to South Ashcot of all things. Something must be up there. We got several calls from residents needing our help."

"Is that common?"

"Not at all. Most unusual. Are you sure you don't want me to get you nine-one-one? They'll pull from wherever they have to."

How foolish would I look? I'd heard Hank leave. What if some real 911 call came second to mine and someone died? "No, just put me on the list. Do you know where Sunni is, by the way?"

"She just called in. She was summoned to a briefing on the robberies at the station down in Stockbridge, but when she got there, no one knew what she was talking about. She's on her way back. Very strange."

"Okay, can you tell her to call me when she gets in?"

"Will do. Take care and call me if you need anything."

What I needed was peace of mind and a briefing with Sunni about Hank Blackwood. A real briefing, not the one that didn't happen in Stockbridge.

I sat back. What was going on? A flurry of incidents in South Ashcot that called North Ashcot's resources away. A summons from Stockbridge that took our chief of police from her station. A call to Quinn that required a last-minute trip to Northampton. All just when Hank Blackwood's car stalled in front of my house and he needed to use my phone. I questioned whether Dyson's friend had called to invite him to pizza, or whether Hank had engineered that also.

I punched in Quinn's number, an exercise that took three tries, thanks to my twitching fingers. Ordinarily, I wouldn't disturb him while he was doing business, but I needed to check out what was happening to my support system.

"Hey, Cassie."

"Are you finished with your business?" I asked. Calmed down a little after hearing his voice.

"Funny thing. I got to the area and it was an ordinary

residence in a somewhat squirrely part of town and no one knew anything about—"

I gasped. "Quinn, please call nine-one-one for me. And hurry back. I—"

A loud crash at the back of my house took my breath away. I dropped the phone. I heard Quinn's panicked voice. I hoped he recovered quickly enough to call for help.

"You need to do something about that flimsy lock on the back door." Hank, with his stubby legs, nevertheless made it into my living room with record speed.

All my self-defense training became a blur. There was no advice when faced with a gun except to duck. My options were limited. My only advantage over Hank was that I was better able to maneuver in the dark living room.

How to stall him while I figured out how to save my life?

"I'm sorry, Hank. I should have invited you in. That was rude of me."

He laughed at my silly, futile ploy. I almost laughed myself.

"You're way too clever, Cassie. When Dyson told me you'd been in his father's office, I knew you'd probably find something. The arrogant, self-righteous Dennis told me he had all he needed to go to the college board. He knew about my little moonlighting scheme with the less gifted but wealthier students."

The headlights of a passing car illuminated his face enough for me to see a sinister smile. And to size up my attacker. Hank was shorter than me by several inches, but heavier. And armed. He stood about five feet away, I estimated, on the long narrow area rug that Quinn had delivered only a week or so ago. I remembered the oval rug, of a similar vintage to the one in Dennis's home, the one I'd searched for bloodstains. Now I imagined my own blood on my rug. The front door was an equal distance behind me. No chance that I could turn, run, unlock the door, and make it outside alive.

"Can't we sit down? Talk this over?" I asked.

"Too late, Madam Postmistress. I came here tonight to quiz you, that's all." He waved his gun at me. "Well, I did come prepared, just in case, but I had no idea you'd already figured it all out. And I knew that this time it wouldn't be just academic sanctions, but a trip to the police station."

"I haven't figured anything—"

He shook his head. "If you hadn't, you would have let me in." He turned toward the kitchen table. "And I just happened to notice what you were working on out there. You saved me the trouble of looking for what Dennis claimed to have on me. Something I'll scoop up on my way out the door. Fortunately, I've amassed enough money for a clean getaway, in case there's a loose end somewhere that I haven't thought of. I'm thinking some place that's warm all year."

And where will I be? On the floor, dead? I realized I hadn't mentioned Hank's name to anyone. Not to Greta, not to Quinn. This seemed the ultimate unfairness. I had to do something, if only to leave a clue as to who had killed me.

I could tell Hank was finished talking, shifting his feet, getting ready to aim and fire. I took one step back, off the rug, leaving Hank at the other end of it, still posturing.

I saw my one chance—when he had one foot in the air. I dropped to the floor and pulled on the rug with both hands, as hard as I could. Just in time to topple Hank. He ended up flat on his back, his gun flung toward my coffee table.

With his thick middle, it took him a few seconds to turn over and search for his gun in the shadows. I used the time to grab on to my only remaining defensive resource, the heavy metal bust of Sir Rowland Hill that had been sitting on my coffee table. The inspiration for my postal history presentation. I picked up Sir Rowland and sent him crashing down on Hank's skull. I kicked the gun under the coffee table, out of reach. Even though Hank wasn't moving, I ran to the door, tripped on the messed-up rug, righted myself, and made it out onto my porch as Sunni's car was pulling up.

I crawled to the top step and pointed toward my front door. "Hank Blackwood," I said, in case they were the last words I uttered.

22

A lot of people spent most of Friday processing criminals, delivering each one to the appropriate department for arraignment or whatever else had been agreed upon by all the law enforcement representatives. In spite of the overload of paperwork, Sunni's office seemed brighter than ever, her officers and others of us walking around with big smiles.

The chatter was all about the many cases that had been solved this week.

Greta was happy because her two favorite people, as she called us, were alive and well. Once Quinn's chain of information had reached Greta, she realized that my intruder had set her boss up. "What was to prevent him from attacking the chief, or having someone attack her?" Her worries over, Greta made countless cups of good coffee and more than one run to the bakery.

Officer Hirsch, from the South Ashcot PD, who had come to help process the bevy of crooks in our midst, was especially impressed by Morgan. "She managed to pull off her cons in eleven states—all of New England, plus five others."

In the end, Morgan had been helpful, in that she ID'd Hank's car, a classic Chevy Nova, as the one she saw leaving Dennis Somerville's home around the time of his murder. "Putting him at the scene," Sunni said. "Always handy for the prosecution."

Greta summarized nicely. "Morgan was surveying her competition, following the other three crooks around town, and therefore she was able to finger our murderer." She tsk-tsked. "You've gotta love this job."

Mercedes and Joyce—who, I hoped, would never know that theirs had been initials in my suspect mnemonic—came to the station to give statements. If the case ever went to trial, character witnesses, or the opposite thereof, would be needed. The two women, and many others in the Ashcots and at the college, would be called on to testify to the animosity between Hank and his victim.

I'd assured Quinn the night before that Hank had never gotten to lay a hand on me. He was still reluctant to leave my side and, at the same time, delighted that his carpet had saved the day for me.

"And don't forget Sir Rowland," I said. "Heavy enough to knock Hank out but not lethal enough to keep him from facing a murder charge."

"I know my antiques," Quinn said.

Sunni gave me only a short lecture about meddling

and safety, and then hugged me. "I don't know whether to lock you up for obstruction or give you a medal for valor."

Embarrassing as it was, I was happy to hear the vote from the station house full of my friends.

"Cassie. Cassie," they shouted. Then, "Medal. Medal."

I felt right at home.

NOW. p. 129 makes sense

Linda arrived in time to help decorate on Friday evening. In another last-minute change, the venue for the dance had been moved to the community center. Apparently, the senior center had a massive plumbing problem that would have made it inconvenient to host an event. The Ashcots had been rehearsing here anyway, and took the opportunity to fit in another brief practice session while we untangled beads and red lights and silvery garlands.

"I can't believe I'm doing this," Linda said more than once while stringing hearts and roses across the walls. "Decorating for an old folks' dance on Valentine's Day weekend."

"Be nice about it," old Moses told her, "or nobody will do this for you when you need it."

"Duly noted," Linda said, trying to contain a grin. At which point, two-thousand-year-old (he claimed) Moses took Linda by the arm and waltzed with her to an old tune.

After a few turns with Moses, and a few more with Ben, who didn't want to miss any action, Linda found me and reminded me, "Shopping tomorrow. New dresses for all. I can hardly wait."

Just when I thought the worst of the week was over.

23

The Valentine's Day dance on Saturday evening seemed anticlimactic compared to the celebration at the NAPD the day before and the decorating party in the evening. Shopping for dresses wasn't bad, either, as Linda and I took breaks for lunch and snacks, and nonstop talking.

Talk of love and romance took a backseat for a while to the scandals at the college, particularly in the math and sciences department. A woman masquerading as a math major as a cover for her robberies, and a professor taking money in exchange for good grades. As far as anyone could tell, there was no overlap. Two separate rings of crime. I had the thought that Gatekeeper Gail must be overwrought, even blaming herself for not picking up on what was going on in her department.

Dyson came by in time to hear the tribute to his father.

His friend Chrissy had driven down from Maine to be with him, and had been coaxed into a solo with the Ashcots when it became known that she was a voice major. Her rendition of "Un Bel Di Vedremo"—"One fine day we'll meet again," I'd been told—had never been so moving.

It was strange to be in the room just one thin wall from my place of business. I pushed away feelings of guilt about my week as absentee postmistress and accepted the thanks of my friends, some old, some new, for whatever I'd contributed to the restored peace in North Ashcot.

"You look beautiful," Quinn said as we twirled around, neither of us very good at dancing.

"Thanks to Linda," I said, fingering the shiny red fabric she'd chosen to clothe me in this evening.

"No, thanks to you." Quinn maneuvered us into a corner where we'd established a makeshift coat check station. We stopped dancing. "I've never been more worried about you than when you cut off that call last night."

"I know." Because he'd already told me a dozen times.

"And never happier to see you. I never want you out of my sight."

I laughed. "That can be arranged."

"I hope so," he said, reaching into his pocket, pulling out a small red box.

I drew in my breath, ready to agree to a new arrangement.

POST OFFICE STORIES

Cassie's connection to the U.S. Postal Service goes way back to when she was a kid and loved to see envelopes addressed to her. She admits to sending away for things just to receive letters or packages with her name on them. "Send for more information" was an invitation she never refused. As a result, she acquired items a little girl had no other use for than to display them. In her room were stacks of seed catalogues, brochures from the army and navy, surveys from the airlines and financial institutions, and pamphlets from colleges and universities from all over the world.

Here's a small collection of her favorite postal stories and facts—some funny, some strange, all very interesting.

POSTAL HISTORY

- The Post Office Department issued its first postage stamps on July 1, 1847, first in New York, then in Boston, then in other cities. Previously, letters were taken to a post office, where the postmaster would note the postage in the upper right corner. The postage rate was based on the number of sheets in the letter and the distance it would travel.

- The B. Franklin Post Office in Philadelphia is the only active post office in the U.S. that does not fly the American flag—because there was not yet one in 1775 when Benjamin Franklin was appointed postmaster general.

- The envelope-folding machine was invented by Warren de la Rue and Edwin Hill at the 1851 Great Exhibition. The machine was displayed at Thomas de la Rue & Co.'s booth.

- During the late nineteenth century, letter carriers' bands were organized and became very popular. Wearing special uniforms, the bands would play at conventions and at public events.

- The first woman to be featured on a U.S. postage stamp was Queen Isabella in 1893. The first American woman featured was Martha Washington in 1902.

- In the days after the Great Depression (1929–1939), murals were commissioned to be displayed in post offices around the country, to boost morale. Examples include a mural of "Paul Revere's Ride" in Lexington, Massachusetts, and one of "Cowboy Dance" in Anson, Texas. The USPS houses more than fourteen hundred murals and/or sculptures from President Roosevelt's New Deal programs.

- From the late 1800s to the early 1950s, mail was sent via a complex series of pneumatic tubes, whisking cylinders full of mail at thirty-five miles per hour to its various destinations. For the inaugural event, a few chosen objects were sent: a Bible, a large fake peach, and, for reasons unknown, a cat. According to witnesses, the cat was slightly dazed but unharmed.

BY THE NUMBERS

- The Automated Flat Sorting Machine (AFSM) sorts "machineable" flat mail at seventeen thousand pieces per hour.

- In fiscal year 2014: Forensics scientists examined more than sixty-two thousand documents, fingerprints, controlled substances, audio, video, digital media, and other items of physical evidence for inspectors' investigations, resulting in the identification of 899 criminal subjects.

- Nineteen billion postage stamps were sold in 2014.

LITTLE-KNOWN FACTS

- The inspection branch of the USPS serves many purposes in the prevention of crimes. They gather clues related to mail fraud and perform laboratory analyses; and they participate in the security at major public events, such as sporting and political events, by screening mail for explosives and for biological, chemical, and radiological agents.

- The smallest post office in the United States is the Ochopee Post Office, a tiny shed, about fifty-six square feet, on U.S. Route 41 in the heart of the Everglades, near Ochopee, Florida.

- Marc Chagall's painting *Study for Over Vitebsk* was stolen in 2001 from the Jewish Museum in New York. It was found in a Topeka, Kansas, dead mail sorting facility, where letters are sent when they can't be delivered and are without return addresses.

VALENTINE'S DAY TRIVIA

- Approximately one hundred and forty-five million valentines are sent in the U.S. mail each year.

- Every Valentine's Day, the Italian city of Verona, where Shakespeare's lovers Romeo and Juliet lived, receives about a thousand letters addressed to Juliet.

- Along with the Valentine's Day postmark craze, each December many people travel long distances to postmark cards from the Christmas, Florida, post office.

FUNNY SHIPMENTS

- This story is attributed to a famous popcorn maker and may or may not be true: Every now and then, someone mails him a single popcorn kernel that didn't pop. He picks out a fresh kernel, tapes it to a piece of paper, and mails it back to them.

- Not unusual among shipments Cassie has handled are livestock and human remains. Perhaps the strangest was a box of human eyeballs floating in a saline solution.

The Postmistress Mysteries

by Jean Flowers

**Cassie Miller returns to her sleepy hometown in the
Berkshires to start over as the new postmistress,
but she soon finds that dead letters are nothing
compared to murder victims.**

Find more books by Jean Flowers
by visiting prh.com/nextread

"Flowers has created a very likable protagonist to head
her latest series...a fresh take on amateur crime solving.
—Library Journal

"The pacing is pitch-perfect. Ms. Flowers understands we
the art of writing a cozy mystery."**—Suspense Magazine**

BERKLEY | Penguin
Random
House